Praise

TIDES *of* H

National Be

"[Graham] has delivered a book that reads like a love letter to a time and place that figures largely in our national identity: Halifax in 1917."

—*The Globe and Mail*

"Fans of Gabaldon and other historical fiction/romance writers will lap this up for the classy, fast-moving, easy-to-read, and absorbing book that it is—with some Canadian history to boot."

—*Winnipeg Free Press*

"Evocative of place and time, a novel blending tragedy and triumph in a poignant and uplifting tale that's sure to leave its mark upon your heart."

—**Susanna Kearsley, bestselling author of**
A Desperate Fortune

"Audrey is a strong female character, a hallmark of Graham's books."

—*The Chronicle Herald*

"Travel back to 1917 and explore a world of suffragettes, Bolsheviks, and the Great War—and the love story that illuminates them all."

—**Jon Tattrie, author of** *Black Snow*

"A moving Maritime story of love, loss, and the human spirit."

—**Lesley Crewe, author of** *Relative Happiness* **and** *Kin*

"A memorable story of love surviving devastation. Set during the dark days of the Halifax Explosion—the largest man-made explosion prior to Hiroshima—a young artist and a wounded soldier are forced to overcome their personal struggles in the face of disaster. Graham examines class struggles and the post-traumatic effect of war with a vivid description of early twentieth century Halifax."

—Pamela Callow, international
bestselling author of *Tattooed*

WITHDRAWN
From Toronto Public Library

ALSO BY GENEVIEVE GRAHAM

Tides of Honour
Under the Same Sky
Sound of the Heart
Somewhere to Dream

WITHDRAWN
From Toronto Public Library

PROMISES
to KEEP

Genevieve Graham

Published by Simon & Schuster
New York   London   Toronto   Sydney   New Delhi

Simon & Schuster Canada
A Division of Simon & Schuster, Inc.
166 King Street East, Suite 300
Toronto, Ontario M5A 1J3

This book is a work of fiction. Any references to historical events, real people, or real places are used fictitiously. Other names, characters, places, and events are products of the author's imagination, and any resemblance to actual events or places or persons, living or dead, is entirely coincidental.

Copyright © 2017 by Genevieve Graham

Map of Nova Scotia. Library and Archives Canada/e007913201.

All rights reserved, including the right to reproduce this book or portions thereof in any form whatsoever. For information, address Simon & Schuster Canada Subsidiary Rights Department, 166 King Street East, Suite 300, Toronto, Ontario, M5A 1J3.

This Simon & Schuster Canada edition April 2017

SIMON & SCHUSTER CANADA and colophon are registered trademarks of Simon & Schuster, Inc.

For information about special discounts for bulk purchases, please contact Simon & Schuster Special Sales at 1-800-268-3216 or CustomerService@simonandschuster.ca.

Interior design by Lewelin Polanco

Manufactured in the United States of America

1   3   5   7   9   10   8   6   4   2

Library and Archives Canada Cataloguing in Publication

Graham, Genevieve, author
Promises to keep / Genevieve Graham.
Issued in print and electronic formats.
ISBN 978-1-5011-4287-1 (paperback).—ISBN 978-1-5011-4288-8 (ebook)
I. Title.
PS8613.R3434P76 2017   C813'.6   C2016-903860-2
C2016-904036-4

ISBN 978-1-5011-4287-1
ISBN 978-1-5011-4288-8 (ebook)

For Dwayne,
mon amour pour toujours

We are upon a great and noble Scheme of sending the neutral French out of this Province, who have always been secret Enemies, and have encouraged our Savages to cut our throats. If we effect their Expulsion, it will be one of the greatest Things that ever the English did in America; for by all accounts, that Part of the Country they possess is as good Land as any in the World: In case, therefore, we could get some good English Farmers in their Room, this Province would abound with all kinds of Provisions.

—News dispatch from Nova Scotia,
   printed in the *Pennsylvania Gazette*,
   September 4, 1755

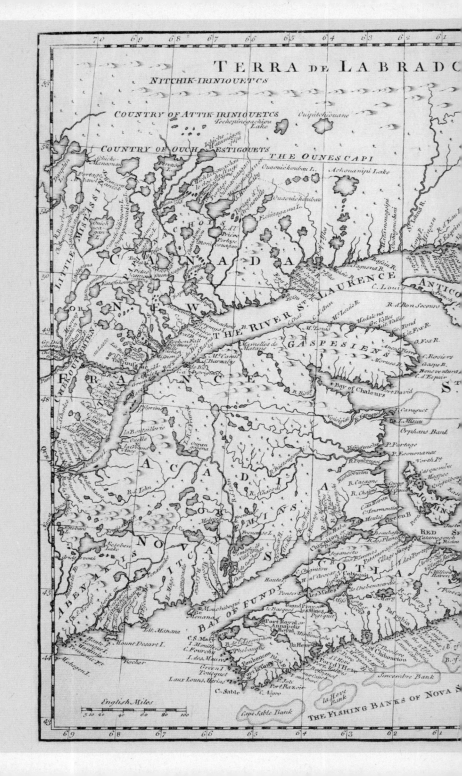

A New & Accurate Map of the
ISLANDS OF
NEWFOUNDLAND, CAPE BRETON,
St. JOHN and ANTICOSTA;
together with the Neighbouring
COUNTRIES OF
NOVA SCOTIA, CANADA &c.
Drawn from the most approved Modern
Maps and Charts,
and Regulated by Astrol. Observat.
By Eman. Bowen.

No 95.

Prologue
1733
Grand Pré, l'Acadie

Me'tekw knew he was dead. The instant his braid was yanked back and a filthy, shaking hand pressed a blade to his brow, he knew this life was over. The fire from a musket had already burned through his thigh, and blood streamed down his chest from a gash on his neck. One eye was swollen shut, and his lips throbbed. He tasted iron on his tongue. He could run no longer, could not slide his broken body out of the soldier's reach. He was dead.

There was barely time to make peace, to thank the Creator Kji-Niskam for giving him this life, to ask for greater wisdom for the next. Forcing his eyes open, Me'tekw stared into the calm, safe distance and prayed to Mother Earth, offering what strength he had left.

The tension on his neck released suddenly, and his cheek slammed onto the ground. His braid landed beside his face, and he noted with surprise that its long black length was still attached to his head. He breathed, inhaling the sun-warmed grass, though it stank of fresh blood. Overhead, the only break in the blue sky was a pair of silent gulls gliding in wide, curious circles.

He was not dead after all.

The British soldier who had hesitated lay lifeless nearby. His death cry had been cut short, the gurgle in his slit throat the only sound he'd emitted after hitting the ground. A second redcoat fell near the first, and Me'tekw rolled away in confusion. Sunlight blazed into his eyes when he glanced up, then Charles Belliveau stepped in front of the glare. The Acadian farmer clutched a knife, its bloodied point aimed toward the ground.

Me'tekw was still staring at Charles when two of his friends arrived and crouched beside him, assessing his wounds. They helped him to his feet, but his leg failed him. He collapsed amid blinding pain that made him long for death—though in truth, it was only a fleeting wish. His life was not his own and never had been. Everything he had and was belonged to the Creator. Evidently, Kji-Niskam had plans for him. If he had not, Me'tekw would be pumping the last of his life onto the ground beside the men Charles had slain.

He held up a hand, asking his friends to wait, needing to get his heartbeat under control. When he was ready to try again, he nodded, and the two Mi'kmaq slung his arms over their shoulders. They began to drag him away from the fallen soldiers, but he stopped once more and looked back at Charles.

Me'tekw was ashamed, not simply for his injuries but for his stupidity. He'd wanted nothing more than to go fishing from his favourite rock, but the warm caress of the sun had lulled him to sleep. He'd been an easy target for the enemy soldiers, who saw him as little more than a plaything to terrorize. They'd treated him as such many times before. He should have known better.

Me'tekw had been born eighteen years earlier without a voice. He had survived by expressing his thoughts and needs through face and hands, and neither his family nor his friends had ever treated him differently from anyone else. Certainly he regretted not being able to vocalize, but he understood: this was a trial given to him by the Creator. At this moment, however, he wished with all his heart he could speak to Charles, to thank the quiet Acadian for saving his life.

"I have known you many years, my friend," Charles said in Me'tekw's tongue. His voice was calm, though it laboured slightly from his exertions. "You have always had a thick head of hair. They were not welcome to it."

Me'tekw's throat tightened. Bracing himself against the pain, he took his arms off his friends' shoulders. He pressed his palms against his own chest then held them up to Charles, offering all he had.

Charles's expression did not change. "I ask nothing of you."

Me'tekw had known him since childhood. This was not the first time the quiet farmer had come to his aid. Once again, Charles had put himself in the way of harm, and today he had saved Me'tekw's life. Charles Belliveau was a better man than he.

As Charles walked away, Me'tekw closed his swollen eyelids and made a promise to himself before all the spirit world. Whatever it took, he would watch over this man and his family for the rest of his life.

PART ONE

The Expulsion

Amélie

ONE

June 1755

The hummingbirds would return soon, tiny warriors marking the true beginning of summer in their frantic, efficient manner, and I smiled every time I saw them. For now I had to be satisfied with the robins, poking their little beaks into the dirt, retrieving what goodness they could find.

How simple for them, I thought, hoisting my second bucket of water. They pulled their food from the earth and drank their fill from the dew, and they had no chores at all. Early summer—*nipk* to the Mi'kmaq, when Nipniku's brought the summer moon— meant the morning mud beneath our clogs would be cold, the stinging flies relentless. At the end of the day we would fall back into bed, exhausted and itchy.

Ah, but the little birds did not have what I had either, I mused. They could not come inside and warm their feathers by a welcoming fire when the rain raged or the wind banged the shutters of our house. They could not keep their tiny feet warm in fine woollen socks or wooden clogs like mine. They could not even enjoy the notion of how fortunate we were to live in this wonderful place with a loving family and so many friends.

I heard Maman singing, then Giselle joined in with her high, happy voice. My little sister was fourteen, but she often seemed younger than that to me. Setting a bucket on the threshold, I opened the door and walked inside, then poured the water into the large pot hanging over the stove. No one had been tending the fire, and I glanced at the others, but they seemed not to sense my annoyance. I thought about mentioning their laziness, but their laughter dissuaded me. There was no sense in dampening their good mood. I knelt and coaxed a flame from the pulsing orange logs.

"Oh! Thank you, Amélie," Maman said. "I don't know where my head is this morning."

"I do!" Giselle said.

Maman shook her head, but she was smiling. "You are a little tease."

Shame washed through me, and I turned so they wouldn't see my embarrassment. How could I have forgotten?

"You were distracted," I said. "Thinking about Claire and Guillaume."

"Aren't you?" Giselle asked. "The wedding will be wonderful! Then Claire will have her own home and her own children, and I will be an aunt! Oh, if only we didn't have to wait until September! But I suppose it is all right. After the harvest we can enjoy it even more. What about you, Amélie? You are seventeen already. When will you choose a husband?"

I abhorred that question, and they loved to ask it. It wasn't that I didn't want to marry. I simply had not met anyone with whom I could imagine spending the rest of my life. When I thought about the hours in a day, then those in a night, I knew my husband would have to be more than just strong and hard-working. He would have to be someone with whom I could talk about anything, and no one in our village had yet reached my standards.

"Hush, Giselle. Don't ask me that."

Maman pursed her lips. "You know, Pierre Melanson—"

"I will not talk about this right now."

"But, Amélie!" Giselle wailed. "There must be someone—"

"Stop! I said I won't talk about it." I yanked the door open. "I suppose I'll get the milk too, since everyone but me seems too busy to do anything today."

The sweet, ripe smells of the barn welcomed me inside, and I breathed in deeply, feeling instantly soothed.

"Good morning, Amélie," Papa and André said, glancing up from their work.

The men in my family have never pressured me to find a husband. Marriage was important, I knew, but they seemed to understand that nagging would do no good.

"Good morning. Maman will have breakfast ready soon."

"Merci, mon ange," Papa said, scraping his rake across the stall floor.

"He told them they need their canoes back for fishing," André said.

I realized I had accidentally interrupted their conversation, and I perked up, listening for clues to the topic. Anything would be more interesting than discussing marriage.

"And said they are losing cattle and oxen to the predators in the woods."

Papa nodded sombrely. "This is true. Now that the Mi'kmaq have moved away and no longer hunt—"

"They moved away?" I cried. Surely Mali wouldn't have gone without speaking to me or saying goodbye!

"Not far, but far enough. Don't worry. Mali will be fine. Go on," he said to André. "What else? The petition? What did he hear about that?" He gestured with his chin. "And work while you talk."

That reminded me I had a job to do as well. I dragged a stool to the cow and leaned my shoulder against her warm, bristled side, letting her know I was there. My fingers closed around her and tugged in a familiar rhythm.

At the other end of the barn André began filling the wheelbarrow, clouding the air with dust. "Governor Lawrence would allow no one to read the petition, Papa. Instead he ordered everyone assembled—all one hundred men—to swear an oath of allegiance to the British Crown, promising to take up arms against the King of France."

Papa and I both stopped what we were doing, incredulous.

"Take up arms?" Papa puffed out a breath.

"But we cannot side with the English in any kind of war," I reasoned. "They can't make us do that, can they?"

What would the Mi'kmaq do if the Acadians were forced to side with the British? Would they have to fight against us? It hurt to imagine it.

"Keep working, Amélie." Papa nodded toward the cow. "She'll get impatient." He turned back to André. "Tell me, what happened when the men heard the order?"

André could only shrug. "Of course everyone said no. They said such an oath would rob us of our religion and everything else we believe in. So Governor Lawrence arrested them all and sent them to a prison near Halifax!"

Papa groaned. "This Lawrence. I've heard terrible things about him, threatening people with his sword, frightening them for fun. A tyrant! Does your friend know what they plan next?"

"No. He ran when he thought the soldiers had discovered him there." He sighed. "There is more to the story, I am afraid."

The oldest of my three brothers was an intense man. Even as a child he had been particular and precise in everything he did. His expression was often difficult to interpret, since he deliberately hid his feelings. This morning he was surprisingly easy to read.

"Governor Lawrence took away the priests," he said, his voice so choked with fury that I feared he might break down. "He then made the church into his command post—"

"What?" I blurted.

"And he himself has moved into the priest's house. Tents have been picketed all around the area for the soldiers. The English flag now flies over our church, Papa, and they are tossing out sacred items as if they are nothing more than a nuisance." He flung his shovel aside. "To make matters even worse, more soldiers have come."

I couldn't speak. What did this mean? What could have prompted the British to behave so? The act of seizing our church was an insult to all of us. We were not a warring people; if they declared war on us, what would we do?

By the time I had been born in 1738, the British and the French had battled over this land many times, but my people had not been part of the fight. We had always called our home l'Acadie, but when the British had finally defeated the French for good, they named it Nova Scotia. It had never mattered to me which country believed they were in charge, because we Acadians lived independently of them all. I was not a Nova Scotian; I was an Acadian. Politics had never touched my life before now.

I set the full bucket outside the barn, then gazed across the land toward our church. The shapes of men moved among the straight white rows of tents where they slept. Certainly I had seen them before, but they had not seemed so menacing until today.

TWO

We were not expecting a knock on the door. Usually approaching voices could be heard before anyone requested entry, but these footfalls had been quiet. The sound startled us, and we stopped what we were doing, glancing up to gauge each others' reactions.

Whoever our visitors were, they were fortunate to find us in the house. It was growing late in the afternoon, and Papa, my youngest sibling Mathieu, and I had only just come in from the fields. Papa had wanted a bite to eat and had just lit his pipe, filling the house with its sweet smoke. Mathieu had carried in another bucket of water for the soup, and Maman and I sat by the window, letting the sun spill light onto our mending.

A knock came again, and Mathieu peeked through the window. "Deux soldats anglais," he whispered.

Why would English soldiers come to our house? They never had before. I tried without success to read my parents' expressions, but it didn't matter. I knew they were concerned.

Nevertheless, Papa wore a cordial smile as he lifted the latch and swung open the door. "Good afternoon, messieurs."

Two red-coated men stood before him. The first was tall and evidently in charge, for the shorter man stood silently behind.

The officer spoke hesitant French, but while he had trouble with our language, he seemed not the least bit confused about his orders. His Majesty, he informed us, had decreed that our people were to hand over our weapons. He said they would be kept safe but that the army needed to hold them, to make sure we Acadians kept our promise and did not take up arms against the British.

"Our weapons?" Papa asked. "I do not understand what you say."

I interpreted the foul order, and he blinked with surprise.

"I do not intend to fight anyone," he objected, as the officer pushed inside.

Papa's two rifles were in plain view, leaning against the wall next to the stove. They were all we had for defending ourselves—besides kitchen knives and fists. Like every other home in Grand Pré, our house was small. We had no place in which to hide our things even if we had considered doing so beforehand. The arrogance I saw in this man's eyes made me wish we had.

"Those are for protecting our farms from beasts of the forest."

The softness in Papa's voice was meant to soothe, but the officer appeared not to be listening.

"It does not matter," he replied in his broken French. "We take them. Move."

After the slightest hesitation, Papa stepped back and gave Maman a subtle nod. Her gaze dropped to the floor and her fingers locked around each other as if to contain her nerves. Beside her, Mathieu took a breath to speak, but Papa's tight look held him back.

As the officer stalked toward the stove, the second man entered our house. He already carried Papa's axe. He must have picked it up outside, by the woodpile.

"Will we have our axe back on colder nights?" Mathieu demanded, putting words to my concern.

Both soldiers stopped and everyone stared at my bold thirteen-year-old brother, including me. But how could he have kept his mouth closed? It was the truth. How would we survive without it?

The officer scowled at Mathieu. "The king will decide."

This was an insult of the worst kind. Maman instinctively grabbed for my arm, but I moved out of her reach and toward the second soldier, the one holding Papa's axe. He had said nothing, suggesting to me he was the easier mark.

"Surely the gracious king wouldn't ask us to live a winter without a fire!" I cried in English.

It was the officer, the one with the sharp eyes, who answered. "His Majesty will take care of all his subjects. It is not your place to question him."

His smug reply was like a slap. Determined not to react, I stepped closer to the quiet soldier. "Trust must be earned," I replied. "What about you? Do you trust the king to take care of us?"

Before he could respond, the officer blustered past, knocking him sideways. "This is all?" he demanded of Papa. "Two old hunting rifles and one axe?"

Papa's anger was quickly veiled by an expression of confusion. He opened his palms and shrugged. "Oui, c'est tout. I am farmer, not soldier."

Evidently disapproving, the officer grunted and started toward the door. "MacDonnell!" he snapped.

"Yes, sir," the other soldier replied, but before leaving he made a quick bow to Papa. "My apologies for the interruption," he said in a cultured French accent. Then he left, closing the door softly behind him.

No one spoke.

"This is not good," Maman eventually muttered.

"They will surely bring back the axe," I said.

Mathieu regarded me closely. "What did you say to them?"

"Only that I could not believe the king would allow us to live without it."

"And they said what?"

"That I had no right to question the king."

"You must be careful, Amélie," Maman warned. "They do not hear a question, they see a beautiful young woman, and one who dares challenge them. You are not as safe as you once were."

"Especially now that they have stolen all our weapons!" Mathieu added. "Papa, can they do that?"

Our father had not grown up as we had. When he was only five, a group of Mi'kmaq hunters had discovered his father, drowned in the Gaspereau. His mother had died the year before, giving birth to his stillborn sister, leaving him an orphan. The Mi'kmaq had welcomed little Charles to their village and raised him as one of their own. He came to know their language as well as he knew French, if not better, and he learned the secrets of the forest. He lived and trained with the other youths, hunted with them, ate with them. I had been told that in a dark forest, he could be mistaken for one of them—as long as he covered his bright gold hair.

I loved to imagine him as the young blond warrior he had once been, strong, courageous, living wild. I imagined he sometimes longed to return to that life, if only for a little while. Now would be one of those times.

He answered my brother through a clenched jaw. "Apparently so."

I needed air. Slipping my apron over my head, I hung it on the hook, then tied my bonnet tighter as I stepped outside. The wind reached for it, but I foiled her attempts. The best she could do was whip at my skirt, but I pressed my palms flat against the material as I stormed barefoot up the slope behind our home. When

I reached the peak, I hugged my arms across my chest, looking down over the fields and watching a stand of scraggly spruce bow and dance with the wind. The crops swayed as well, though their rich ocean of green buds was shallow, still swelling in adolescence.

I came to this place when I needed to be refreshed, to escape my family's expectations, to clear my thoughts. In my life I'd never gone beyond the limits of Grand Pré, but from here I could see past the golden rises of the dikes and let my daydreams ride the Atlantic. The prettiest sight of all was at the end of the day, when the fishermen's white-sailed boats returned home, riding the spill of sunset on the water. They had been joined recently by a number of much larger, unfamiliar ships, and we all wondered at their business. Until this morning, I had enjoyed the anticipation of one day finding out why they were there. Now I knew from my brother that they brought only more soldiers. I was no longer happy to see them.

A patch of darkness skimmed over the fields as a lone cloud passed overhead, and I looked up. Claire always said cloud shadows warned of darkness yet to come, but I chose to ignore her superstitious words. I liked the clouds.

Another gust of salty air washed over me, tacky on my lips, and I closed my eyes. My favourite afternoons came before a storm, when I stood in the wind and watched rolls of hungry clouds swallow the sun. When the sudden darkness folded around us—a last-minute warning to bring in drying laundry and gather children—its power made me shiver with anticipation. Even more wondrous was when lightning cut through the sky, diving down to split the water. Those storms were rare, making them a gift in my eyes. When hurricanes blew in autumn, I stayed out of doors as long as I could, welcoming the impending madness.

Today I felt no rain on the wind but a tension in the air, as if the clouds waited with me to see what might happen next.

A small child cried out, and I searched out the Labiches' home. I knew the sound of little Jacqueline, and when I squinted I saw her stamping tiny feet in the grass. Angelique and Suzanne stood with her, their mother behind. Monsieur Labiche was in their doorway, staring down the same two soldiers who had just left our home. Another man I hadn't spotted before sat beyond on a wagon bench, holding his horse's reins and watching over a load of seized weapons. Monsieur Labiche was a big man with a temper, and I wondered at the fortitude of the soldiers, since I probably would have turned and run if faced with his wrath. Then again, I imagined they had faced worse.

Curiosity led me down the hill toward the little group. I already knew the soldiers' mission; Monsieur Labiche would eventually be forced to surrender his weapons. About halfway down the slope I stopped and listened, wanting to hear how they would persuade him, but all that came to me was the officer's terrible nasal attempts at French. His tone was disrespectful, making me angry all over again, but I would not interfere. I paused twenty feet away, and the other soldier—MacDonnell, I recalled—looked my way.

I have seen a rabbit freeze in place, trying not to be seen though it was in plain view. That was my instinct as well. But like the rabbit, I had stopped too late. MacDonnell glanced from me to his commanding officer, assessing the situation, then stepped toward me. At the wagon, he removed his coat and set it on top, partially covering Papa's rifles and our axe. His white shirt was stained with exhaustion, and I wondered who was tending these men—doing their wash, cooking their meals. They were only human after all.

I saw no hostility on MacDonnell's face; his expression was one of curiosity. Even so, I shifted my feet, on guard. He must have seen my inadvertent movement, for his mouth curved in response, adding an unexpected gentleness to his expression. When he was about six feet away, I stepped back.

He stopped and held out empty hands. "You've nothing to fear."

I lifted my chin in denial, strangely pleased that he'd chosen to speak French. Still, regardless of the language, he and I were strangers, and I did not mean for him to pretend otherwise.

"That's not what we've been told."

His mouth twisted slightly. He found this funny? "No, I suppose not," he said. "The British army does not make friends easily, does it? What I mean is that you, yourself, have nothing to fear from me."

I crossed my arms. "No? Why not?"

"I will not hurt you."

It was a bold statement. I decided the test was not over. "Will you give me back my family's weapons?"

"I cannot. You know that."

"At least our axe?" Any pretense of bravado faded from my voice.

"I cannot. I am sorry."

"Then you lie," I said, turning away. "Without that axe you not only hurt me and my family, you kill us." I climbed back up the slope, my head held high. I didn't want him to see defeat in the set of my shoulders.

But he seemed disinclined to end our conversation. His feet shushed through the grass behind me. "Wait! Mademoiselle, wait!"

I paused but did not turn around. "Is that an order?"

"Please, mademoiselle, I am sorry. Truly I am. But if we gave back your axe, we would have to return them all, and the whole point is to ensure your people will not carry weapons which could be used against us. I do know you will need firewood. We all know that." He hesitated, then his voice lowered. "I will do what I can to help you and your family when that time comes."

I nodded but continued up the hill, feeling his eyes on me the whole way.

THREE

Papa was waiting for me on the other side. He was turned toward the west, his face glowing orange under the beginnings of a sunset, and my step faltered, seeing him there. As much as I welcomed spending time with him, not having to share him, I had thought I was alone.

"Papa," I said. "What are you doing here?"

He turned his head to smile at me. "I came to find you."

Of course he knew where I would go, needing to escape. "I was so angry . . ."

"As was I."

"You didn't look angry, Papa."

He nodded, facing the sun once again. The oranges were fading to pink, washing into purples as they sank slowly into the sea. The wind had died down and the night was calm, marred only by the occasional whine of a mosquito. The dulled surface of the sea was still, and my father's quiet strength settled over me like a warm blanket.

"No, ma chérie. I did not look angry. Come. Walk with me."

The day's heat had risen toward the darkening sky, but the dusk was not yet too cool for a stroll. From their soggy homes in the marshes, frogs sang lullabies to the birds and other creatures of the sunshine as they bedded down, and a bat swept silently across our path, enjoying a winged feast. A wolf cried in the distance, but his call went unanswered.

Papa lifted his hat so he might scratch his head, then set it back down. He walked to the edge of the hill, just before it descended to the crops, and I followed his gaze beyond the dikes, beyond the water, to the red cliffs of Cap Batiste where Glooscap lived.

"Sometimes, my dear Amélie," he said, "it is better to hide your anger."

I thought of my brief conversation with MacDonnell. "I'm not good at that."

He chuckled, and the warmth of the sound rippled across the sunset. "No, you are not good at that." His smile faded. "But I think maybe it's time you learned."

"Claire says I am impulsive."

"You are. Like running out here tonight and speaking with the soldier just now. That was foolhardy. He could have been dangerous."

I said nothing, only flushed with shame.

"You are a fortunate young lady. You have spent your whole life with a family who loves you very much. You have been sheltered from the ignorance and violence of men, and you are naive." He gnawed on his lower lip. "I am to blame for that, so it is up to me to set things right."

"I don't understand, Papa."

"Maybe not, but I shall tell you why. You know, my daughter, that a long time ago I was a different person."

I nodded. Of course I knew that.

"My Mi'kmaq family loved me as we love you; however, we lived differently. And when I was one of them, I was treated as one of them by outsiders." He hesitated. "I have done things of which I am not proud—"

"You are a good man, Papa!"

"Yes, yes. I am a good man. I know myself to be honest and moral and a man of God. But even good men may be called to do bad things, and I . . . well, I was called."

I had never heard him speak this way. He rarely spoke of his days in the Mi'kmaq village, though he occasionally shared his favourite memories. This was something else.

"What did you do?"

He folded his arms across his chest and inhaled slowly. "I will get to that in a moment."

My father had lived as an Acadian for twenty years, but I still saw the Mi'kmaq in him, in the way he carried himself. Though he was a few years past forty, he was a strong and handsome man. Most of the other men his age were losing hair and gaining pounds, but not my papa. Maman too appeared younger than she was. She was fine boned and looked fragile compared to many other women, but she could keep up with any of them, I knew.

"I believe the tides are changing again," he said, "like they did years ago. Maybe it will be even worse this time. No one will speak openly about the growing anger in the air, but when they took our rifles and axes today, the British rendered us helpless. André tells me more soldiers have come. They are fortifying their ranks. There is still war between them and the French, but I had hoped we would be allowed to avoid it. I no longer believe we can."

War? What was he talking about?

"You must step lightly," he warned. "I do not want you to say what is on the tip of your tongue or to act impulsively. You need to be prepared to suffer the consequences if you make a wrong decision. And yet, should the time come, I want you to believe in yourself." He took my chin in his hand. "You are special, Amélie. Since you were small, I have known you were strong. God has plans for you, I am sure. Promise me, Amélie. Promise me you will be smart, and you will take care of yourself, whatever happens."

My throat swelled, but I would not cry. I did not want him to know his words frightened me.

"You have never had to ask yourself if what you're doing is right or wrong, but I fear the time is coming when that will be unavoidable. I need you to understand that sometimes doing what is right is not the same thing as doing what is good."

His meaning was unclear. "I know when it is Giselle's turn to do something," I tried, "and she forgets to do it, what is right is that I should tell her to do it since it is her responsibility, but I often decide it is easier and nicer of me if I simply do it myself. But that is not what you're talking about, is it?"

He shook his head. "It is a question of using your judgment, yes? And you are a kind, hard-working young woman. By the way, I want you to tell Giselle it is not your job to collect the eggs for her. She is small for her age, and she is using that to her advantage."

"Yes, Papa."

A softer look came into his eyes. "I need you to know, dear Amélie, that I once killed two men." After his confession the air seemed to still around us, the crickets and tiny frogs hushing. I could hardly breathe. Even more shocking than his news was the smile which came to his lips. "And I do not regret it."

I did not know how to answer. He seemed suddenly to be a different person.

"I can see what you are thinking, Amélie, and that is something you must learn to hide. Emotions can betray you. They can get you into trouble. But I will explain so perhaps you will not judge me too harshly." He sighed. "Yes, over twenty years ago I killed two men. They were going to kill a friend of mine who could not defend himself, and when I heard the noise, I rushed to see what was happening. I had only a few steps in which to decide what to do, so I followed my heart. I did not make a conscious decision. When I saw my friend and I saw the wickedness of those men, God forgave me the sins I was about to commit; I felt His hand on my knife."

Never in my life could I have imagined hearing these words. My father was a gentle, kind soul, not a killer. "What . . . what happened afterward?"

"My friend survived and escaped back to his village. I have not seen him in many years. I came home to your mother, and I learned to build a wall around my thoughts, for if they were known, there would be grave consequences. My family needed me, and though I am not ashamed of what I did, I have not told many people. The men I killed were soldiers. If my actions were to be discovered, I would be punished to the full extent of the law. This is what I need you to understand about judgment. If I had felt what I did was wrong I would have turned myself in, but to this day I know I did the right thing."

"Does Maman know?"

He nodded. "And André."

"Why are you telling me, Papa?"

"Because war is all around us. It is closing in." His words grew urgent. "If our world is turned upside down and we are forced to fight, I want you to be able to tell the difference between what is right and what is good. I want you to trust your instincts."

"Of course, Papa," I whispered, afraid to disappoint.

"If you trust your heart, Amélie, you will always do what is right."

I had no idea what he was saying. I could only hope it was true.

FOUR

August had always been my favourite month. The Mi'kmaq called it Kisikwekewiku's, named after the Fruit- and Berry-Ripening Moon. In addition to the seasonal beauty, the air was bereft of most stinging insects, and the simple act of lying on the grass under the caress of the summer sun felt so good it was almost sinful. As mornings began to cool, we were welcomed by fog so thick we could barely see the neighbours' homes. It eventually burned off, and the days came alive with sudden storms and waves of heat, flooding the red soil and feeding the thick green crops. The harvest of corn was already safely stowed for the winter, and the rest of the gardens exploded with colour, awaiting our busy hands. While we worked, we sang the songs of our ancestors, and when the nights descended, we danced around open fires.

Today, as I had many times before, I would bring some of our crops to the British. Lately we had done it under orders, not simply for generosity's sake. The soldiers I had once visited as friends were wary of me now, almost suspicious. I was uneasy about being in the midst of them, but not enough that I asked my brothers to come with me.

After I'd finished the day's chores, I went to the gardens and dropped some of the late-summer bounty into my basket. The rows were thick with growth, and when I yanked out a weed, a couple of juicy earthworms came with the roots. I carried the wriggling creatures toward the chickens, earnestly pecking and scratching at the side of the yard. At sight of me, the flock raced over, wings spread, their feathery little haunches pumping so hard they lifted off the ground. When all twenty or so had grouped at my feet, their necks stretched optimistically, I was sorry I didn't have more to offer. I pinched the two worms into as many pieces as I could, then held them out for eager beaks.

"I'm sorry," I said, rubbing my hands together to loosen the dirt. "That's all I have."

They weren't satisfied, but unless I spent the rest of my day weeding—which I did not intend to do—those were the only worms I'd be bringing today. The chickens jostled for position, squawking, but I held out empty hands.

"See? Nothing."

A few of the hens followed me back toward the garden, eventually giving up when a bug or bit of grain caught their attention.

When I was on my own again, I headed toward the tents. A gust of warm, salty wind sent wisps of my dark hair flying, tangling outside my bonnet. I tucked in the ends and waded the familiar path through the tall grass, swinging the basket of beans and peas at my side. The wind brought me a whiff of the fresh loaf of bread I'd packed as well, in case I needed something sweet to facilitate my visit, and the smile I wore out of habit grew wider. After two weeks of merciless rain, this was a day made for happiness. I would not let my concerns dampen my spirits.

I could have taken the direct route to the church, but today I chose one which wound under apple trees and over knee-high rocks and grass. This path saw less traffic, meaning there was less chance of my running into anyone along the way. I had no need to walk past the cruelly misappropriated church and its meadow of tents, its arrogant wooden fence. Nor did I feel the urge, as I had in times past, to slow my step and gaze up at the familiar stained-glass windows. As beautiful as they were, I could visit them anytime I chose. Today I wished to ease my feelings of frustration by enjoying the glorious day blazing around me.

A hummingbird darted past, its wings loud as a hive of bees, its ruby throat shining like a jewel in the sun. I paused to watch the tiny green creature hover at a flower, then dart off to the next source of food. Like the bird, I was drawn toward a stand of raspberry bushes, branches bowed under the weight of their fruit, and I decided to add some to my basket.

As I neared the thicket I noticed a man seated on the grass beneath an apple tree, his red coat neatly folded beside him. I checked but saw no other soldiers, so I began picking berries, taking care not to disturb his peace. Then he leaned back and tilted his face toward the sun, and I almost dropped the fruit in my hand.

Curiosity has always been my downfall. Despite my stubborn insistence to myself that I had only come to bring food to the soldiers, the truth was I had hoped to catch another glimpse of Corporal MacDonnell. We had begun a conversation of sorts, and I was interested to see how that might continue. Nevertheless, seeing him here sent a flurry of nerves through me, and I doubted my next step. Both Maman and Papa had warned me against speaking with these men, and I did understand their concerns. In the end, however, my curiosity won, as it always did.

I took a breath then stepped out from behind the bushes. "Good afternoon," I said in English. I refrained from laughing at his surprise when he leapt to his feet, hat in hand.

"Forgive me, Mademoiselle Belliveau!" he said. "I didn't hear you approach."

His embarrassment bolstered me. "Why should you apologize? You have done nothing wrong, have you?"

"Not today," he admitted. He spoke differently from the other soldiers, with a thick, curling accent that was sometimes difficult to understand. I liked the sound of it.

"I have intruded on your peace."

"I can think of no one else with whom I would rather share it." He gestured toward the ground where he'd been sitting. "Join me?"

I was unsure how to react. He was a stranger, yet he behaved as if we had known each other a long time. I dared myself to be as courageous as he.

"I brought a picnic," I told him, settling onto the grass.

He waited until I was comfortable, then sat beside me and leaned toward my basket. The movement startled me, and I drew away, tipping the basket accidentally. He caught the handle and rolled it back toward me.

"Are you hungry?" I asked. "Please help yourself."

"Mademoiselle, I am in the army. It is understood that I am hungry."

He grinned and plucked a handful of pea pods from the basket, his fingers accidentally brushing against mine as he did so. Heat rushed to my cheeks at the contact, and I hoped he had not noticed. To hide my embarrassment, I bit into a pea pod and tried to chew quietly. He had no such concerns. He dropped three into his mouth and crunched, giving me time to collect my thoughts.

"Thank you," he said. "These are delicious."

I could not hold his gaze and focused on the basket instead. "It's been a good year in the fields and gardens. God willing, next year will be as good."

"God willing," he echoed. He motioned toward the basket. "May I have a few more?"

I spread my skirt on the grass between us and poured some pods on top, wanting to avoid his touching my hand again. We did not speak for a moment, and I scrambled to continue the conversation.

"The peas are sweet, are they not?"

"Delicious."

We supped in silence on as many of the greens as we could, then I brought out the bread. He used his knife to cut off little sections, doling them out between us.

"You speak English very well, if you don't mind my saying so."

The question—for it seemed a question to me—took me slightly off guard. "Thank you. I learned from the British soldiers. We have not always been at war with the English." I smiled shyly. "You speak excellent French."

"Merci, Mademoiselle Belliveau," he said, tilting his head in a Gallic bow. "My mother was French, and she'd be pleased to hear you say as much. She believed it important I learn her language as well as my father's. She was my teacher."

"Your mother is French?"

I was sorry to see his smile fade. "She was. She and my father are no longer with us." He hesitated. "They were killed, ironically, by the English."

"What? But . . ."

"It's odd, isn't it? How I ended up here, I mean."

"I don't understand."

"I am not English," he said bluntly.

"You look English enough in your coat."

He studied the red wool on the grass beside him. "Aye. I know. I am a soldier in the British army, but I am not English." He took a deep breath and let it out slowly. "My home is Scotland, but Scotland was taken by the English."

I began to understand. "I'm sorry."

"So am I." Nevertheless, he shrugged. "War between England and Scotland has been going on a long while. Ten years ago Scotland finally lost, and many of us were either killed or sent here, labelled as criminals."

"But I do not understand. You were sent here as a criminal? Ten years ago you would only have been a child."

"Aye. I was ten. They'd already killed my parents." He didn't bother to disguise the bitterness in his voice. "My crime was that I did not agree with the English."

I did not press him further; to do so seemed cruel. Nevertheless, my thoughts dwelt on what he had just said. How terrifying that must have been. In silence we watched a small white butterfly land briefly on a bloom then take to the air again. How fortunate for the little fellow, never to have to contemplate such wickedness.

"I am so sorry, Corporal MacDonnell. I cannot even imagine what you have lived through. Let us speak of happier things. The day is too beautiful to darken it with sad tales."

"I agree. We have had much rain of late, and these precious hours of sun must be allowed to shine without clouds of any kind."

"We do get a lot of rain here," I admitted. "But I do not mind. I enjoy the storms and the wind."

"As do I."

He slapped at the back of his neck, then showed me a large horsefly, flattened in his palm.

I dutifully admired his kill. "Lucky for you. Those creatures are mean."

"They are indeed." He flicked the insect into the tall grasses with one finger and peered toward my basket. "Pardon me, mademoiselle, but is the bread gone?"

"You ate the last piece and all the peas as well. Perhaps I will bring more another day."

One corner of his mouth curled, and he inclined his head. "I should like that very much. Even if it were raining, you would bring out the sun for me."

"You are a romantic, sir," I replied quickly, biting my lip against a traitorous smile, "but despite today, we are still strangers, and your army is my enemy."

"You are right, of course. Would that we were in a different place at a different time. I would welcome the opportunity to show you how romantic I can be."

I squirmed inwardly, uncomfortable with what I suspected to be an overly familiar suggestion. I did not know how the British were used to speaking with women, but his gentle teasing seemed inappropriate. At the same time, it had not escaped my notice that he was a very handsome man. The glint in his eyes only made him more so.

I changed the topic. "Do you have brothers or sisters?"

"There is only me. I was always envious of large families like yours."

"Mine is a blessing, although the house can get crowded at times."

"Still, you always have good company. I imagine you are quite protective of each other."

"Oh yes. I would do anything to be sure my family is safe and happy."

"Of course you would."

He sounded so melancholy I rushed to change the direction. "Do you wish you could go back to Scotland? Is it safer there now?"

A smile flitted across his face. "No. I doubt I will ever return to Scotland. It isn't the same country it was before. The English have made sure of that." He hesitated, and when he spoke again, his voice was sombre. "I must be honest, mademoiselle. I do not believe your land will be the same when they are done either."

"You are wrong about that. This is our land, not theirs."

"I understand that, but the army does not."

"They will see, certainly."

He sighed. "Your people need to understand that the English are not to be underestimated. They are determined and ruthless, and they mean to win this war."

"I'm not afraid," I replied.

"No," he said. "I can see that. But I am suggesting that perhaps you should be."

I stared at him. "I do hope that is not a threat."

"Not from me, of course. I am concerned, however, that the Acadians do not know the extent of the threat offered by the British army."

"We will be fine. We have been fine for a long time."

He shifted slightly on the grass and folded his arms around his knees, taking his time. In that moment, a blackbird dropped onto a branch and snatched up the little white butterfly. Perhaps the creature had never known wickedness, I mused, but in the end it had not escaped it.

"That does not mean it will always be that way," he said quietly. "My life was good when I was a child. I had a good home. I ate well, I had friends, I was loved. Then everything changed. I had not expected any of it. And I can tell you, mademoiselle, that since then, nothing has been fine. Nothing."

I lowered my chin, and my fingers skimmed the tips of the grass blades. "I am sorry for you."

"There is no need for that," he said. "I am alive, and I am fed."

"I should have brought more bread."

"What you brought was generous. Thank you."

His simple acceptance of an unhappy life saddened me. "What do you miss the most? If you could have one thing—and only one thing—back, what would it be?"

The suggestion of a smile returned to his lips as he thought that over. I expected, considering that he now lived in the rough confines of a tent, he would mention comfort. A house, a bed, perhaps his family.

"My friends," he said finally. "I have little in common with the English in my camp, and I do miss laughter. Conversation. I am enjoying this afternoon a great deal."

He did not say it to flatter me. His loneliness was genuine, as was his appreciation for my simple act of sitting there and speaking with him.

"As am I."

I was no longer uncomfortable with his friendly gaze. Speaking with him was both confusing and welcome. I looked forward to the next time.

"I must be leaving," I said, rising and brushing grass from my skirt. "My family will be expecting me. I would not want them to worry."

He stood as well, then leaned down to retrieve the basket for me. He was taller than I remembered.

"Thank you for this afternoon," he said. "For the food and the company."

"It was my pleasure."

I no longer had any offerings for the soldiers by the church, so I started toward home again. After a few steps I stopped and looked back. To my surprise, he was still watching me. I needed to say something.

"Corporal, I . . . I want to say again that I am sorry that you long for friends. If you and I were not presently on opposite sides of this conflict, I would be quite happy to be your friend."

He bowed slightly. "And I would be honoured to call you my friend. Good day, Mademoiselle Belliveau. I wish you a pleasant evening."

FIVE

I roll onto my side, expecting to see the sleeping profile of my little sister. She is not there. I rise to look for Claire, who I expect is already awake and stepping into her skirt. She isn't there either.

In the next instant I am in our garden, breathing in morning fog as it seeps between lush rows of lettuce and beets, soaring vines of peas and beans. I pluck a twig of lavender from the small herb garden next to the door. I am asleep, yet I know how the lavender smells, how it will reach like caring fingers into my senses and soothe any worries which might have festered within me.

I have had this dream before, I think.

Beyond the budding fields stretch the salt marshes and the long walls of dikes, holding back the sea. Livestock dots the green, scattering in mindless ebbs and flows at the command of a gleeful dog. Over a hundred houses and a hundred barns stand around me, each with an identical garden, each sharing my glorious view. Pale smoke rises in soft white plumes from every stone chimney. I know every brother, sister, mother, and father within those walls. We have worked side by side for generations, cultivating this paradise. Together we have played and cried, laughed and died. We are a family.

But in this dream I see no one. I stand alone. The voices are silent; the helping hands are nowhere to be seen.

Perhaps I have not had this dream after all.

I gaze past our world toward the sea, shading my eyes against the brilliant blue. As a child I waded in the warm waters and reeds of the Gaspereau, squeezing delicious red mud through my toes, sinking with pleasure as the ripples touched my arms, then my waist. Sometimes I dropped my head beneath the surface, losing myself in the push and pull of the currents. It was bliss. It was escape. It was lovely.

But the dream shows me a different sea, one in which I no longer see freedom. It rolls in a frothing black anger, its fury far more powerful than our dikes. I watch helplessly as the water crashes over the fields and climbs higher, flooding the gardens, claiming our homes.

When all else is gone, the sea comes for me. I cannot outrun it, but I cannot stop running. It seems right that Corporal Mac-Donnell stands just ahead, a vivid image in red, calling to me. He holds out his hand, but I cannot reach it. The water licks at me, drags at my skirt, sucks me into a whirling, crushing eddy. I flail and scream, though there is no sound but the water. I cannot fight, I cannot breathe—

I awakened with a gasp, though it was a moment before I realized where I was. Part of me still felt as if I were anchored beneath the sea. To my relief, Giselle lay beside me as she should, her soft pink lips open slightly in sleep. Claire had already tied on her apron, pulled her long blond hair into a tail, and was tucking it under her cap.

"Come on, lazybones," she scolded. "We have a full day ahead of us."

My heartbeat slowed as I adjusted to being awake, and I reminded myself it had only been a bad dream. I was not alone after all; this day of hard work would be shared by everyone. We would plant, we would fish, we would mend the dikes, and we would do it all together. We would be tired, but we would be happy.

I nudged Giselle awake. "Come on, lazybones," I echoed Claire.

She groaned but dressed quickly beside me, and soon she had settled into her usual incessant chatter. When our bed was made, we followed Claire down the narrow stairway and into the main part of the house where the pine walls shone golden, lit by the sun streaming through the window. Maman stood at the end of the room by the clay bread oven Papa had built for her a year before, setting the morning's loaves within. As she always did, Claire went to the closet and fetched the broom. Two empty buckets waited for me by the door, so I swung them down. From the noise outside the door, I knew I would find Papa there.

He didn't hear me; both his concentration and strength were focused on his work. It was still early, but already he sweated through his shirt, and his hair was slick against his brow. I never tired of admiring his skill at crafting masts for ships. Whistling to himself, he leaned against the long, tapered trunk of the white pine he and the other men had laid out beside our barn, and the muscles of his arms flexed within his rolled-up sleeves.

Over the past few days he'd completed the most difficult parts using his hammer and froe to slice off the bark and shape the length of the pine into four sides, hacking away the general roughness with the pendulous swing of his adze. He'd cut the four into eight and eventually into sixteen, whittling away until he got to the hard, straight core of the tree. Now he was planing the edges into curves, which meant the mast neared completion. When it was at last sanded to a smooth finish and the men came to carry it away, I would picture it adorned with sails, the proud bow of its ship cutting through Atlantic swells. In my mind, my father's masts always guided travelers safely home.

I did not wish to interrupt Papa's work, so I set off for the well instead. Along the way, I glanced up the hill toward where the Mi'kmaq village had been. Subtle as the change of seasons, they had vanished into the forest to avoid the soldiers, whose commandeered section of l'Acadie increasingly buzzed with activity. We had not seen the Mi'kmaq in months. I longed to be with them, and more than anything I wanted to be with Mali. While I loved Claire and Giselle, Mali was my true sister. Since we were toddlers taking our first steps together, we had understood each other without words—though we never had a shortage of those. Nor did we lack laughter. Of the two of us, Mali was the wiser, and she became more so the older we got. When the day's work was done, we often used to lie side by side on the cool grass, staring at nothing. I would tell her about the dreams I had, the ones in which I travelled beyond our land. Mali always listened with a smile, then helped me understand that what I truly needed was to discover the world within me, that it was more important than what was beyond. She was right, of course, but her words didn't stop me from dreaming.

My brother Henri, who was one year older than me, was the dark opposite of our oldest brother, André, and in our family he was the most like me. He preferred the Mi'kmaq way of life to the more rigid ways of the Acadian village, and we shared a best friend in Mali. Like Papa had years before, Henri had learned to hunt and fight the Mi'kmaq way, and he knew every one of their legends better than he knew the Bible stories. He had even joined the Mi'kmaq youth in their sweat lodge.

The Acadians had always been close to the Mi'kmaq. Some even married and raised children of both worlds. The only conflict which ever arose stemmed from some Acadians not approving of how the Mi'kmaq retained their gods even after they had accepted our Christian God. To those Acadians, there was only one God.

I had never understood their criticisms. Of course our family went to church every week, and the Bible said we should not worship other gods, but in my mind the Mi'kmaq religion was something different. The Christian God was all-powerful, a force never questioned or doubted, and Jesus died for us, to save our souls. If I lived a good, Christian life, I would eventually join God in heaven. But before I died, while I still existed in the world, the Mi'kmaq spirits were all around me, filling my mind and body, keeping me alive. They were a part of my living world. The Christian God would look after me when I died.

There were discrepancies, though. The Bible taught me that Adam was the first human; however, the Mi'kmaq said Glooscap was the first *osgijinew*, the first man to stand on *wesgit*, the earth.

Papa said it was for me to decide what I believed. He said it was a question of *faith*. "Do not worry, Amélie. As long as you believe in God and give him your soul after death, I see no problem with believing in Glooscap as well. God is not selfish."

Mali's father, Tumas, was like my second father and just as wise as Papa. He was also more blunt. "The Mi'kmaq lived on this earth before Christianity began. Glooscap was the first god, and he will be the last god."

The Mi'kmaq story of Creation was much more vivid than the one in the Book of Genesis. Glooscap had been created from dirt, stones, wood, plants, and feathers; a bolt of lightning had brought him alive. On the day Glooscap declared he wanted to take a bath, Beaver built a dam so the water would cover him. A mighty whale came by and, unhappy to find her path blocked, she knocked the dam down. From their disagreement came the tides that rose and fell twice a day, every day, in our Bay of Fundy. I suppose that was what made it easier for me to believe the Mi'kmaq stories: God was everywhere, but the Mi'kmaq spirits were right here, doing things I could see.

I dropped one bucket at a time into the well and hauled them up again, then I turned back toward home, the rope handles rough on my fingers. After I brought the water to Maman for her soup, I would do my chores in the barn, return to help with the meal preparations, weed in the garden, then go out to the weirs to bring in the fish. Our days were always full. If only Mali were here to brighten them for me.

Summer flew by. This year it was made even more busy by the impending wedding of my sister and Guillaume, which would happen in September. Surrounded by my family and Acadian friends, I had less time to wallow in the loneliness which had settled over me since the Mi'kmaq had withdrawn. But there were moments when I was not consumed by work or conversation. I did not bid them to do so, but when they could, my thoughts went to the conversation I had had with Corporal MacDonnell under the trees that day. I told myself that my desire to seek him out and talk with him once more came purely from my lack of companionship now that Mali was gone. I had felt comfortable with him, and his intriguing—though sad—tales of Scotland gave me the opportunity to learn about one of those faraway places beyond the horizon. But even though I visited the camp twice more, I did not see him. Nor could I differentiate him from any of the other redcoats I spied from a distance when the activity by the church drew my eye.

On a beautiful night two weeks before Claire and Guillaume were to be married, we gathered to celebrate the anticipation of their wedding. Despite the unfamiliar tension the British had wrapped around our people, we seized the opportunity to remember what it was like to live. We lit the evening with bonfires—though we took care to be frugal with the wood. We had no idea how long the British might keep our axes from us, and we would need firewood once the cool nights arrived. With our cups filled with cider, we danced to fiddles and flutes, kicking up our heels after long, hot days, staying near the fire to keep the hordes of mosquitoes at bay. Claire and Guillaume danced the night away, and I wondered if they even noticed the rest of us. My friend Evangeline Bellefontaine spent the evenings with her beloved, Gabriel Lajeunesse, and while I did miss our time together as friends, I was glad to see the contentment on her sweet face. Though it was true I had no intention of marrying anytime soon, I did long to carry that same light of love in my eyes. Both Claire and Evangeline practically glowed with happiness, as did the men at their sides. I tried not to give in to the sin of envy.

Maman brought over two more cups of cider as I bent over, laughing at Giselle. Too much spinning had sent her sprawling into the cool grass, and her grin shone in the moonlight.

"Ah, my silly girls," Maman said. "Which of these boys will be lucky enough to earn your affection?"

I hid my annoyance behind my cup, but Giselle was happy to chatter away. "Maman, does Jean Dupuis not look handsome tonight?"

"He does indeed. He has grown into a man this summer. And look, he is coming this way!"

"He was already a man, Maman. He is sixteen."

"So he is. And you, my beautiful daughter, are only two years younger. Will you dance if he asks?"

"Of course." And she did when he appeared before her.

The fiddles' notes danced through the air like the sparks leaping from the fire. It was a perfect night, sent to us from God as a reward for our courage through these uncertain times. Maman and I watched Giselle spin around with Jean, and at the speed she was going I hoped she would not tumble again. Then he took her hand and put another on her waist, and she blinked up at him in such a perfect imitation of Claire's flirtatious expression I could not help but laugh.

"She is happy," Maman said warmly. "That is all I have ever wanted for my children."

I knew what she meant, what she had not said. "We are all happy. You need not worry for me."

"It is my right to worry." She put an arm around me and pulled me close. "I love you very much, Amélie."

I was the same height as she was now, and I wondered when that had happened. We were almost cheek to cheek, so I had only to turn my face to kiss her.

"I love you too."

⁓

The next morning arrived before any of us were prepared, and though I had awoken at our rooster's imperious cry an hour before, I had coaxed myself back to sleep. I could not do the same after a sharp knocking came at our door.

Claire made a disapproving grunt when I climbed over her and pulled my cloak from the hook on the wall. "Your curiosity will be the death of us all," she murmured, but I knew she was only teasing.

"Go back to sleep. I will tell you who it is later."

Papa stood at the door with Mathieu at his side. Papa eyed him. "Do not cause trouble, Mathieu. Stand back, out of the way."

With a scowl, my brother stepped behind him and toward me.

"Who is it?" I whispered.

"Soldiers."

The door creaked open, and we saw two red uniforms waiting in the morning mist. Corporal MacDonnell stood just behind his commanding officer, who he had told me was named Sergeant Fitch. Both men's coats were beaded with rain, and their faces were pale from the chill. I smiled in welcome at MacDonnell, but he kept his eyes averted from mine. The action surprised me, as he had been so friendly before. Was it because of his sergeant? Perhaps he had forgotten this was my house. I cleared my throat to draw his attention, but all he did was frown and stare at the floor. So his rudeness was deliberate. I was surprised by how much that hurt. *Silly girl*, I chided myself. *Thinking he was special. He is just one of them after all.*

"Bonne matin," Fitch said in his terrible French.

"Bonjour. Puis-je vous aider?" Papa asked.

Clearly uncomfortable with speaking French, Fitch turned from Papa to me. "We are here with orders from His Majesty."

"What orders?" I asked. "We have no more weapons, as you know. We have nothing more your king could want."

MacDonnell's jaw was clenched tight. Memories of our happy afternoon were all I had left of that day, and I pushed them from my mind whenever they showed themselves. I no longer felt any pleasure at the sight of him.

Fitch's narrow gaze slid past Papa and paused on Claire, who could not resist her own curiosity, it appeared. At sight of her his nostrils flared slightly, and he smiled in a way I can only describe as carnivorous. The man made my skin crawl. Claire made a small noise of disgust in her throat and turned away, hugging herself, but Fitch was undeterred. His repugnant gaze came my way next, and I glared back, though I know not why I was so foolish. I should not have baited him; I did not know what power he might wield. Fortunately, he said nothing, though his thin lips pursed with annoyance.

All this happened in the space of a few seconds. While Fitch had been ogling Claire and me, André and Henri had melted into the walls, staying out of sight. Papa had told them they should, for we all knew my brothers would not hesitate to raise their fists if they felt we were in danger. They could not win against well-armed soldiers, and Papa feared the soldiers would try to antagonize them to that point.

Fitch cleared his throat. "I have been directed to inform you that all men, including lads over the age of ten, are to attend a meeting at the church this Friday, the fifth of September at three o'clock in the afternoon."

Three days from now. My father squinted at Fitch, and I could tell the officer's words had been too quick. I lifted to my toes and whispered the translation into Papa's ear, unpleasantly aware of Fitch's attention on me.

"Why we come to church?" Papa asked.

"Colonel Winslow will address all the men in the village." Fitch rubbed a wet sleeve over his face, mopping rainwater from his skin. He looked irritated, as if he had expected to be invited in.

He waited for me to translate, then Papa crossed his arms. "Yes? You call and we come like dogs? Maybe we do not."

"Then you forfeit your home and all goods to His Majesty."

"What?" I cried. "How—"

Papa seethed. "His Majesty already take almost all."

Fitch's smile was cruel. "Almost."

How dare he speak this way? I stepped closer to the door, but my father held out an arm to restrain me.

"But, Papa—"

His lips narrowed. "Hush, Amélie. Remember what I said before," he said in French. "Think first." His attention returned to Fitch, and he jabbed a thumb at his own chest. "You tell me more."

Fitch merely shrugged. "I don't speak your foul language."

In his most cordial voice, Papa unleashed a string of French that made us all blanch.

"Excuse me, Sergeant," came another voice. MacDonnell stepped into the doorway, and I remembered his fluent French. He would certainly have understood every one of Papa's expletives.

"I do not require your assistance, Corporal."

"I can speak their language, sir. That will make it easier for you."

Sergeant Fitch grudgingly stepped to the side, giving MacDonnell a dark look as he did so. Water dripped from MacDonnell's tricorne as he gave Papa a quick, respectful nod. "I apologize for this intrusion," he said. "My name is Corporal Connor MacDonnell of His Majesty's army. Sergeant Fitch and I have been tasked with delivering this message, but I am afraid we were given no other information."

Papa was—and rightfully so—still annoyed by the demand no matter in which language it was made. But it is easier to be plain-spoken to a rude person than it is to take out anger on someone with manners. Some of the bluster left his sails.

"Bien," he said. "We will be there." He narrowed his eyes at Fitch. "But it is highly irregular to be summoned in this way."

"Yes, sir. Merci bien," MacDonnell said. "Again, I apologize." He angled his body slightly and gave my sisters and me the same sort of bow. "Good day, madame, mademoiselles, monsieur."

When he straightened, his eyes flickered quickly around the

house, and I worried he saw my hidden brothers. He said nothing. If he had spotted them, he showed no sign. He simply turned and left.

Maman clutched Papa's sleeve before he'd even turned from the closed door.

"What is this now?"

"Perhaps it is a good thing that they want to address us all," he suggested. "Maybe this time we really will learn what is happening."

The soft tan of her brow wrinkled. "Oh, if they would only leave us alone!"

"And yet they will not, ma chérie." He drew her against his chest and looked over her head at my brothers, who had reappeared. "Do not worry, Sylvie. The Lord will see us through this. We have three days. Then we will know more."

"I say we should not go," Henri declared. "This is our land—"

"It is not our land," Papa reminded him. "We are on His Majesty's land."

Even Giselle joined the conversation. "We were here first!"

Maman's attention switched from Papa to Giselle, and she laid one hand against my sister's blond curls. "Hush now, ma petite. Papa will take care of everything."

My doubts were reflected in my brother André's eyes, and I wondered why he kept them to himself.

Henri didn't hesitate. "I will not go," he decided, folding his arms and looking like a younger version of our father at his most defiant. Of course Henri would bluster at this, ready to declare war. This kind of battle cry appealed to him. "They cannot tell me what to do. I will stand up for our rights!"

I heard again the advice Papa had given me and remembered the wisdom of keeping my emotions hidden, yet I saw a hint of concern in my father's expression.

"You will do no such thing. We will all go," Papa said after a moment, laying an arm over Maman's shoulder. "For your mother's sake."

"They cannot—"

Papa raised his voice, though it was was not quite a shout. "They can indeed, Henri, and I do not believe it is an empty threat. Tell me, my brave son, what would your mother do if they burned our house to the ground?"

"They wouldn't!"

"They would."

Henri closed his lips, but I could imagine the thoughts roaring through his head.

The following day, Papa left the house before the sun had risen. September was Wikumkewiku's, and evenings were lit by the moose-calling moon, but the darkness would not bother him. I was sleeping when he left, and he was still gone when I awoke. When I asked Maman where he had gone, she wouldn't say.

"Don't worry," she assured me, trying to put a stop to my questions. "Your papa is fine. He will probably come home with a nice venison meal for us all."

But I could not imagine how this was possible, since he could not hunt without weapons. When Maman left the house as well, heading to the garden, I pondered what she had said. I was aware my father often found solace with his old family just as I did with Mali's. Papa had no weapons, but Tumas did. Papa had hunted with the Mi'kmaq before; maybe he hunted with them today. What kind of conversations might they have in the cool, silent refuge of the forest?

SIX

Henri remained emphatic that he would not attend the meeting, and I could not blame him. The soldiers had not seen him—unless Corporal MacDonnell had caught a glimpse the last time he'd been at our house. I secretly encouraged my brother to do what his heart told him. I even suggested I might run to the forest with him, but André overheard and forbade it. When André spoke, everyone knew he'd deliberated over every word. I would never purposefully disappoint him. Still, I urged Henri to run.

An hour before the men were required to go to the church, we could find no evidence of Henri. His clothes were gone as well. In truth, I was relieved. I wanted him to stay as far from trouble as possible. But I was astonished to discover that Henri was not the only one who was missing. André was nowhere to be found.

Oddly, neither of my parents seemed concerned about their absent sons. All Papa said was, "Eh bien. If they are not at the meeting, they can at least watch over the house from wherever they are."

Something in his tone made me wonder if he too wished he could flee the unknown. If he'd been young and without responsibilities, he might have gone as well. But he was not a twenty-year-old blond Mi'kmaq warrior anymore. He was my papa and a leader in our community. He knew his responsibilities, and he would never shirk them.

Claire, however, was frantic. "How could they do this? They cannot just have disappeared! Oh, Amélie. Do you know where they are? Do you know what has happened?"

Though my face raged with heat, I answered with all honesty that I did not. I prayed they were with Mali and her family. I even wondered if that could have been the motive for my father's disappearance the other morning. All I knew for sure was that my brothers were safer with the Mi'kmaq than they were with the men in red coats.

Claire did not believe me, but she didn't accuse. The tension was high enough in the house that she didn't want to upset anyone even more. She waited for Maman to walk away before she leaned in to whisper in my ear.

"Will they return?"

Their absence felt strange, and the house seemed empty. "I don't know. I don't know anything."

"Are they in the forest?"

"Probably. Maybe they will return in a day or two," I whispered, assuring us both. "They cannot simply leave without a farewell, can they? It would break Maman's heart." *And mine.*

Fitch had said even boys over ten years must attend. The only one left was my little brother, Mathieu. Maman stood tall, determined to be brave as he and Papa prepared to go.

"It is just a meeting, Maman," I said.

"Amélie is right," Papa agreed. "I will be home soon." He folded her into his arms and kissed her brow, then looked over at Claire and me. "Take care of Maman."

"Of course, Papa," we replied.

Uncertainty kept us active for the rest of the day, and we did what we could to ease Maman's mind. Maman, however, did not want us to tend to her.

"Outside!" she ordered, shooing us out the door. "I cannot breathe through all your fussing."

I wanted to give her comfort, but I was glad to escape. The house was sweltering, the air unmoving though the windows were open. Lush, golden acres of wheat stood waiting in the salt marsh, ready to be harvested, scythed, then piled into messy thatch roofs on the *barges à foin*, but I could see no one working. The quietness was eerie; it reminded me of the dream I'd had, in which everyone was gone and the sea was coming to swallow me up.

But these haunting thoughts were no help. I must not indulge in fearful imaginings. The truth was, I assumed, that everyone was simply too caught up in wondering about the church meeting to think of farming.

Claire smiled when I stepped inside the garden fence, but I would have had to be completely insensitive not to see how anxious she was about her betrothed. There was nothing any of us could do but wait. The men would be full of questions and answers when they returned, and they would be hungry as well. The Bible said idle hands were the devil's workshop, and I agreed. If I could keep busy, my mind might allow itself to be distracted, so I set to work sawing at a large cabbage while Claire squatted and reached for a turnip. We didn't know how many of us would be home for supper; surely the meeting would be over by then.

We worked without talking for a while, and after I'd set the cabbage aside, I reached for the pole beans, which had grown so heavy they had toppled their wooden supports. I began to fill my apron, but without a breeze it didn't take long for the heat and the marsh's humidity to bring sweat to my brow. I leaned against a post, propping myself up while I wiped a sleeve over my face.

"How is Guillaume?" I asked, hoping my question would not add to her distress.

His name roused a smile, though it was fleeting. "The last time I saw him he was very happy. We've been waiting so long for our wedding, and now it's only a few days away." She sat still for a moment, lost in thought. "A wedding will be wonderful, don't you think? I mean even more than usual, since so many other things are happening."

I could not answer her pleading expression at first, so she looked down, pretending to search under the thick green leaves for weeds. Claire didn't like to speak of unpleasant things. In that way she was much like André, though she wasn't nearly as clever as he was.

"Of course," I eventually said.

I swatted at a horsefly just as Claire popped up to her feet, shielding her eyes with one hand. "Did you hear that?"

"What?"

"Voices. I heard them yelling in the church. You didn't hear it?"

I started to shake my head, then a sound cut through the air. "Can you hear what they're saying?"

The tone was angry, but the words were unintelligible. Hundreds of our men and boys had crowded into the old building, but even with that many, I wouldn't have expected to hear them from here. People always kept their voices down in the church. Then again, it was hardly a church these days.

"No, but—" She stopped at the sound of another outcry, but we still couldn't understand what was being said. "I'm sure Papa will tell us everything when he gets home."

But Papa and the others did not return that night or the next day. It made no sense. What were they doing? How were they sleeping, with so many people crowded into a place with no beds? What were they eating? We went to the church with some of the women, demanding answers, but the soldiers would tell us nothing.

For two days we waited. Finally, on the third morning, Mathieu burst through the door, his face and clothing filthy. We flocked around him, cooing like doves, and he held on to Maman, looking as if he were trying hard not to cry. I hadn't seen him cry in years. When at last we had all held him and remarked on how hungry he must be, Maman bade us sit around the table. She brought him soup and shushed us so that we might hear what he had to say.

"Tell us now, Mathieu," she said, pressing bread into his hands. "Where is your papa? What is happening?"

Mathieu devoured the food as though he hadn't eaten for days, and I wondered if that could truly be the case. When the last morsel was gone, he dropped his head into his hands.

"That is why I have been sent here. Twenty of us were sent out as messengers, and I must return to the church in the morning. And they have asked that the women come as well and bring food."

I stood and moved to the larder, planning to collect what I could, but Maman waved me back. "Come, Amélie. Sit and listen first. We will go when we learn what has happened." She leaned in, touching Mathieu's arm. "Tell me, my son."

I handed my little brother an apple and sat down to listen. He gave me a gratified look and bit into it with a noisy crunch.

"It is very crowded in the church," he said through a mouthful. "The windows cannot be opened because the soldiers have nailed timbers across them. It smells like pigs have moved indoors."

My heart broke for them all. Papa, I knew, would suffer in silence, keep his fury hidden.

Mathieu's eyes flicked to Maman. "All the men and boys are there except for some like Henri and André."

She nodded but said nothing. Since Papa and Mathieu had left, we had not talked about our two older brothers. For the hundredth time, I wondered if Maman knew where they were.

"At first we all sat and listened," he continued, "then some of the men, like Monsieur Melanson and his brother, they started to speak on our behalf, saying we wanted our livestock back so we could start on the fall harvest. That was when Colonel Winslow stood and motioned for everyone to be quiet. More of our men spoke up, demanding to be heard, but Winslow told them to sit down. Papa and Monsieur Melanson said they had heard enough and they went to the door, but guards stood there with their muskets. They will not let anyone out."

Maman looked ready to cry. So they were truly prisoners, then.

"Winslow wants us all to sign an oath," he said. "Neutrality, he says, is no longer an option."

Of course they had refused. Taking that oath could put them in a position where they would have to carry arms against the French.

Mathieu choked on a sob and covered his eyes. "There is more, Maman. Much more. And it is so much worse than this."

My body tingled with fear at his words. They held our men prisoner without food or rest, demanding they sign a piece of paper which would in effect be a declaration of war against the French and the Mi'kmaq. What could be worse than that?

Maman echoed my thoughts. "More? What more can we endure?"

A tear glinted at the corner of one of his eyes, and he swiftly wiped it away. "Colonel Winslow read us the king's orders. He told us that what he must read was not in his nature but that he had no choice but to read it to us."

"Yes, yes," Maman said. I nodded with her. Mathieu seemed to be stalling, and we wanted to hear the truth.

He took her hands in his, surprising us all. It seemed such a grown-up gesture.

"All our land and livestock are now forfeit, and we are to be removed from this land, Maman. The Acadians are to be put in ships like cattle and sent away. Not just the men, Maman. The women and children as well. Some ships have already come. They are only waiting for more so they can take us all."

My mouth fell open. I could not speak. Maman and Claire too stared at him, speechless.

Only Giselle could find words. "What does that mean?"

"They are sending us away from here. All of us. We can take what things we can carry, but no more."

I was outraged. "They cannot—"

"Where?" Maman whispered, clenching her hands together. "Where are they sending us?"

"They didn't say, but they will make sure families remain together."

"That is small comfort!" she cried. "They think—"

Claire spoke for the first time, her eyes round with horror. "But other families? We will be separated from them? What about Guillaume and his family? Will we—"

"When Papa gets home he will explain everything, I am sure," Maman said, trying to gain control of the situation. "He will know what it all means. We must wait until he is home and be patient until then. Do you know when they will release the men, Mathieu?"

Mathieu looked away, then slumped in his chair. "I do not know any more than what I said." No one else moved. "I am so tired, Maman," he finally mumbled. "And in the morning I have to go back. I must sleep now."

So many questions still hung over us, but he was exhausted. We made sure he was well fed before he collapsed into bed, then the long, slow breaths of a little boy fallen to sleep filled the room. I watched him briefly, then returned to sit with my mother and sisters. Their cheeks were wet with tears.

Mine were dry. I suppose I simply didn't believe the story. It couldn't be possible that we would be forced from our homes, from our lives, and shipped off to another land. Even if it were true, I was not ready to give up, to let the English destroy everything I had.

I got to my feet. "I will bring food, and I will speak with Papa. He will know what to do."

"Now?" Claire sniffed. "You think they will let you?"

"I will not leave without an answer."

Maman and my sisters helped me fetch what food I could find. With my arms full, I headed toward the church. If I could not speak with Papa, I would insist on speaking with Corporal MacDonnell. He seemed my best hope of hearing the truth.

SEVEN

The guard stopped me by the fence and took the food, then he told me to go home.

"There is nothing for you here," he said.

"Of course there is," I told him, speaking in English. "My father and brother are here. I wish to speak with them."

"You cannot."

I planted my feet, folded my arms, and glared up at him. "Is Colonel Winslow afraid to talk with the women?"

"What? That is preposterous!"

The word was unfamiliar. "Prepos . . . ?"

He sneered at my ignorance. "Ridiculous."

"Everything about this is pre—" I blurted, then stopped, sounding out the word in my head. I had to get it right so I did not appear the fool. "This is *all* preposterous. I need to speak with my father."

"You cannot."

"Then I would like to speak with Colonel Winslow."

He closed his eyes, then slowly opened them, looking at me as if I were a foolish child. "That, mademoiselle, is not going to happen. Thank you for the food. Now go home."

I felt a little like Giselle, standing there and carrying on, but what choice did I have? "I will not! I deserve an explanation."

He set the food basket on the ground and curled his fingers around the handle of his musket. "Do you mean to force my hand? Because I—"

"Excuse me! Soldier!"

I knew that voice, and something in my chest gave a little hop. Corporal MacDonnell rounded the corner and strode toward us with authority. Maybe I would get some answers after all.

He frowned at the soldier. "Is there a problem?"

"No, sir. This woman brought food for her menfolk and was just leaving."

"You are mistaken, sir. I am not going anywhere." I rolled my shoulders back. "Not until I find out what is happening to my brother and my father."

The two men regarded each other, then MacDonnell hooked his hands behind his back. "Carry on, soldier. I will speak with the lady."

Once he was gone, Corporal MacDonnell gave a small but formal bow. "It is an unexpected pleasure to see you, Mademoiselle Belliveau," he said in French. "Despite the circumstances."

"Circumstances indeed." This was no simple picnic of peas and bread. "I came to see my father."

The welcoming smile faded. "Of course you did. I understand, and I'm very sorry, but only the men are permitted inside, and no one is permitted out."

"Except the messengers."

His smile was contrite. "Yes, except the messengers. Your brother, Mathieu, was one. Am I right?"

I nodded, unsure. Why did it please me to learn that he knew Mathieu was my brother?

"Mademoiselle, allow me to assure you that your father and

brother are well enough, though I know they would be much happier in their home with you. Unfortunately, that is not possible at the moment." He hesitated. "Could we . . . would you walk a bit with me?" He must have seen the doubt in my expression. "I wish merely to speak with you where no one can hear us."

"Where?"

"Wherever you'd like. But what I want to say is for your ears only." He glanced around, then announced, "I shall walk you home," so anyone could hear.

Trust must be earned, and yet despite what had happened, I gave him what I could of it. I led him away from the church, away from the houses, and toward the fields. We would not stroll there, for the ground was always wet, but I knew a safe place where we could talk, unmolested by others. When we reached the trees, I stopped and crossed my arms, waiting.

He kept walking, hands linked behind his back. "You are wondering what I could possibly have to say to you."

When I trotted up beside him, he slowed so I could keep up.

"Why are they doing this?" I demanded.

He rounded on me, and I stopped short. "Really? You do not know?"

I was surprised by his tone. He sounded exasperated. As if *I* had upset *him*. "No," I snapped. "I do not know. That is why I am here, *soldier*."

"This is war," he said.

"We want nothing to do with war or with anyone else. We have lived here for generations, hurting no one. Take your war somewhere else."

"This is exactly where they want it to be. Look at all this." He waved at the dikes and fields before us, the ocean beyond. "Do you know how valuable your homeland is? Do you have any idea what you have here? The fishing and hunting are wondrous. The crops are plentiful, and the ground so fertile you could coax the dead to life. How could the English not want this land for themselves? They have found heaven on earth, and they will not stop until they have it."

I had never been anywhere but l'Acadie. I had known nothing but this place. I suppose in my naiveté I had believed everyone lived the way I did, that the whole world was as happy as I was. Thinking of someone else claiming our land as their own filled me with an unfamiliar rage.

My voice shook. "It isn't theirs."

"Nor was Scotland," MacDonnell reminded me. "But it is now. And now that France and England are at war, they are battling over this place as well. I say again: You must not underestimate the British army."

A cloud washed over the sun, casting a long shadow, and I thought of Claire's superstitious warnings. As if he knew I needed solace, he touched my arm, and I looked up.

"I understand your anger. I know how it feels, and I'm sorry for you and your family."

His compassion was obvious, but I did not accept it. This man was not my friend. He was the enemy. I wanted to sweep the comfort of his hand from my skin, but I did not. My eyes burned, I quickly blinked the tears away. I hadn't cried when I'd heard our lives were about to be stolen. Why would a simple act of empathy move me?

"Thank you," I said. "That is kind of you, I suppose."

"You suppose?"

I moved away from his touch, and he dropped his hand. "You are one of the men who is making us leave."

"I am aware of that. And I regret it deeply."

He took off his tricorne and held it between his hands. The line of his jaw was taut and he had been sweating; I could see the wet line where the hat had pressed. Frustrated, he ran a hand through his dark brown hair, messing it inadvertently. Without the hat and with his coat slung over one arm, it amazed me how normal he looked, as if he were no different from the boys with whom I had grown up. Of course his clothing was nothing like their plain linen shirts or short wool trousers, but without the severe uniform he seemed much more human.

"It's not something you can help," I replied. "I understand. There is nothing you can do about it. But you should know that we will survive this. We are a determined people, we Acadians."

"I can see at least *you* are."

"I'm sorry?"

"It's only that I saw no other women storming up to the church just now as you did."

"Plenty of women will come with food," I objected. "Especially now that we know our men are captives."

He stooped as he walked, picking up something in the grass that caught his eye, then he flicked it away. With his face still toward the ground, he asked, "Do you have other brothers?"

For a moment I couldn't breathe, then we both stopped, distracted by a sound behind us. He turned to face it, and I watched, but his eyes showed no sign of alarm. Still, he was careful. With his face set, he gave a little bow and swept my hand into his.

"Tell them to stay away," he whispered, raising my hand to the level of his lips as if he meant to kiss it. "I saw your family before this madness began but have told no one. You have two other brothers who did not come to the church. I don't know where they are—"

"What are you—"

"—and I don't want to know. But if you love your brothers, tell them not to come back."

Shaken, I stepped away and tried to pull my hand from his.

Instead, he seized my other hand as well. I felt truly afraid for the first time.

"Why are you doing this?" I whispered.

"If they are caught, they will be arrested."

I shook my head. "I don't understand. It is your job to find them and arrest them. Why—"

He seemed unaware that his hands had closed far too tightly around my fingers, and I did not move. Instead of backing away, he stepped closer and slowly raised our joined hands so they were against his chest. I should have objected, should never have spoken to him again.

"There is no reason you should trust me," he said, "and I have no expectations that you will. Regardless, I offer this information so that you might understand I am telling the truth when I say I mean you no harm. The British army is your enemy, but I am not."

I had never been so physically close to a man unrelated to me, except for when I had danced with my friends. This was entirely different.

"Corporal MacDonnell—"

"My name is Connor. Connor MacDonnell, if you'd do me the honour of using my Christian name."

I hesitated. "Connor."

"Aye. That is what my friends call me."

Our hands were still pressed against his chest, and I was suddenly uncomfortable. Despite feeling sorry for him, I pulled away. I understood he was unhappy being in the army, that these same people had done to him what I now knew they planned to do with us. But it did not change the fact of who he was, or who I was.

"Mathieu told us the British will be sending us all away from here. All of us. You cannot possibly believe I would want you as a friend after learning that."

"I understand," he said, standing taller. "And I do not question your resolve. But you should not question mine either. I am determined to prove to you that I am not the demon you see when you look at this uniform."

"Why? Why should it matter to you what I think?"

At my question his expression softened, and his steady gaze intensified.

"It simply does," he said quietly. "I will prove myself to you. And I swear to you that when the time comes, I will take care of you."

EIGHT

One week later, the doors of the church swung open and our fathers, sons, brothers, uncles, cousins, and friends stumbled into the light of day. Hearing their voices, we ran to greet them, to welcome them back, but the soldiers stood before us, as solid as any barrier. We tried to push through, but our men were kept away from us.

Maman's eyes were swollen from days of weeping when she'd thought we were not listening, and now her sobs changed to cries of relief. She clung to Claire's sleeve, weak and grasping for balance. She had barely eaten while the men had been gone, and I worried for her health, but she had brushed my concerns aside, reminding me that our fears should be for my brothers and Papa, not for her.

"Papa!" I yelled, spotting him in the crowd. "Over here, Papa!"

Exhaustion melted from his face when he saw us, and I imagined he reached deep into his soul to find the strength to smile and wave back. Mathieu stood beside him, looking practically dead on his feet. Beside him, Claire's beloved squinted into the sunshine.

"Guillaume!" cried Claire. "Oh, Guillaume!"

"Mathieu! Mathieu! Nous sommes ici!" I called.

My little brother spun toward me and made as if to run, but as soon as he took one step in my direction, he was grabbed roughly by a soldier and shoved back into the ranks. He blinked up at the man, not understanding, then looked back at me. Tears rolled down the dirt on his face, and I know he saw them on my own cheeks as well. I couldn't hide my pain any more than he could.

I couldn't see Corporal MacDonnell—Connor—anywhere, though I scanned the area for any sign of him. His commander, Colonel Winslow, observed from his post near the church. Though I had never seen the man before, I could tell who he was by the way others approached him, the way they ran to do as he bid. When would he issue the order that would release Papa and my poor brother? The prisoners seemed barely able to stand on their own feet. We needed to tend to them, to feed them. Winslow was wasting time. I stared hard at the stocky, middle-aged man, willing him to look my way, needing him to see my rage, but he was oblivious.

"Sergeant Fitch!" he shouted, snapping everyone to attention. "Formations!"

I remembered Fitch, the officer with the cruel smile and hungry eyes. It only seemed right that he should be a part of this horrendous day. He repeated Winslow's command to his subordinates, and more English voices rang out, echoing his orders.

At first I couldn't make out what was happening since all seemed utter confusion, then I surmised that the English had formed a rough formation around the prisoners, like a hastily constructed wall. What for? Did they think the weeping women would attack them? The orders continued, and I watched in bewilderment as Guillaume and my wide-eyed brother were herded into a line with a group of other young men and boys. Papa was led to a different group, one made up chiefly of older men. Their separation from each other sent fear racing through me. Did they intend to keep some captives here after they'd released the others? What would be the purpose of that?

Like Maman, the women around us fell into hysterics as the men were shifted around, and this evidence of our helplessness in the face of such evil was terrifying. Women I had known my whole life, women who had toiled in the fields, at the weirs, and in their homes without complaint, now leaned against each other for support, weak with despair. Claire cried out desperately for Guillaume, and Evangeline pressed up behind me, waving and crying for Gabriel, who looked back at her with agonizing sorrow. I wished I could give her some kind of comfort, but I could find none. Not even for me.

"What does this mean?" Claire cried. "Why are they doing this? Guillaume! Oh, Guillaume!"

"Gentlemen!" bellowed Colonel Winslow.

All eyes went to the commander. I was surprised to see Connor at his side, standing tall and stiff, and I couldn't take my eyes from him. He didn't see me, since he stared straight ahead, hands behind his back. I remembered those hands holding mine. I remembered the folded red coat on the grass, the sweat-stained marks on his white shirt, how his eyes lit when he smiled. That Connor was nothing like this man I saw before me, standing like a statue by Winslow.

"Messieurs!" Connor said, addressing the groups of men. "Votre attention, s'il vous plaît!"

His voice rang across the field—the same voice which had called me "friend"—strong enough that there was no need for him to yell despite the noise. It was then that I realized he was to be the translator for the crowd. He would be the one telling us what awful, undeserved future we faced. Knowing the words would come from his mouth made everything we'd shared before feel like a horrible, traitorous lie.

Again he called out for attention, and the people ceased shouting. They contained their sobs as well as they could, needing to hear what was being said.

"It is the king's command that we march today," Connor continued, his steady voice giving nothing away. "Five ships wait at harbour, and fifty men shall be boarded upon each one. Those not boarded today will await ships which are currently at sea and en route here."

For the space of one breath, no one said a word. Maman, my sisters, and I exchanged a stunned glance, then the space erupted with agonized cries of protest. Some women fell to their knees, praying and crying, and I wondered how my dear little brother could bear this nightmare. He stood stock still, trembling hands hanging by his sides, looking so much younger than his thirteen years.

Papa's eyes, dark with lack of sleep, were on me. *Be strong*, they commanded. *Remember what I said.* But I couldn't remember anything. What had he said? What did he expect of me? I remembered how he'd faced Fitch in the house, how he'd kept his anger in check, and how he said I must learn to do the same. But how could I possibly hide the anguish I felt?

And now that I saw him here, hungry and helpless, I wondered what good his strength had actually done him.

"Papa!" I yelled. "I don't know what to do!"

His stare never wavered. He nodded slowly at me, his face set. *You will.*

Maman had collapsed onto the grass, and Claire stooped beside her, cradling her head in her arms. I did not. I had to see what would happen next.

"Sergeant Fitch!"

Smirking, Fitch nodded at Winslow, then strode toward my brother and Guillaume, who huddled with others in a confused line. When he stood at the group's head and ordered, "Forward march!" no one moved. It wasn't for lack of understanding his English, since the physical command was obvious. It was simply a belated, doomed attempt to rebel. My heart raced, witnessing their act of defiance, and everyone's attention focused on the ragged group of young men standing bravely against their oppressors. *Too little, too late*, I thought miserably.

"Attention, gentlemen!" Fitch ordered again, raising his nasal voice. "March!"

"We will go nowhere without our fathers!" yelled Giselle's dashing young Jean Dupuis. Most of the others—my brother included—cheered their agreement.

I couldn't help myself. I looked toward Connor, pleading, and saw him staring at me. Sympathy was in his expression, but contempt clogged my throat. How dare he offer such a useless apology? He was not in charge, but had he even tried to stop these foul orders? A last second spark of hope ignited, and I wondered frantically if there was a possibility he could change any of this because of his position. Could he use his ability to speak French and order the Acadian men to rebel? Could he save us?

"Please!" I cried, though I didn't know if he could hear me.

He did. He shook his head in the smallest of movements, and his lips moved. "I'm sorry."

I looked away, denying him forgiveness.

Colonel Winslow strode toward Papa's group and stared down one of the men until he was forced to drop his eyes. Tears blurred my vision, but I watched nonetheless. I had never before witnessed such brutality. Had these men been born cruel or were they trained into it? How did one man look in the eye of another and inform them they had no choice, that some unseeable force had deemed him superior, that he had the right to take everything away?

"Gentlemen!" came Winslow's voice.

The rolling tide of rebellion stilled at his authority.

"Hear me now," he commanded. Strangely, the colonel's expression was not angry; he looked . . . disappointed. As if we were recalcitrant children, nothing more. "I will have none of this insolence. I do not understand your use of the word *no*. You have been living here under the king's generous allowance. The king's command is absolute and must be absolutely obeyed."

He scrutinized the captives, and they stared blankly back. Did he even realize that only a few understood his English tirade? Did he care? Connor did not step closer to his commander, did not offer to translate.

Winslow apparently didn't see the need. He shook his head, lips tight with disapproval. "It goes against my temperament to use harsh means; however, I will not abide these arguments. Sergeant Fitch!"

Fitch's nostrils flared. "Sir!" he replied, then he bellowed, "Company will fix bayonets!"

As one, the soldiers reached into the scabbard on the left sides of their belts and slid out thin metal spikes. Gripping the rifle barrels with their right hands, they lifted the weapons so the butts could be placed between their worn black boots, and I watched in silent, horrified alarm as they readied themselves. With practiced efficiency, they fitted the spikes over the mouths of their weapons then waited. At Fitch's next command, the soldiers proceeded to march toward our brothers, sons, and friends, the lethal blades aimed directly at them.

I am certain I was not the only one to scream at the sight, but all I heard was my own voice. As the wall of steel marched closer, the fragile line of defence crumbled and four of the five lines—one of which included Papa—began to march. The once-strong farmers of Acadia were docile as lambs, a straggling herd shuffling helplessly toward the harbour.

Mathieu looked so small, walking with the group of men. I panicked when I lost sight of him, but he fell out of line and looked back.

"Papa!" he cried.

Papa remained tall and stoic, the sturdy oak for us all. "I will see you soon, son." We heard a crack in his voice as his resolve weakened. "Listen to Guillaume and do as he says."

"Papa! I'm afraid!" Mathieu sobbed, then he looked over at us. "Maman! Help!"

"Oh, Mathieu!" Maman wailed, reaching into the empty air as if she might draw him to her breast again. "I love you, my son! We will be together soon. God bless you. Be brave!"

Claire's lips formed silent, earnest words, and I knew she was praying, her reddened eyes on Guillaume. I could no longer claim to be strong. Tears poured down my cheeks, and I choked for air along with the other women.

I hadn't believed any of this could happen. To me it had been the worst of threats, nothing more than that. Connor had warned me that the British would eventually follow through with their evil plan; he had told me more than once that we should not underestimate the enemy. I'd paid him no heed.

"Come, Maman," Claire said, gently tugging our mother to her feet. "We shall follow, and later we shall bring food."

The mothers and wives, daughters and sisters clung to each other as they followed the forced march, stumbling through their grief. Unlike the men being herded before them, the women were not hushed. The mournful shrieks of gulls circling overhead on that beautiful September day were drowned out, overwhelmed by the sobs and prayers of the families left behind.

NINE

For the next two weeks the atmosphere around our home was subdued but determined. Even Giselle was quiet. We agreed we would not grieve—at least not when any of the others were watching—since no one had died. The ships still bobbed at the docks, jerking at their ropes like impatient horses, burdened by the captives in their bellies. We would see our men again, we told ourselves.

"God will protect them," Maman assured us.

I performed my part as best I could: I limited my tears. But I was hard pressed to share her faith. Connor had told me the English coveted our land, and I knew he was right. If they wanted it as their own, why would they ever let our fathers, husbands, and sons go free? If our men posed such a threat, the army would never release them. Would we ever see them again? And if we did not, what would become of us—the women and children?

For two weeks Maman carried baskets of food toward the harbour, a resolute silhouette marching into the light of every sunrise. She would not allow us to either replace or accompany her, and every morning my sisters and I knelt in the doorway of our house, praying as we watched her go. By the time she returned it was always dark, and she did not want to talk. She told us she never saw Papa or any of the others; she was forced to give the food to the guards to pass on. The only other thing she mentioned was the reek of the ships.

I realized I was a hypocrite. At the same time as I cursed the foul English for their unthinkable cruelty and begged God to destroy them, I peered toward the docks or the churchyard, seeking a glimpse of one particular redcoat. Despite everything—despite knowing everything between us was based on a lie—I missed Connor. Whatever the reason, he had worked his way so deeply into my thoughts that I found it difficult to think of much else.

He was a soldier, I reminded myself, bound to follow orders.

And yet it was I whose mind was at war, constantly condemning him, then seeking out an excuse. Papa had said I would know what to do when faced with making a decision, and that the difference between "right" and "good" came down to judgment. With that in mind, I tried to put myself in Connor's position.

As a soldier, the right thing would have been for Connor to walk away from me in the very beginning. If he had, he would have said nothing to me of the terrible plans which were being made for my people. I would not have known, so I could not have blamed him. But he had not walked away.

As a friend, the right thing would have been for him to help us escape, taking us deep into the forest where we might elude the army's reach. Then again, if he'd told me everything from the beginning, we would have told all our friends and family in turn. Since we had no weapons with which to defend ourselves, we would have run from our homes, seeking safety and a new life in the woods and beyond. But if there had been a mass exodus to the woods, the army would have been alerted to it. They would have come after us, and I was convinced their wrath over our attempted escape would have been met with even more despicable punishments. Would they have bothered to load us all onto ships and send us away? Or would they simply have imprisoned or killed us, along with our Mi'kmaq families?

As a man, he had been trapped. I clung to the fact that he had committed something close to treason when he'd warned me to keep Henri and André away. If he had not, they would be on the ships as well, or punished in an even worse way for trying to hide. I had to believe he had done the best he could. I had to.

One night as we were falling asleep, Claire whispered through the dark, "You're so quiet. What are you thinking about?"

"Papa, Mathieu, and Guillaume," I replied. "And our other brothers, of course."

"Really?" The mattress crackled as she rolled to face me, but her expression was invisible in the night. I imagined I could see it, the suspicion plain in her eyes. "So why do you smile when you're thinking about them?"

"I don't."

"Yes, you do," she said. "Our men are prisoners, our world is upside down, and yet you smile."

Her words stung, but my guilty conscience hurt so much more already. I covered the pain with a snort of laughter. "That's ridiculous. You can't even see me."

"Amélie, I have slept beside you for more than ten years. Do you think I cannot sense what you feel?"

When I did not answer, she sighed with exasperation. "You have a secret. I promise I will not tell."

She was warm to me now, her voice sweet as honey. She was thinking of Guillaume, locked away for God only knew how long, and she wanted to know what I knew. I knew nothing, so I said nothing.

In the morning I was determined to focus on my chores and banish Connor—whom I had not seen in two weeks—from my mind. Try as I might, his smile still came to me. I decided the only way to cleanse my thoughts of him was to confront the source. From the pantry I retrieved a sack of apples I had gathered earlier that week, then placed a dozen in my basket, careful not to bruise them.

"I'll be back by dark," I told Claire, who stood by the fire, sampling fish soup.

She glanced up. "Where are you going?"

"I'll be back."

"Can I come?" Giselle asked. She had been my shadow recently, craving diversion.

"Not this time. Claire needs your help here. You should make an apple pie for when Maman returns."

Then I was off, striding toward the rows of white tents, trying to look as if I were in no rush, though apprehension roared through my veins. Tenacious white willows at the water's edge clung to their festive coats, shimmering with colour whenever a breeze stirred, and the autumn sun blazed, bringing the yellows and oranges to an almost liquid gold. My clogs slipped on the rain-slicked leaves already loosed by the maples, but I kept my balance and continued up the hill. The air was warm enough that I could have left my shawl on the hook at home, but I had brought it in preparation for the later hours. In truth, I hoped to find Connor and be away from the house at least until sunset. In that time, the cold might sneak in, as it had lately, and I would be grateful for warmth.

I rarely saw many soldiers when I came up this way, though I supposed their presence depended upon which duties had been assigned to them that day. Today a few lingered in the area when I arrived, but they didn't seem busy. Most gave me a cursory glance and returned to whatever they'd been doing, but a few eyed me openly, making me uncomfortable. Concerned now, I kept my eyes straight ahead and looked for an officer in charge—even if it wasn't Connor—assuming I'd recognize one by his uniform. The coats I saw now all looked equally dingy.

"Oy! What's this, then?" A young soldier stepped in my path, giving a cheeky grin. When I said nothing, he squinted and stepped a little closer. "What do you think you're doing, mademoiselle, marching in here like you own the place?"

I heard another man chuckle, but I remained mute out of both fear and reluctance to reveal the extent of my English. I used my knowledge of their language like a secret weapon, listening in on conversations when they thought I could not. I didn't know this rough-looking man, and I wasn't about to tell him anything.

"Asked you a question, didn't I?"

Wide-eyed, I held up the basket and offered an apple. He stared at it, frowning, then cocked his head and peered more closely at me.

"Me, I likes apples," he said, coming impossibly close. His breath, thick, heavy, and sour, puffed against my face. "I likes *all* sweet things."

He reached for my neck, and I thrust the basket into his face. He shoved it sideways so hard an apple bounced out and hit the grass, but I kept holding the basket handle between us, maintaining a shield of sorts.

I shouldn't have come. My parents, my neighbours, Connor—*everyone* had told me to stay away from these men. I was impulsive, naive, and stupid, and the reality made my eyes burn. I turned to run but crashed into another, taller soldier who stood like a leering pillar. The first soldier grabbed my arms, twisting them behind my back and anchoring me in place. I shrieked with panic.

"Hello, mademoiselle," said the taller man. "Ever been kissed by a New Englander?"

They laughed when I tried to wriggle away, mimicked me when I shouted in French for them to let go, but the fingers of the New Englander dug into my shoulders, holding fast. He leaned toward me, and I turned my head . . . then suddenly found myself falling to the side. I hit the hard earth and scrambled sideways, staring with confusion at the two soldiers, now crumpled and groaning on the ground a little way from me.

A hand appeared, offering assistance, and when I looked up I nearly cried with relief.

Connor's eyes were dark with concern. "Are you all right, lass?"

I nodded meekly and took his hand.

The rest of the soldiers who had gathered seemed eager to escape the scene, but Connor demanded their attention.

"Perhaps you have forgotten Colonel Winslow's orders that no man from this camp is to interfere in any way with the inhabitants of the land." The men at his feet dropped their eyes. "No? So you do recall. In that case, I reckon you'll not be overly surprised at the punishment." He nodded briskly at two other soldiers. "Bind them. Bring them to the church. I will deal with them when I return."

"Mademoiselle Belliveau," he said to me formally in French. "Would you accompany me, please?"

I stooped to pick up my basket, then followed him away from the grumbling men and along a narrow path lined with fallen leaves, their sweet, cloying smell thick in the air. When we were far enough from the others, I saw him flex his right hand. The knuckles were smeared with blood.

"You're hurt," I said.

He glanced at his hand. "It's nothing. Come away now, mademoiselle," he said. "I think I know why you're here."

TEN

We picked our way across a wobbly path of large rocks, their silver-grey curves bumping from the surface of the river like a dragon's tail. Pebbles and haphazard piles of driftwood littered the dark sand on the other bank. I had been to this place often enough in the past, but it felt entirely new now that I shared it with him. A hidden enclave awaited us in the willows, just down the shore, where a birch had fallen years ago. Its trunk was still sturdy, even comfortable enough to be used as a bench after Connor spread his long, black cloak like a blanket for us both. I could not sit, though.

"Are you warm enough?"

I nodded, not only warm enough, but blazing hot with embarrassment at what I'd done, coming here with him. "I am sorry. Thank you for helping me, but I should go."

"What? Why?"

"I shouldn't be here. You are a stranger, and—"

"But—"

"Please," I said, close to tears again. I could see by his expression that I was making everything worse, but I couldn't help myself. "Take me home. I should not be here."

He gestured toward the log. "Mademoiselle Belliveau, please sit down. You don't have to stay, but at least rest a bit. Get your breath back. You've suffered a shock."

He'd moved a little farther down the tree, away from where he'd first been sitting, and I appreciated the space he'd given me. I ignored the voice of reason screaming in my head and did what he suggested.

"I do think I know why you came," he said quietly.

I almost laughed at the irony, since I was flustered to the point where even *I* hardly knew why I'd come. I glanced at the basket. "To bring you an apple?"

"They look good. May I have one?"

"Of course. Let me—"

We reached for the basket at the same time, and our heads collided with an audible thud. We sat up quickly, both of us pressing a hand to our brows.

"I'm so sorry!" I cried.

"Are you all right? I didn't mean—"

He reached reflexively for my face but dropped his hand when I pulled away, and I maintained a respectable distance.

"I'm fine," I said, handing him an apple. Nervous laughter bubbled behind my lips, but I kept it inside. The poor man already looked so concerned, it would be cruel of me to worry him further. "I'm sorry for making this so difficult."

He bit into the apple, taking almost half of it into his mouth with one bite. "You need not worry over that."

"Thank you for what you did back there."

"You shouldn't have had to go through that. They shall be punished, I promise. I'm only sorry I wasn't there faster."

"You were there in time; that's what matters. I hate to think—"

"Let's not, then. Let's talk of other things. Like why you came here."

"In truth, I don't know," I admitted, shy once more. "It was foolish. I should—"

"But you did anyway."

He stared at me, willing me to speak; I feared I would say the wrong thing, so I said nothing.

"Perhaps I could speak first," he offered.

I nodded, grateful for his assistance.

"I do not want to seem presumptuous, but I . . . well, I have thought of you often of late. I miss our conversations. Circumstances being what they are now, it has not been possible, and I regret that—among other things."

"I feel the same way," I admitted. "But holding private conversations like this cannot be appropriate. I know very little about you."

He reached for another apple, having finished the last, core and all. "True enough. Please allow me to remedy that situation. What would you like to know?"

A mosquito buzzed past my nose and circled toward my hand. As soon as it landed I planned to slap it—except Connor had seen it too, and his hand whipped out. He crushed the bug before it could reach its destination.

"Well," I said, watching the tiny corpse fall to the ground, "judging from your expertise against horseflies and mosquitoes, I am fairly sure you've seen combat in your past."

"Oh, aye, but not how you'd think." He grinned. "I mostly learned to stand up for myself when I was a lad."

I imagined he'd charmed everyone with that smile. Thinking of him as a boy reminded me of the story he'd shared before, of the violence that had brought him here in the beginning. I tried to picture this strong, confident man as a helpless little boy on his own. How did a child survive that sort of thing?

"Will you tell me what happened when the English sent you away from your home?"

I shouldn't have asked. From his expression I knew that immediately, and I regretted being so bold. I opened my mouth to apologize, but he held up a hand.

"It's all right. You want to know who I am, and that will tell you a lot, I suppose." He gazed across the river. "I told you I was ten when we were put in the hold of a ship similar to the ones where your father and brother are now." He took a deep breath. "Some weeks later we landed in North Carolina."

I thought of Mathieu, lost in the crowd of men, and realized Connor had been even younger than my brother. His terror would have been unimaginable.

"Once we arrived there I was sold off the docks in Charleston."

"Sold?"

"Aye. I didn't have the money to pay for transport, so the captain of the ship sold me, along with most of the others."

He spoke calmly, but his expression was hard. He told me about the farm where he'd worked for seven years, tending his master's animals. It had been an adjustment, he said, living the life of a slave. Especially since his father had once been a well-respected man of some wealth in the Highlands of Scotland.

"I'd grown up in my da's stable, working with his horses, so that was the same. Living rough was not much of a challenge, but I was not used to being treated like dirt. That was difficult. After seven years I was released from that service, and I joined the army."

"But why join the army after everything they did to you and your family?"

For the first time I saw frustration flare. "Because I had nothing else I could do. I had no money, no training, nowhere to live. I did what I had to do."

"I can't even imagine having to live that way."

He shifted on the log and faced me again, his expression hard.

"When a person's world changes, he must adapt. You need to understand that your world is changing as well. Your story may not end up being so different from what happened to me."

"What do you remember of Scotland?" I asked, changing the subject.

He frowned. "But I need to tell you—"

"No. Tell me about Scotland."

Every one of my days was filled with dread at what might happen to us. From sunrise to long after dark I worried. Connor would tell me more about that in time, I was certain. For now I needed to think of something different.

His eyes narrowed, but I insisted.

"I remember working hard." He exhaled, giving in. "And I remember a lot of rain. And laughter."

I nodded. "When Papa and my brothers were at home, we laughed more."

We stared at the clear water of the river, sparkling with sunshine. It was a perfect day, a perfect place to be, and his was the company I wanted. Yet I was still uneasy.

"Do you not think it strange that you and I are talking together when we should be enemies?" I asked.

He blinked, evidently hurt by my question.

"I'm sorry," I said quickly. "I should have said the *army* is my enemy. But you are a part of that army, whether you like it or not. The truth is, you and I should not be friends."

He leaned down and picked up a handful of pebbles, then tossed them one by one, thinking over what I'd said. They plonked into the water with tiny splashes.

"You insist upon that; however, I disagree."

"How can you? We are on opposite sides."

"Amélie," he said, "our countries are at war, but you and I need not be."

I was startled to hear him address me by my first name, but I did not object.

"Have you not been listening?" he asked, leaning toward me. "I do not believe your father and brother should be imprisoned. I do not believe the English deserve this land. I do not want you to be unhappy." Frustration drew his brow, and he reached for my hand. "I am *not* your enemy."

"I know," I whispered. "Still . . ." I slipped my hand from his and rose. "I should go."

He stood quickly. "It's not dark yet," he objected.

"No, but it will be soon, and I must get home to make supper."

"Suddenly you're in a hurry. Have I said something to upset you?"

"Not at all," I assured him, but the emotions I had tried to smother suddenly swelled to the surface, making it difficult to think clearly. Yes, I was upset—and I was afraid, though I did not know why. Was I intimidated by the exasperation in his voice, his insistence that I need not fear him? Was it his talk of war? Certainly that was frightening, but my fear ran deeper than that. Panic had struck unexpectedly when he had said my Christian name, and it had worsened when he'd held my hand.

"I need to get back."

"Don't go," he said. "I'm sorry I said the wrong thing. I don't want you to leave. Please stay."

"Why?" I demanded. "I do not understand. You insist we are friends, that you will protect me. You tell me things about this war that you should not tell me. You say my name as if we are close, but . . . You do not know me. Nor do I know you. This makes no sense."

"To me it does. I am fond of you, and my affection grows with every one of our meetings. In my grey world, you shine like the sun through fog. I admire your courage, the way you demand truth even when it is being firmly denied. This place is being pulled apart, but you will not permit that to happen without a fight. I will even admit to being impressed by your stubbornness, though it concerns me at times. You seem unafraid."

I laughed and shook my head. "You think I am unafraid? You truly do not know me."

"I said you seem that way, but I know you are not. We are all afraid, Amélie. Every one of us. But we do not have to surrender to it."

It was difficult to imagine his being afraid, but I could not bring myself to argue. "You are the boldest man I have ever met."

"I imagine I am," he replied, chuckling. "But I am an honest man as well. One you can trust."

A cloud drifted past the sun, the first I had noticed all afternoon, and I shivered despite the warmth of the day. Recently, without Papa and my brothers, and without my Mi'kmaq family, I had felt very alone. Thoughts of Connor had kept me company. Here was an offer of friendship, one I truly desired. It would be simple to blame social propriety and deny us both that simple pleasure. On the other hand, what would happen if I chose to trust him?

Surprising us both, I reached for his hand and gripped it tightly. "Connor, I . . . I get afraid at night, wondering what might happen," I blurted out. Once the words began I found I could no longer contain them. "I remember my brother's face as he was taken to the ships, and I think of the soldiers with their bayonets . . ."

I willed the images away, but they remained, dark and terrible as ever.

"I cannot bear the fear that comes of uncertainty; I have never felt that before," I told him, trying not to crumble into sobs. "All my life I have known what the next day would bring, and I knew I was safe. My life has gone from being paradise to being unpredictable and cruel. I am so afraid, I cry at night when everyone else is asleep. I think of you and dare to hope I will be all right, that you will protect me somehow. Then I wonder . . . if they send me away, will I ever see you again?"

He lifted my hands and slowly, gently pressed his lips to them. The rugged lines of his face had relaxed, and I knew my words had moved him.

"Amélie, I cannot predict the future, but as God is my witness, I promise I will do everything in my power to keep you safe."

Connor

ELEVEN

Connor sat in the doorway of the empty church, his thumb absently stroking nail holes from the boards the army had used to barricade the windows and doors. Those should have been enough, but they were not. Having blocked all escape routes, Winslow had then installed nervous soldiers around the perimeter of the crowded room, smothering any possible rebellion. The soldiers wouldn't have been able to do much within the small confines of the church, but the goal of intimidation had been achieved.

Connor understood the theory behind holding them captive. Without the men—usually the ones to stir up trouble—the women and children would be without anchors. They would be as quiet as church mice, frantic to see their men delivered safely home.

It had taken a full day before the Acadians had been subdued into the uneasy state of recognizing they were trapped. There was nowhere to go, there was nothing they could do. Food had been sparse, though they had had water. Not enough to wash, of course, and as a result the air had clouded in a miasma of unwashed men and boys, hostility, and fear. Exactly the atmosphere Colonel Winslow had wanted.

What the English wanted, what they always wanted, was for their enemies to be submissive. Once the vanquished bowed before their conqueror, the English would go that step further to prove they were the more powerful. In Scotland, they'd destroyed the ragtag Jacobite forces at Culloden, then carried on around the countryside, arresting, raping, burning, and killing without paying heed to any sort of law. His homeland had been torn apart until it didn't retain anything of its past glory, and that was *after* the Scots had admitted defeat. It took a special sort of people to get pleasure from that. The English enjoyed it, obviously, since they were doing it here as well.

The Acadian men were gone from the church now, herded to the ships. All had been bitter; most had seethed; others had seemed disoriented, unable to fully grasp what was happening. Few had been entirely broken. Charles Belliveau had not given in easily. Not at first. But as soon as young Mathieu had returned from his messenger errand, Fitch had grabbed him, threatened harm to the boy if his father did not comply. The wind in Belliveau's proud sails dropped to nothing in that instant. He had assumed his seat without another word, gazed levelly at the other Acadian men, and they'd sat as well. His eyes returned to his son and stayed there, offering silent encouragement to the boy. After a while, Fitch's interest had been piqued by something else, and he'd forgotten about his small captive. Seizing the opportunity, Connor had led Mathieu discreetly back to his father's side.

As Mathieu sidled back into place, Connor had felt Belliveau's scrutiny. Amélie's father would recall him from the unwelcome visits he and Fitch had made to their home, following Winslow's orders to steal anything and everything from the local people. Perhaps he also remembered Connor's attempts to be civil, to apologize for his commanding officer's insolence.

It had been impossible for Connor to look at Belliveau later on, when he had stepped up beside Winslow and taken his position as translator. His role that day, he knew, would forever brand him in their minds as the enemy. There was nothing he could do to change that.

Since the captives had been crowded into the holds of the ships, temporarily put out of the army's minds, the windows and doors of the church had been opened wide once again, the floor and benches wiped clean. Winslow's desk and chair had been returned to the rectory, and the overall atmosphere became as close to regimented military as it could get. Life had moved on.

Except Connor couldn't think of much else besides the men in the ships. Ten years had passed since he had lain on the slippery boards of a ship's floor, their cold clamminess bleeding through his skin and pooling in the marrow of his bones. Ten long, hard years.

Time had not dimmed the memories of his own incarceration. Nor could he forget the little boy he had been, scared and haunted by the sense that he had been abandoned by the rest of the world. Like these innocent Acadians, hundreds of Scots had been packed together like kindling, stuffed into a creaking, swaying coffin, a dark world of confusion. Once they'd sailed from the only shore he had ever known, they had rolled over waves for weeks without respite, the ocean rising and falling beneath and around them with treacherous irregularity. Throughout the voyage he'd prayed for death yet clung to the brief promise of sunshine peeking through the hatch. He'd witnessed the damage that chains could make on men's wrists and ankles, how those tight, inflexible manacles eventually hung loose over emaciated limbs. Gnawing, agonizing hunger had ravaged his young body as he awaited shrinking rations of maggot-riddled mush. And when men died and their bodies were tossed like offal into the sea, the survivors had greedily laid claim to the dead men's meagre portions.

He could still recall the moment when his will to live had begun to rot along with his insides.

When the ship had finally anchored offshore and the captives staggered into the light, not one of them could claim to be the man he'd been before. Connor's hunger barely registered anymore, it had become so profound. Over time the humiliation of slavery was softened by the assurance of fresh air to breathe and clean water to drink, and he found comfort in a bed of straw. For years, he had worked hard and earned his release—one which resulted in his being bound by a different set of chains.

Being a soldier was Connor's job. Being here at Grand Pré, doing what he was doing, reeked of irony. It hadn't been the posting he'd had in mind when he'd decided to join His Majesty's army. When he'd picked up his money and boarded the ship from Boston as a free—though enlisted—man, he'd imagined battles and adventure . . . and an actual enemy. Instead he was tearing families from their homes and each other.

The troops had set sail for Canada in April and dropped anchor in late May. The trees and shrubs of the Annapolis Basin had been in full, glorious bud, and Connor had stood on deck with the others, cheering the welcome sight. As the tenders rowed into the harbour, millions of tiny, voracious insects, having been encouraged to hatch by the balmy air, descended upon them. They floated about like specks of dust, landing on the men's cheeks, necks, brows, scalps, and wherever else they could find vulnerable skin. As the men set up camp, they slapped at clouds of black flies, a bittersweet reminder to Connor of the midges back in Scotland. When at last the tents were up and the exhausted men formed a line for food, they were informed they would not be receiving their rum allowance that day, prompting angry complaints.

Three days later the disgruntled troops set off to Chignecto, destination Fort Beauséjour. Connor was among the first of the troops who crossed a hastily built bridge assembled near a collection of small buildings. As soon as they neared the other side, the quiet of the pathway erupted into chaos. Howls and shrieks filled the air, and as the terrified men wheeled in confusion, they were faced by French cannon and muskets. Panic made them clumsy, but they prepared their own four cannon and returned fire as best they could. Their adversary was visible through the smoke, some wearing the blue uniform of the French, some in leather clothing Connor had not seen before. Could these be the Indians of whom he'd heard people speak? It seemed so, for when one raced through the trees nearby, he caught a glimpse of ink black hair and a naked male chest. So it was true: the native people were united with the French.

"Look there!" shouted the corporal beside him.

He was pointing at the same man Connor had just seen. With a grin, the corporal lifted his musket to eye level and focused on the Indian. Connor looked away, unimpressed. A musket rarely hit anything it aimed for. Aim it at a wall and there was a chance it might strike something, but the only way to truly hit a target was with an arrow. Just as Connor turned, the corporal gave a sharp grunt, then crumpled to the ground. Connor dropped beside him, sickened by the rush of blood spurting from the man's throat. An arrow pinned him to the cool green grass.

"I'll get help," he told the gasping man, scanning the area for the medical officer.

"Keep moving!" roared his sergeant.

"But sir—"

"He's already gone. Keep marching, Corporal!"

A well-aimed shot from one of the English cannon ignited a redoubt near the enemy's front line, and flames soon shot out of other buildings as well. The undisciplined, inexperienced British forces pressed on, driving the defenders back, surprising Connor and many of the others with their own success. Their battle instruction had been limited, their actual exercises even more so, yet the French fled before them, surely hoping to find safety in numbers at the nearby fort. The Indians went as well.

Bloodied but victorious, the troops settled into what remained of the small village, celebrating around campfires with a meagre meal and—finally—a taste of rum.

Similar altercations followed as the English worked their way toward the fort, but now they were better prepared and less liable to fall prey to surprise attacks. Hostages were taken by both sides, a small number of men were hurt and even fewer killed, but for the most part the process was a determined forward march. When the British finally reached the fort, the command "Fire!" was given, and the result was astounding. Any surviving French turned and ran.

That night the fort was renamed Fort Cumberland, and the English flag was hoisted. Connor wound his way through soldiers enjoying the fort's rich store of brandy and wine, but he was not in the mood for celebration. It had not been a glorious battle, and the last few weeks had not been easy. Certainly this was a victory they'd earned, and as a member of the army Connor was entitled to revel in the win.

But he could not. Once again, the English had taken someone else's home. This time they had named it after the Duke of Cumberland, the man who had ordered English troops to slaughter Scotland.

Two weeks later the British arrived in the beautiful land of Minas, which the local people called Grand Pré. Connor was mesmerized by the poetic, undulating land with its copper red sand and sheer rock cliffs. If the slowly climbing hills had been taller, they might have reminded him of the Lowlands back home, though it had been a long time since he'd seen them. This little village, with its humble houses and fat cows, its endless wild game and seafood, seemed idyllic. There was something about the way the sun poured onto the land here, feeding the shining leaves, bringing the wildness alive.

When he first saw the Acadians' unusual dike system, he didn't understand what it was. All he knew was that their plentiful crops were a deeper green than he'd ever seen before. He watched the villagers work, mused over their strange choice of land, and wondered how they had harnessed the sea.

One of the other men claimed to have seen this sort of system in France before, and he explained the process.

"This marshland belonged to the sea for thousands of years," he was told. "Every time the tides receded they left behind a thick deposit of salt which made the land useless for farming. These Acadians are like the French I saw. Perhaps they are even related." He shrugged. "Anyhow, they did not see a desolate land. They saw possibility."

To prevent the sea from returning, the Acadians built massive dikes all along the edge of the land using sod from the original marsh. Since those particular grasses were used to being covered by salt water for hours at a time, they were able to withstand the sea when it battered the dikes. Within those dikes the Acadians built aboiteaux, which contained a wooden sluice. Inside the sluices were small wooden valves which were angled in such a way that they opened to allow any fresh rainwater to escape from the field, but they stood strong against the seawater. For a couple of years the Acadians had left the fields completely alone, letting natural rainwater wash through the marshland and escape through the aboiteaux at low tide, carrying the salt deposits with it. What was left behind was layers of silt and soil which created the most fertile land imaginable.

It was an incredible undertaking and surely required constant upkeep, but the concept was amazing. Connor longed to visit the people of the land, to speak with them about the system, but Winslow's order prohibited any soldier from leaving camp and heading down the street of the village without special permission.

Summer here was so much hotter than he'd expected it would be. When the wind stopped and the cicadas screeched from their perches on towering oaks and maples, his heavy woollen uniform was torturous. More than a few soldiers took to removing coats and stockings when they weren't required. Sleeping at night was a challenge. The stink of sweat and dirt mixed with the waves of heat in the stuffy tents made it nearly impossible to breathe. Connor prayed for rain—though when it eventually came, it hit with a vengeance.

Then Winslow had made everything worse. Feeling the need not only to establish the English presence but to protect it, he ordered pickets to be set up. The barricade was to enclose not only the church but two other buildings as well, stretching out a distance. It was difficult work and hardly seemed necessary, considering the near helplessness of the villagers, and most of the soldiers grumbled their disapproval. Sergeant Fitch, however, revelled in the plan. He took a sort of perverse delight in yelling orders. Having armed his battalion with the axes they had taken from the Acadians as well as a number of bucksaws, he lined the men up and marched them into the forest. The air within the trees was somewhat cooler than in the direct sun, but the insects were no less ravenous. While some men cut trees, others prepared three-foot-deep holes for the pickets, alternating between pick axe and shovel, breaking their backs in a whole different way. At least Fitch allowed the men to leave their coats in their tents. After four days of chopping, sawing, and carrying the trunks to the holes, the barricade was completed. The area looked almost like a proper fort, but Winslow wasn't satisfied. He sent them out again, this time to extend the fence around the church cemetery.

Now the English had a fort; the battle could truly begin.

It seemed impossible that something so ugly could happen in a place this beautiful.

Connor suddenly needed air. He got to his feet, wanting to be far from the misused church, and sought a private, quiet place where he could think. The farther he went through the lush grass, his eyes on the world around him, the calmer he felt. From a nearby tree came the call of a songbird, cheery and bright and welcoming to all. A moment later the little thing flitted before Connor's eyes and disappeared into the trees, but he still heard its song. And why wouldn't it sing? There was nothing here that might steal the feathered fellow's happiness or his melody. The land all around them was as close to perfection as he could imagine anything being.

Amélie had called Grand Pré paradise, and Connor thought she was most likely right. No wonder the English wanted it.

His feet led him to a familiar spot, and he smiled in memory. The last time he'd sat here, she had come along with her little basket. Her presence had been an unexpected gift, and ever since then he had hoped against reason to see her again, to hear her thoughts. The girl was courageous to a fault and fiercely beautiful whenever she disagreed with him. Not belligerent, though. Never ill-mannered. Before their conversation, he had considered the army's position to be wrong on many levels, and now he was more opposed to it than ever. Since speaking with her, he'd daydreamed more than once about changing the minds of the men in charge, convincing them to let the Acadians remain in their homes. After all, they had caused no trouble; they had pledged not to fight for either side; they had even fed the army from their crops.

More than anything, Connor wanted to be the one who made it possible for Amélie to stay in the home she so obviously loved. He agreed with almost every one of her arguments and reluctantly accepted that she was right that the two of them were on opposite sides—though he hated that fact. He would not agree, however, that they should be enemies.

The air had come alive with trills and calls of other birds, and from somewhere far away came the continuous shush of the ocean. With a sort of guilty relief, he yanked off his boots, rolled his stockings down over his feet, and curled his toes into the tall grass. He held in a sigh of contentment, not wanting anyone to hear him and disturb his peace. He craved this kind of quiet.

Now that Winslow's army had no battles to wage, no target for their cannon, its general condition had declined. Morale was low all around. The men were whipped or otherwise punished almost daily for stealing, being drunk on guard, or some other idiocy. One fool accidentally shot another through the ankle, necessitating his friend's having a leg cut off. A number of soldiers had succumbed to illness, and the lucky ones were sent home.

He wondered what it was like here in winter. Would he still be here?

A girl and a black and white dog appeared in the valley below the fort, walking from barn to field. *Does Amélie know her?* Even from this distance, Connor could see the dog's tail wagging madly. It danced around the girl, who stooped under a fence with her basket, happily going about her daily life. How long before she could no longer do so? How long before she must bid farewell to her little dog?

These people had lived here for generations—not as many as his own family had been in the Highlands, but enough. This was their home, and everything about this impending eviction felt morally wrong.

A dark blade of grass waved to him from between his feet. He plucked it from the ground and slipped it between his teeth, letting it hang from his lips in an arch, like a bow. That made him think of the local Indians—the Mi'kmaq, they called them. Governor Cornwallis's bounty for scalps had been abolished three years previously, but he'd noticed the natives wisely remained hidden for the most part.

"Nice view, innit?"

He knew the voice before he turned, and he managed a weak smile of welcome as Sergeant Fitch slunk out of the shadows of the trees. Thumbs in his waistband, he strode to where Connor had been relaxing and stood beside him. Fitch was the last person on earth Connor wanted to see. The tall, gaunt officer had developed into something far beyond a simple irritant. He was an obnoxious, patronizing louse who took great pleasure in the fact that his purchased commission had put him in charge of better men than he. He was also, as was made obvious by his rough speech, ill-educated. It was a mystery to Connor how he had been able to afford such a payment. It could not possibly have come from his own pocket.

"All done for the day?" Fitch asked. He bent slightly and spat a wad of something into the grass near Connor's hand.

Connor resisted the urge to flinch. It was difficult enough to understand the man's thick accent, but did he always have to speak through a mouthful of something?

"Shouldn't you be busy somewhere, Corporal?"

"No, sir. I've completed my work for the day."

Fitch seemed to consider this, then he spat again and eased down beside Connor. "I'll be glad when we're done here," he said snidely, his gaze fixed on the horizon.

"Do you not fancy the countryside?"

"Not a bit. Too . . ." Fitch narrowed his eyes, searching for a word. When it finally came to him, he nodded. "Too quiet."

Connor resisted the urge to roll his eyes.

"And the women, well, ain't seen but a few what aren't mop-seys. All these big, strong farmers ought to produce more females is what."

Connor was impressed by the stupidity of the comment. "Families here are large enough. I've seen homes with more than ten children, and I expect half of those are lassies."

Fitch rocked back and let out a knowing bark of laughter, catching himself with one hand on the grass when he lost his balance. "That's true enough. Rutting Frenchmen everywhere. Disgusting, really." He hesitated. "Not to say I'd not relish a good romp should the opportunity arise."

Connor was glad the night was closing in on them. He didn't want to watch Fitch's face, and he didn't want the sergeant to see his own.

The man jabbed Connor in the ribs with his elbow. "I'd not walk away if I found myself alone with one of those young French things."

Connor refused to take the bait, though his thoughts had gone directly to Amélie.

"Come to think of it . . ." Fitch lifted a sparse eyebrow at Connor. "I should very much like to get my hands—"

Connor pushed to his feet, carrying his boots with him. He was simply unable to remain a moment longer in the man's presence. "If you'll excuse me, Sergeant. I'm to meet Corporal Brandt—"

"Now? Must you go *now*? I only just arrived!"

"Afraid so, sir. He'll be waiting."

Connor had no such appointment, but he strode hastily from the little spot, ducking under a low hanging branch. He was distracted, imagining Fitch's rage at being abandoned, so he didn't hear the swishing of grass growing louder behind him. Before he could make a sound or lift a hand, he was wrestled behind a shrub, far from any suggestion of help. He landed flat on his back, a knife pressed to his throat. A familiar face loomed over him.

"André Belliveau," Connor exclaimed, astonished.

He had assumed the two missing Belliveaus were far from here, hiding in the forest with the Indians, but Amélie's oldest brother wasn't dressed like a Mi'kmaq. He wore a white coat with blue trim, marking him as a French fighter.

André added weight to his blade. He straddled Connor, pinning his arm to the ground with one knee.

"It is good you remember who I am, because I know who you are as well, Corporal MacDonnell." André's eyes narrowed. "I have seen you with my sister."

Connor swallowed, and he felt the knife's sharp edge ride the movement.

"I have a decision to make, soldier," André informed him. "I could slice your throat and leave you here—or not." The Acadian's blue eyes were hard, his brow slick with sweat. Connor doubted he was bluffing. "Fortunately for you, I am a good Christian. Because of that I will choose the second option and hope I am right. But in return, I demand a promise from you."

The sharp pain of the Acadian's knee on his arm was distracting, and Connor could not wriggle free. "What is it?"

"You know my sister." André waited, but Connor did not speak. This was uncertain ground. "Fine. You do not need to confirm that which I already know. What you do need to know is that I detest your army with every drop of my blood. It has come here and torn my family apart, and I would be happy to see it destroyed. But you . . ." He drew in a breath, and Connor heard the effort it took. Emotion was creeping into the young man's voice though it did not show on his face. "Well, you have caught Amélie's eye, which tells me you might not be entirely wicked."

Connor held so still he barely breathed.

"We all have options in life," André continued. "Yours are clear. You are in a position where you can can either protect my family or you can follow your colonel's despicable orders. I am asking you to do the right thing, Englishman. In return for your life today, you will look after Amélie and the others. Keep them safe since I cannot do it myself."

"That decision has already been made." Connor's voice was hoarse. "I swear it to you, as I have already sworn to Amélie. You have nothing to fear from me."

At that, André's pale eyebrows lifted. "That I do not believe. You speak Winslow's words, and those are words which must be feared."

"But they are not mine. Right now, as I look you in the eye, I speak the truth. These words are my own."

André hesitated, giving Connor a brief opportunity to study him. He saw Amélie in the thin line of his lips, but more than that, he saw their father.

The knife lifted, and a moment later the agonizing pressure eased off his arm. André stood, staring down at him.

"If you fail, MacDonnell, I will hunt you down and I will kill you. Do you understand?"

"I do."

They held each other's stare a moment longer, anchoring the vow between them. Then Belliveau was gone, vanished into the tall grass.

TWELVE

Connor awoke with a sense of apprehension. Other than the clang of tin cups and the shuffling of boots, the camp was oddly hushed, the usual protests over having to get to work muted. He stared up at the blackened seams of the canvas, listening for clues. At last someone came near enough for him to make out a few words.

"—stupid bastard," he heard.

"The arse had been warned more'n once. He deserves what he'll get." The voice laughed. "And I hope it's a lot."

The speakers edged close enough that Connor could hear the rustling of their coats when they moved. He rolled to one side, curious.

"She's a bonny thing, though," the first voice mused. "I can see why—"

Alarm shot through Connor's veins. *Please don't let it be Amélie.* He rolled to his feet, dressed quickly, and pushed through the flap of his tent, but by the time he poked his head out, the men were gone. Nothing seemed amiss around the camp, so he wandered farther, lured to the church. There he might find answers.

"Terrible business," Winslow grumbled, greeting him at the door.

"I'm sorry, sir?"

The colonel's expression brightened, and he slapped Connor on the shoulder. "But it is a most excellent day for you, *Sergeant* MacDonnell."

He was utterly confused now. "Sir?"

Winslow shook his head so his jowls wobbled slightly, then stepped toward a small table, where he served tea to Connor and himself. "So you've not heard yet. The camp's gossips have not yet risen from their beds, I gather. Well, today's news is that the former Sergeant Fitch gravely overstepped the boundaries of his position." He took a sip, then pressed his lips together with distaste. "Indeed, he overstepped the boundaries of moral responsibility."

Connor's fingers tightened around his cup.

"The man overindulged—as far too many men around here seem wont to do," Winslow said. "Then apparently felt he was within his rights to hunt down a young Acadian girl." He cleared his throat. "Have his way with her, as it were."

Connor's stomach filled with ice. "And the girl, sir?"

Colonel Winslow glanced up at him. "Oh, she is fine. She escaped the creature's clutches before he could . . ." He chuckled. "Well, suffice to say she now has an adventure to tell or keep to herself, however she should wish. She's a pretty young thing and is now under my protection."

"Does her family know?"

"Good of you to think that way, MacDonnell. Yes, yes, they have been informed." He frowned. "Of course her father and brothers are being held, but the Doucet women have been here, and we have spoken. Since the girl was frightened but no one was harmed, we decided not to inform her father."

Doucet. Not Belliveau. It was all Connor could do not to slump with relief.

"As a result of Fitch's idiocy, you have been temporarily pro-
moted to sergeant. You'll be pleased with that?"

"Yes, sir. Thank you, sir."

"You'll arrange for the flogging."

"Sir?"

"The flogging. As interim sergeant that will be your responsibility, of course."

⟶

Connor couldn't deny the satisfaction of seeing Fitch led forward
in chains, snivelling in fear, but a small part of him felt sorry for
the wretched creature. By the time this day had arrived, the man
had already been incarcerated for two days. He looked leaner and
dirtier than ever.

Seeing Connor, Fitch gave his approximation of an endearing
smile. He'd lost a tooth, Connor noticed. He hoped the girl had
kicked it out of him.

"Up to you, then, is it?" Fitch's usual cockiness was still there,
but it lacked his customary confidence.

Connor said nothing, only waited stiffly. Two guards tied
Fitch to the pole and removed his shirt, revealing a pasty white
back and the outline of ribs. The tail of Fitch's hair quivered with
fear, but the coward soon put a stop to any of Connor's reserve.

"It were almost worth it. If she'd just stopped fighting, I'd
have got what I came for," he muttered, giving Connor a sideways
leer. "But I'll tell you what, if I were to do it again, I'd go after that
young doxy I've seen you with. Tell me when you're done with
her, would you?"

Connor swallowed bile and gave the guard a grim nod. The
order was called, and the flogging began.

⌐

Other than better rations and less abuse from his superiors, what was the point of having a position of authority if there was nothing he could do with it? Certainly Connor could issue a few orders, but matters of importance were completely out of his control. He handled Winslow's mail—orders for a milk cow or a better horse— and the troops' constant whining about the shortage of rum and molasses, repeated complaints of how cold the army's tents were, how greatly they were suffering at these inconveniences . . .

Would it not be better for everyone if the English army simply returned to England? If only they could abandon the need to possess every region upon which they landed, there would be no cause for such grievances.

Connor reached for a quill and scowled at his own bright red sleeve.

Where was Amélie? Was she all right? He hadn't seen her in some time and was aware that some of the residents had been vanishing quietly into the woods. He wondered if she might do the same. He wanted her to escape, to flee the nightmare he knew was coming, but the thought of her being gone was more difficult than he'd thought it would be. He forced his mind back to the work at hand, going over the commander's missives of the day, filing what needed filing and taking care of what needed taking care of. Only after that could he head out to tend to other, more physical aspects of his position.

The monotony of this post was driving him mad.

Sept 13. Orders of the Day

That all officers & Soldiers Provide them Selves with water before Sun Sett for that no Party or Person will be admitted to go

out after Calling the roll on any account what Ever, as many bad
thing have been done Lately in the Night Season, Distressing the
French Inhabitants in this Neighbourhood and that in the Day
Season when the Companys want water a Serjt or Corporal to
go with the Party who are not to Suffer the men to Intermeddle
with the French or their Effects. These orders to be Publishd at
the Head of Each Company at Calling the Roll and Strickt obe-
diance paid them . . .

At times Connor marvelled at the cool, proper tones of the
officers' missives, the often good-natured, even lighthearted sig-
natures that occasionally accompanied a shocking order. Direc-
tions and explanations sounded more like instructions given to
merchants taking wares to market, not to soldiers driving families
from their homes. But as he stared at the latest *Am in receipt of*
your kind letter, at the *I long to be with you I am Tyred of the . . .*
and at the ever present *your most obedient Humble Servant*, he understood the men writing the letters had little choice but to write
in this detached manner. Their only option was to think of their
duty and the job at hand. If they allowed themselves to feel sympathy for the Acadians, the cause in which they so passionately
believed would surely be lost.

Flipping through the morning's papers, he came across a listing of all the inhabitants of Grand Pré, and his finger skimmed
down the names until he spotted Amélie and her family—or at
least those who had not mysteriously disappeared before they
could be recorded. From what he'd seen, they were a close family;
then again, everyone here seemed that way.

The thought prompted an unexpected wave of homesickness,
and the dark chill of his childhood home stirred in his mind. The
stink of peat returned—both miserable and comforting—and he
shivered reflexively. The raw air of the Highlands had often forced

his family to huddle together by the fire, to warm each other's hands, to tell stories to distract themselves. For a brief moment he closed his eyes, welcoming back the half memories of cold, rainy days and nights, then the days spent outside when the sun finally braved a visit. A song whispered through the reminiscence, and he missed his mother with an unexpected pang of grief. The faces were fading; the longing remained.

Winslow appeared at his side and cleared his throat. "Have you the missive from Osgood? I believe I gave it to you this morning."

Connor straightened, blinking away his thoughts, then rifled through the pages and produced the one in question. "Yes, sir."

Rubbing his bristled chin with forefinger and thumb, Winslow made no move to take the document from Connor's hand. "He was in agreement with my recommendation?"

This was rarely a question, since the men with whom Winslow communicated generally bowed to his wishes. Still, since Winslow was obviously waiting, Connor read the original letter and its reply out loud.

Grand PRE Camp, Septembr 15th, 1755.

A Court Martial to be held this Morning for the Tryal of Simon Bloode of Lievt Colo Winslows Company & Ephraim Parker of Capt Hobbs Company for Unlicensed Interference with French Civillyans Last Night and of Jonathan Gould of Capt Hobbs Company, for that he being Postd on Centry at the North Gate Suffered the sd Parker & Blood to Pas and Suposed to be Confederate with them, and make return as Soon as you can

Members: Captain Osgood, Lievt Smith, Lievt Crooker, Lievt Wheeler, Enn Gay.

John Winslow

And the reply:

In obedience to the within warrant we the Subscribers have assembled and Sent for the Prisoners, upon Examanation do Finde Simon Blood & Ephraim Parker to be Guilty of the Crime aledged against them, and do award them Thirty Lashes apiece well Lade on and do Finde Jonathan Gould Not Guilty.

Phineas Osgood

Winslow nodded, pensive. "Thirty lashes apiece. Right. Answer for me, would you? My hand is stiff with the rheumatism this morning."

Connor pulled out a fresh page and dipped his quill.

" 'Sentence confirmed and ordered to be executed at the relief of the guards.' Then sign for me, if you will."

Supply requests, minor criminal sentences, the occasional note of gratitude—all passed under Connor's scrutiny, but most failed to rouse any interest in him. None of the news was good, as far as the Acadians were concerned. Recently, missives specifying actual ships, numbers of passengers, supplies, and destinations had begun to pass through his hands. The Acadian names had been reduced to no more than scratchings on a list of goods. Just another package to be shipped. But no matter how this parcel was wrapped, the corners would always be sharp, the contents fragile. And those responsible for its transport were already careless.

Yet another chart of names and numbers lay on the desk before him. Resigned to finishing as much as he could for the day, he began to work through it, comparing it to other charts, marking names and numbers as other villages were being emptied. Over time, the lists and letters on Connor's desk drew closer to Grand Pré. The noose was tightening. The women and children of the village seemed to sense it; they now regarded the uniformed men—including him—with a tight wariness. Would Amélie look at him as they did? After all, as she had said, he was the enemy. He knew well from the letters he handled and wrote that more ships would soon crowd the harbour. She would be driven into those rocking boxes along with the others, trapped by the hundreds in the darkness. How would she live?

He felt sick with helplessness. Despite everything, he would be one of those charged with pushing the Acadians onto the ships. With musket in hand, he would give them no choice but to cross the gangway. Would he see her? Would she even look for him? Could he bear to meet her eyes?

He paused, his quill poised over the words. When Grand Pré became part of one of these final lists, those pages of numbers and names would come to Connor just as precisely as this one had. He would see her name here. He would know where she was being sent.

When the time comes, he'd told her, *I will take care of you.*

That moment was coming. He was running out of time.

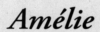

Amélie

THIRTEEN

The weir was full, a dozen or so shiny silver tails splashing in the low tide and protesting their confinement. My feet slurped through the thick, knee-high mud, but I'd hiked my skirt high enough that it wouldn't need washing right away. I plopped ten wriggling fish into my basket, set the rest free, and stared reluctantly down at my captives. In truth I had grown weary of eating seafood. Unfortunately, without the men here to hunt, I had no choice. Our livestock was forfeit to the crown—as were our weapons, of course—and I was reduced to setting snares. I'd managed to bring in one rabbit and two squirrels in four days. Not enough by far. Lately, our entire existence seemed to have been reduced to worrying about food. Most of the fish I'd just caught would end up in pies for the men in the ships.

The last thing I expected to see when I walked into our yard was a small slaughtered deer, enough to sustain us—and others—for some time. What we couldn't eat right away we could hang in the shade and enjoy for the next couple of weeks.

As soon as I saw it, I knew whom to thank for the gift. I hadn't seen my best friend for months, and the separation had been difficult. I had been used to being with Mali almost on a daily basis, and I longed to speak with her about everything that was happening. I even wanted to share my confusion about Connor, though thinking about that conversation made my palms sweat.

I had told myself all this turmoil with the English would pass, that the French would return and drive the army from our land, but that was not happening. I was reluctantly getting accustomed to the idea that the Mi'kmaq were gone as well. At least they weren't gone for good, as evidenced by the deer. Maman exclaimed joyfully over the bounty, and I told her I was going to visit Mali, to thank her for thinking of us in these lean and dangerous times. She was nervous about the idea of my walking in the woods alone, but it was only right that I go. She bade me bring an apple pie and some bread.

"I will be back later to help you with the deer," I promised.

"Don't worry. We can do this," Claire assured me. "Go now. Tell her hello from me."

As I knew she would, Mali found me before I could get lost. She bounded out of the trees, beaming, and we swung each other around in an enthusiastic embrace. The relief of being able to speak and act freely was almost overwhelming.

"*Wela'lin*, Mali!" I said, thanking her and smiling wider than I had in months. "I am so tired of eating fish!"

"How I have missed you!" she cried. "I have been so afraid for your family. Are you all right?"

"We women are fine. We can take care of ourselves. But we're so worried we can hardly sleep! Oh, Mali. It's so terrible." I clenched my fists, wanting to scream from frustration. "Those ships rock in the harbour, going nowhere, and the men inside hardly get to see the sun."

Mali's eyes narrowed. "The English are terrible. They understand nothing."

"At least you are all safe up here."

"They cannot find us. You almost could not!"

"I knew you would find me." I threw my arms around her neck again. "Oh, Mali. I feel almost normal when I see you again."

"Me too. Can you stay?"

I shook my head. "Maman will worry. Besides, I am having venison for supper tonight!" She grinned; my pleasure made her happy. I handed her the basket of pie and bread. "We wanted to say thank you."

"I love your maman's apple pie." She bit her lip. "I'm glad you came. I have another gift for you."

"Another? Oh Mali! I don't need anything more."

She took my hand. "Come."

We followed a deer trail, brushing dry autumn branches out of the way as we went. I inhaled the musky odour of fallen leaves, appreciating the smell of something other than saltwater air for a change. The familiar sight of a birchbark wigwam appeared in the next clearing, and I could see it had been recently built. That meant Mali's family had been moving, intent on staying hidden.

"Ansale!" called Mali. "We have a visitor!"

A pair of noisy dogs raced toward us, passing Mali's older brother, who stood by a stack of wood, cutting it into kindling. He wore only his breechclout, and his long black hair was tethered into a tail, for it was hot work despite the chill of the forest. He stepped back from the pile, wiping sweat from his brow with the back of one arm, and grinned.

"Amélie! My long-lost little sister!"

I didn't mind his sweaty hug, in fact I welcomed it with open arms. His smoky scent was reassuring, reminding me that as long as I was with Mali and the rest of the family, everything would be all right.

"Have you come to—"

"Don't spoil my surprise," Mali scolded. "I told Amélie I have a gift for her. Do you know where it is?"

"I think I do. Shall I get it?"

"Yes, please." She waved her hands at him. "Go! Hurry up, lazy man."

I frowned, watching him go. "Is it heavy? Will I be able to carry it back to Maman?"

"Yes, it is heavy, and no, you will not be able to carry it. This gift must remain here. We must keep it safe with us."

"A gift for me that you get to keep?"

Mali beamed. "Exactly!"

"Hmm."

The dogs sniffed around my feet, and I crouched to pet them. I didn't remember seeing them here before, but that wasn't strange. Mali and her brothers were often joined by stray dogs. The animals were excellent warning systems.

"Here we are!" Ansale called, reappearing. "I come with your gift!"

Henri walked behind him, looking sheepish but healthy. With a cry of relief and happiness I ran to him, and tears rolled down my cheeks as his arms closed around me.

"You are all right! Oh, Henri! I was hoping you were here!"

He was shirtless like Ansale but wore leggings, and the two men could have been brothers. Living in the outdoors had darkened my brother's skin and brightened his eyes. He looked perfectly at home.

"I've done better than you, I think," Henri said. "How is Maman? Claire and Giselle? Have you spoken with Papa?"

I started to respond, but Mali stepped in. "Come and sit. I've already made you walk all the way here. You have plenty to talk about, and I want to hear everything."

Though it was too warm for a fire, we sat around the ashes as if it were a table. Mali surprised me by shuffling close to Henri. So close, in fact, that when she'd settled on the log beside him, their legs were pressing against each other. Aha! My brother was doing more than hiding out here!

"Why did you not tell me you were coming here?" I asked my brother.

"Papa came here the night before the meeting at the church," he explained. "He spoke with Tumas and Mary. It was his idea."

"Does Maman know?"

"Of course."

It was a relief to know I had been right. She had known all along.

The forest was quiet. "Where is André? With you?"

There was no teasing in Henri's expression. The faces of Ansale and Mali were equally blank.

"He was gone that morning," I said. "Just like you. I thought—"

"We thought he was with your papa and Mathieu," Mali told me. "On the ships."

"No, he's not there. Just Papa and Mathieu . . . and they were put in separate ships! They aren't even together. At least Mathieu has Guillaume with him, but I know he must be terrified." I hesitated, but I could not keep secrets from them. Especially this one. "I have not told you all the sad news."

"More than this?"

"So, so much more." I dropped my chin, pursing my lips together to try to contain my tears, then I took a deep, shaky breath. "It is not just the men who are going to be sent away. All the women and children will go as well. There will be no more Acadians left!"

My brother stared at me, his mouth hanging slightly open.

Then he appeared to make up his mind. "I'll come back with you, Amélie. I should be with our family. I'm safe here, but it's irresponsible and selfish. I know that now. Papa said—" He shook his head. "This changes everything. I didn't know whether to run or fight, so Papa chose the coward's route for me."

"I don't think it's cowardly," I assured him, sniffling. "I wish I'd done it."

"I'll come today. I shouldn't have left Maman."

"No. Don't come home."

"But why not? I can't leave you alone."

I hesitated, unsure of how to convince him without saying too much. "I was told by someone in secret that you should stay away."

"In secret? What does that mean?"

I ignored Henri's question. I would never betray Connor's confidence, not even to my beloved brother. "My friend told me that people who have run away will be punished and imprisoned." I took a deep breath. "Please, Henri, you must not come home."

"But, Amélie, this cannot be right," Mali said. "Henri needs his family, and you need your brother."

My vision blurred with tears. When would I see Henri or the others after tonight?

"Nothing is right these days," I said, "but that is the way it is. I am only glad Henri is with you." I held out my hands and waited for my brother to offer his. When I had his warm, familiar fingers in mine, I squeezed them. Then I reached for Mali's hand and placed Henri's in hers. "I love you both so much. Please promise me you will take care of each other. And, Henri, you must promise you will not come home."

"Stay here with us," Mali said, her eyes sparkling with tears.

"I cannot. The soldiers know me and would come looking. Besides, I couldn't leave Maman and my sisters."

We looked at each other, wishing we knew what to say. This could be the last time we ever spoke, but we were lost for words. After a moment Mali lifted a string of beads from around her neck and placed it over my head. It felt like a final gesture, and I was lonely already.

"For your courage," she said, speaking softly into my ear. "And so you will remember me if you ever have need."

"I need nothing to remember you by. I would never forget you." I touched the necklace, remembering how often I had seen her wearing it. "Thank you for this. It is beautiful and will be a comfort."

The forest was growing darker, closing in on us, and the mosquitoes had multiplied into noisy, whining clouds. I got to my feet.

"I must get back."

Henri took hold of me. "This feels wrong," he said. "I should be going with you."

I pressed my face into his chest, forcing my emotions back. I couldn't appear weak now; if I did, he would insist upon coming with me.

"You're better off here," I whispered. "Besides, Mali would never forgive me if I took you from her!"

"I'm going to marry her."

"I hope your babies look like her and not you!"

"I will name our first daughter after my favourite sister. My Amélie."

Tears surged into my eyes despite all my attempts to hold them back, and Mali took my arm. "Let's get you home before it's too dark," she coaxed. "You don't want to miss out on that meal, do you?"

Our trek back through the forest was sombre. I could remember no other times with her that had been like that.

When we neared the farm, she asked, "Who told you Henri should not come out of hiding?"

"It's a secret. I cannot tell."

"It's me, Amélie. You can tell me anything." She frowned. "What is it? Why do you look afraid?"

It felt like forever since she and I had spoken as sisters, and the shame of my connection to the enemy devoured me. But Mali would not judge me.

"I met a man," I admitted, "and I am confused about my feelings for him."

She smiled, and though it filled me with happiness to see that expression again, her teasing was a poignant reminder that the time had come for us to put aside our childish ways.

"Oh, that's common enough. What don't you understand?"

"He looks at me as if he has always known me. He says he wants to protect me, and he . . . he tells me things he should not say."

"Who is he? Is he handsome?"

I wanted to deny it, but the lie would have been obvious considering the heat in my cheeks. "The most handsome man I've ever seen."

That made her laugh. "Is he tall?"

"Not as tall as Ansale."

For a moment we allowed ourselves to enjoy our conversation, to chat about boys as we had before, as if there were nothing more important to talk of. And by letting her interrogate me, I delayed the necessity of my inevitable confession.

"Does he have lovely golden hair?" She had always had a fascination with blond hair.

"His hair is almost as dark as yours, but it only reaches his shoulders. He usually wears it in a tail."

She sagged a little. "His eyes are blue?"

"Sorry," I said, laughing. "They're brown. But you would like his smile. It reaches his eyes every time, and he has all his teeth."

"And why do you love him?"

"I never said I loved him!"

"No, but I can see that you do. Why? What makes him special?"

It was disconcerting, hearing her say these things, and yet I was eager to share the answers. "He is different from anyone I have ever met," I admitted. "He has led a difficult life, and yet he is not defeated. His courage inspires my own. He wants to know about me, and he seems to seek me out as I do him. He makes me nervous, but I do not believe that is because of him."

"Why then?"

"Because . . . because I want to see him despite any terrible news he might bear. I think of him when I should not." I looked away. "And yet I cannot stop."

"Ah." She hesitated, and I could tell by her half smile that she wasn't sure if she should laugh or not. "What has you confused?"

"He is a British soldier."

Her smile faded slightly, then she took a deep breath and shrugged, her eyes deep with understanding. "He was a man before he became a soldier. Tell me his name. I will keep him safe in my heart along with you. And I will not tell a soul."

FOURTEEN

October 1755

I had hoped someone else would be on duty today. I had spoken with this one before, and I didn't like him. He always scowled down his nose at me. Today his cheeks were red from the wind, and his lips were cracked, but I felt not a shred of pity for him. I wore a heavy woollen shawl and was also wrapped in my long black cloak, but despite its hood, my face and hands felt nearly frozen.

"Why must we always argue?" He looked bored. "You cannot come in, and I will not help you find anyone."

"We argue because you are obstinate, sir."

"That is the pot calling the kettle black."

"It would require no great effort for you to call a messenger to find him."

"Yet I choose not to do so. Sergeant MacDonnell is a busy man. He has no time for . . . little French girls."

His arrogance was infuriating. The way he shaped his mouth when he called me a "little French girl," made me well aware that he was biting his tongue, resisting the urge to label me with a worse epithet.

"You are insolent, sir. You have no right to abuse me in this manner."

"To the contrary. I have every right. This is the king's land. It belongs to the English, not your people."

"How dare you? The land belongs to no one, and we have always lived peacefully alongside—"

"Go away before I make you go away." He leaned closer, until I could smell the ripe wool of his coat. "Are you too stupid to understand that?"

"What will you do? Shoot me?"

I shouldn't have suggested that, for he pushed his sleeve back and tightened his fist, his eyes boring through mine. "Too much noise. I'm tempted to—"

"Mademoiselle Belliveau!"

I spun toward the voice but was too flushed from the argument to give Connor the smile he deserved.

"Good afternoon, Sergeant. I was just telling this soldier I needed to speak with you."

The other man cleared his throat. "I told her you were busy, sir."

Connor caught me scowling at the guard. I dropped my eyes, embarrassed that he'd seen me acting childishly, but I saw the corner of his mouth twitch.

"Thank you," he said. "As it happens, I have an appointment with this lady. You may leave us." He bowed toward me. "My apologies for my tardiness, mademoiselle."

After the man was gone from my view, I met Connor's eyes. He was smiling.

"A pleasure to see you, mademoiselle," he said formally in French. "It has been a while, and for that I am sorry."

"That man has no manners."

"You are correct." He was laughing at me, I could tell. While I wanted to be taken seriously, I did like the way he looked when he teased. "And yet you honoured him by speaking his language," he said. "How charitable of you."

I crossed my arms under my cloak. "I wanted to be understood."

"Of course you did. I will speak with him, introduce him to the idea of polite conversation. In the meantime, I apologize on his behalf."

"Why? You cannot apologize for another man's lack."

"No?"

I shivered at the next gust of wind. "No."

"Still, I am sorry you have been forced to come out here on such a foul day," he continued, keeping his voice impersonal for the benefit of the soldiers milling around. "How may I be of assistance?"

The possibility that he could help me with my request was slight, but I had to try.

"A while back," I said, then I snapped my mouth shut, ashamed of how my voice trembled. I hoped he would believe it was due to the cold, not my emotions. "A while back," I tried again, "you said you would do what you could to help my family. It was a generous offer, and I am afraid I must ask for that help now."

He lowered his voice. "What do you need?"

I wouldn't complain like a child. To tell him we were hungry, that Wikewiku's should have been the month of slaughter and preparing meat for winter, then to remind him that we no longer had any livestock to fatten . . . That would accomplish nothing. He could not help with any of those complaints. Instead, I would ask him for something I believed he could give.

"We need our axe. Winter is nearly upon us, and we've no wood for cooking or for heat."

"I shall bring it today. Can I help you with anything else?"

I didn't want to leave him, but I could think of nothing more to ask. "I . . . I do not think so."

The wind whipped our coats and hair, and I clutched at my hood. Concern filled Connor's eyes when he saw my red, chapped hands, though I quickly shoved them back under the cloak.

"I will get the axe, then I shall walk you home," he said decisively. "Come along."

Uncertain, I looked where he'd indicated: beyond the picket fence, toward the church. "In there?"

"I'll not leave you alone in the cold. You'll be safe with me."

The sky rolled in an ominous grey, warning me of the impending season with its shrieking blizzards, frozen water supplies, and food shortages. Soon we would be crunching through snow instead of withered grass. Connor pulled up the stiff collar of his winter cloak, shielding his jaw from the wind. How would he fare here when the storms came? I imagined he was used to more temperate weather.

"This is hardly cold. Wait until December," I said, lifting an eyebrow. "And January will chill you straight through. We'll need more firewood here than you would need in New England, I am sure."

He hesitated mid-step as if he'd remembered something important, but then he continued over the dry, yellow grass, moving with purpose. The easy smile he'd worn earlier now looked forced.

"What did I say? Did I scare you with talk of our winters?"

He glanced at me but said nothing as he continued toward a large tent across the field. He bid me wait a moment while he went in to retrieve our axe, and when he came out, he looked even more grim than before. More than a little concerned now, I hooked my fingers onto the thick black sleeve of his cloak, pulling him to a stop.

"Connor?"

He wouldn't look at me. His eyes went instead to the line of trees bordering the forest.

I scrambled out in front of him. "What aren't you telling me?"

Not long ago he and I had spent a warm, blissful afternoon by the river. He'd disturbed the perfection of the day by suggesting I might someday be forced to live a different kind life, one in which I would do what I must to survive. It had been summer then. Now our breaths formed little clouds that vanished into the grey of the day. Leaves that had once danced in reds and golds over our heads had long since died and fallen to the earth. I knew him better now. Seeing him like this, closed in with secrets, I was frightened.

"The truth, Connor. I want the truth."

He still wouldn't look at me. "You won't like it."

"Of course I won't. I haven't liked *anything* since all this began."

My words hung between us, and I wished I could take them back, for they were in part a lie. Had none of this happened, I never would have met him.

His shoulders sagged with surrender. When he finally turned to me, I couldn't look away even if I'd wanted. His gaze was hard and intense, but behind it swirled a world of concern.

"You said before that you were afraid," he reminded me. "That you didn't know what to expect and that's what scared you the most."

His brow creased into deep lines as he searched for the right words, and I was tempted to put up a hand to stop him. If he was so afraid to speak of it, I did not think I could bear what he had to say. But I needed to hear. I needed to summon my courage and finally face facts. My world was changing, and from the expression he carried, I gathered that courage had become more urgent.

"Time is running out, Amélie. The English are impatient to settle in, and they cannot do it while the Acadians are here."

"There is plenty of land here to share."

He closed his eyes briefly, the line of his jaw tight with exasperation. When he looked at me again, I was sorry. He was no longer teasing, no longer regarding me with affection.

"They will not share. You know that."

The arms I had wrapped around myself in determination now tightened, protecting me. I had asked for the truth—demanded it even—but now I was afraid it would be too much for me to accept.

"But we're . . . we're farmers. We are more of a help than a threat," I blustered.

"I know that, and you know that. I imagine the English know as well. But they no longer want Acadians here." He reached toward me, but when I did not move, he dropped his hands back to his sides. "Amélie, the rest of the ships are almost here."

I stared at him, unable to speak. Everything in me wanted to deny his words, to accuse him of lying, but how could I do such a thing when I knew it was the truth?

His miserable expression drew me from my state of shock. "It is not your fault, Connor." Once those words were out, others followed, rushing like water through the narrows. "It won't be so bad. They will see we mean them no harm, and they will change their minds. I'm certain this is all a mistake. They will let the men off the ships and we can go back to what we were before. That will happen. It must. It would not be Christian of them to carry through with this terrible plan."

He cupped his hands under my elbows. "I'm sorry, Amélie."

Run, stupid girl! my heart screamed. *Go to Mali and be safe! Run now while you still can!*

"Where? Where will they send us?" My voice sounded very small, even to me.

"I don't know. South."

"When?"

"Soon." He closed his eyes. "The truth is you won't need much firewood."

FIFTEEN

After Connor's warning, I thought long and hard about spreading the news among the women of Grand Pré, shivering in their homes without firewood. I climbed to the peak of the hill, needing to find peace in my head and heart so I could think clearly. I could not go to Maman or Claire, because I didn't know how to tell them about Connor. That was another, separate problem crying out for a solution.

If Papa had been there, he would have helped me find the answer I sought. Twenty years ago, he had faced a moral crossroads as I did now. But he was gone. He could not help me.

I stared into the vast greyness before me, its sleeping beauty sectioned into three: the dikes, the black grey of the ocean, and the stark lines of the mountains before they faded into sky. God had created all this, and the Mi'kmaq spirits had made it real. God had introduced grey to the world, and the Mi'kmaq spirits had painted it on every tree, every ripple of the sea. Where did human beings fit into it all? Why were we here? And why were we *exactly* here in this place? I had always considered myself to be a part of this land, as rooted as the willows my ancestors had planted almost seventy years before—but no one was slicing at *their* trunks, ripping out *their* roots.

Connor had given me information no other Acadian knew. He'd wanted me to be prepared so that when I stepped onto that ship I wouldn't be overcome with shock—as if being informed could ever have prepared me for that. But was there anything I could do with that knowledge to save my people and myself?

The *right* thing, I supposed, would be for me to reveal to everyone that I was friends with a British soldier. That I might even have fallen in love with him. I could tell them what he had told me, and maybe we could work toward some sort of last-minute resistance. With that admission, though, the women I had grown up with would surely hate me, as would their children. They would judge me for my weakness and call me a traitor. And if anyone informed Winslow about what Connor had told me, he would likely be both punished and demoted.

After all that, would they even believe me?

Seeing no other solution, I eventually did what I thought Papa would have called the *good* thing. I knocked on the doors of the houses around me and was welcomed in. The first conversations were difficult, since I wasn't sure how to begin, but I became more confident as I spoke. Without saying how I knew, I told the women the ships would be here soon. I watched their eyes, hoping to see a spark of rebellion, but those were few and far between. Instead, I was met with hostility. My dire warning was not welcomed. Most wanted to know where I'd come by such "vicious rumours," and when I was elusive in my response, they walked away, shaking their heads. Some did believe me, and I was pleased to notice that some of those disappeared without another word, vanishing into the forest like my brothers. I said a prayer that they might be safer in the trees than on the sea.

At least Maman and my sisters believed me, and they did not

ask how I had come by such terrible news. Their faces had paled, but they would not take my suggestion that they run to the forest. In the end, they would never leave the men they loved. So I could not save them, and they did not want me to anyway.

Oh, Papa. I tried.

⸻

We didn't need much firewood, as Connor had said. Less than a week later the English came to our doors in the blackest of mornings, jabbing muskets at our sleeping bodies. They stole us away before the sun could catch them at their foul act and reveal them as the cowards they truly were.

Without the sunrise the cold was even more shocking. We huddled in our cloaks, wrapping blankets around ourselves and the bewildered children. Then we allowed ourselves to be marched to the ships. The mud path was our only witness, collecting a pattern of clogs and moccasins of all sizes. Soon even that would be gone.

I had never been so afraid of our harbour. In the past it had given me such happiness to look out and admire the majestic ships anchored there. Sometimes the crafts seemed to dance, bobbing bow to stern when the wind skimmed over the water and coaxed waves to the surface. Once I had even dreamed of being aboard one, bidding my family farewell and sailing into an adventure. Now an ominous grey light leached off the sails of twenty lurking transports, and their hulls creaked with impatience. I felt as if I were entering a floating cemetery at night. The urge to flee was strong, but Giselle's cold fingers gripped mine, and I knew she could never keep up with me if I ran.

We had been told to bring what we could carry, but when we arrived at the docks, our things were stripped away and stacked in heaps. Bodies pressed against me as we were funnelled toward the gangplank, but out of terror and confusion, we did not raise our voices. I longed to cry out, to remind the others that silence implied consent. *We did not consent to this!* But the soldiers carried muskets across their chests, and I had seen them fix those horrible bayonets before. Once we had spoken as friends, exchanged pleasantries, lived in harmony. Now we meant nothing to them. They would not hesitate to still our pitiful rebellion.

A freezing gust cut across the dock and we tucked our chins against our chests in reflex, hiding from the hungry salt wind. Children huddled close to their mothers, their little voices hushed.

"Will Papa be on the ship with us?"

"I do not want to go there, Maman. I want to go home."

And even, "This is an *adventure*, Maman! Remember you told me it was an adventure? Why are you crying?"

I eyed the line of ugly cargo boats. It was obvious to me that they were too small to hold the waiting crowd. Yet we were being steadily loaded onto them. Like the rest of my people, I opened my coat upon request and shivered helplessly while the soldiers searched everyone—including the children—for any kind of weapon. I carried nothing of the sort. None of us did. If anything, I longed for a candle or lantern, since I knew the hold of the ship would offer only blackness. Would we even be able to see the faces of the others? Would we ever see sunlight again?

I knew most of the people around me, though some had been brought from other Acadian villages. Families clung together if they could, but ours had been split apart months before. At least I had been able to assure my sisters and Maman that Henri was safe in the forest. There was no such comfort to provide about André. He still had not surfaced. All I could do was pray he was all right.

I reached the edge of the gangway and froze, holding up the line. "Wait. This is the wrong ship," I said. "This is the *Pembroke*.

We are supposed to be with our family. They are not on the *Pembroke*!"

"We should be on the *Hobson*," Claire agreed behind me. She had not understood my English, but she had seen the painted white letters on the bow at the same time I had. "Or the *Elizabeth*. This is a mistake!"

"Sorry, miss," a soldier said. "Our orders is to put you here. Now up ye go." His nonchalance was chilling. It was as if he were welcoming me to a party or something. He even *smiled*. "Once you're at the hatch, kindly go down the ladder and find a place to sit. There we go."

"But this is a mistake!" I cried in English. "Take us to the *Hobson*."

"No mistake. Come along, miss."

I blinked up at him, my feet anchored on the mud-splattered boards of the dock. How could I blindly go up that ramp? *I am not a sheep!* I wanted to cry, but in truth I had become exactly that.

"Move along now."

He flapped a hand, then absently adjusted the strap across his chest. My eyes followed the blackened leather around his body and stopped at the mouth of the musket peeking over his shoulder. Would he point it at another human being—a woman? a child?—and shoot? Of course he would. He was a soldier, trained to kill whomever he was told to kill.

I was expected to step lively, like all the other sheep. So I did. Before I stepped onto the gangplank, I peered down the dock at the other ships, aching for Papa and Mathieu. Would I ever see them again? Would they at least send the ships to the same destination? Oh God, let it be that way!

Then it was my turn. The girl in front of me was already halfway up the walkway, and the soldiers were urging the crowd behind me. I inhaled the salt air as if I were about to dive into the ocean, filling my chest and holding my breath as long as I could. Then I left Mathieu and my father behind. The sea rose in a ravenous welcome as I stepped onto the gangplank, lifting the boat. I lunged for the thick rope strung along the small bridge and clung to it with both hands, waiting for the wave to subside, then I reached behind for Giselle's hand. It was damp with sweat despite the winter chill. I took another careful step.

"Don't touch her!" I glanced back with surprise at the hostility in Claire's voice. One of the soldiers had taken Maman's arm, and she'd turned to stone. The soldier released his grip, but Claire's glare held. "She does not need your help, *Englishman*."

I didn't recognize either of the soldiers at the gangplank. Those waiting on the ship were strangers to me as well. Where was Connor? What of his declaration that he would watch over us? I swayed with the motion of the ship, feeling dizzy with betrayal. Perhaps he was on another ship. With all the confusion, it was possible even for the soldiers to be loaded onto the wrong ships, I supposed, and my heart twisted at the possibility that he might be close yet not arrive at all. My eyes roamed the crowd, skipping over dozens of small white kerchiefs. From a distance I looked exactly the same as every other girl there. Would he even see me if he was here?

A woman I did not recognize stopped at the hatch and flailed out, fighting the soldiers who restrained her. They pulled her back and tied her hands together; then they forced her, screaming, through the hole. She was swallowed into the black belly of the boat, and the sounds she made were piteous. I promised myself I would not cry.

As Giselle and I walked up the gangplank, I looked back at Claire and Maman. My sister was frowning, her gaze uncertain, and though she was by nature a quiet girl, it was discomfiting to see her this way. After Papa, André and Claire were always the ones in control, the ones to maintain peace in the house. But André was not here. Neither was Papa. At times, Claire did not seem to be here either. She was with her heart, swaying and starving on the miserable *Hobson*.

Our clogs shuffled over the wet deck until it was our turn to stop at the hatch. I still had not spied Connor amidst the seamen. All I saw were rough strangers preparing for the voyage, and the rest of my people stooped with submission. The longer I searched the deck, the more convinced I became that he was not coming. He had lied to me. If only his words hadn't felt so real, so honest, they might not have hurt so much, but I had been gullible and let myself believe in him. I wouldn't be so foolish next time.

The hole in the deck offered no hint of light. Surely they would send down lanterns. The alternative was too terrible.

"What's going to happen?" Giselle whimpered, pressing up against me. She'd been in that position almost the entire walk from our village to here.

"Be brave, Giselle. We will be fine," I repeated for the thousandth time.

"Look!"

As one, we turned and gawked at the furious red glow lighting the sky behind us, and our sobs began anew. Our homes and farms had been set ablaze, and the crackling orange glare made the billowing smoke leap like monstrous ghosts. Like the branches of willows, the women swayed against each other, striving to stand strong against the punishing winds of change, but I could hear their branches breaking one by one.

I stared in silence, wondering why the British would do that. The homes were empty now, the farms easy pickings. Why destroy them?

Giselle's fingers clawed my arm. "Where will Petit Chat go?"

Up until now she had existed in a childish stupor, protecting her heart with the illusion that she had been dreaming. Now that wall was being burned away, and she witnessed the physical truth blazing on the horizon. They would have thrown torches on the roof, and the embers would have tumbled onto our table, our chairs, and our beds, igniting the pillows where our sleeping heads had rested hours before. The window curtains would twist into flaming ribbons, our clothing would flare, then melt into clouds of white smoke. Giselle's question haunted me. What of the animals? What of her cat? What of the dogs, who felt like members of the family? Who would feed them, tend to them? Were they burning as well or had they run?

No, dear sister, this is no dream. This is a nightmare from which we will never awaken.

My gaze moved from the orange glow toward the dark, cool security of the forest. Where were our brothers? Could they see us? Did they weep as we did?

"Farewell, Grand Pré," I whispered.

"Nonsense," Claire snapped. "We will return one day. And when we do, we will take it from these English devils and rebuild it all. They can burn our homes, but they cannot destroy our spirits."

As much as I wanted to believe she was right, I knew deep in my soul she was wrong. Though I could not hear the fire, the noise of breaking hearts was deafening. The English had done what they had intended all along. They had crushed us, the people of Grand Pré. Now the land truly belonged to them.

Connor

SIXTEEN

Connor resisted the urge to wipe at his burning eyes, choosing instead to let the tears cut paths down his grimy cheeks. His mother had said tears were the body's way of cleansing both eyes and emotions. Today they were doing both.

Shame crippled him. He had been part of this obscenity. The command had finally been issued, and it had come as no surprise to Connor that the long-awaited release from inactivity had intoxicated most of the men, filling them with a mad sense of power. Out of duty, he had marched with the others to the quiet homes, his boots crushing the frosted grass, but he had hung back from the task itself. He was a helpless witness to the scene as soldiers burst through splintering doors, roaring and poking muskets at the sleeping inhabitants. Fitch had been in the middle of the debacle, whooping with triumph as he shoved a weeping family of women and girls from their home, dressed in nothing but shifts and cloaks. Some of the prisoners clutched blankets to their chests. A number carried hastily assembled baskets of food. He could only hope they would be allowed to keep some of it.

Connor had purposefully avoided going anywhere near the

Belliveau house. He had gone to different doors, let the other soldiers carry out the contemptible directive while he did what he could to maintain order. She was gone already. Her home was ablaze. Soon every house would be reduced to a pile of smoking ash, along with the barns and gardens and any treasures left behind.

He was glad she was already gone. He couldn't have borne the look of betrayal in her eyes.

He'd warned her today was coming, and she'd listened to the plans he wasn't supposed to divulge, but the words couldn't have been real to her. The idea that she and her family and friends were going to be shut in the bowels of a ship and sent God knew where . . . Of course it had been too much for her to accept. But the truth had now been shoved down her throat.

Hours later, ashes still clung to the air. Every breath Connor took was laboured, but the constricting pain in his chest had little to do with smoke.

"Good day's work, aye, *sir*?"

The momentary relief Connor felt when he closed his eyes couldn't clear the distaste from his mouth. He didn't respond, hoping Fitch would keep walking past, but that only accomplished the opposite. The man had been a terrible superior officer and somehow managed to be an even worse underling. He was a thorn in Connor's side, constantly attempting to impress and move back up the ranks. That wasn't going to happen on Connor's watch, nor on Winslow's. Fitch kept trying, though.

Evidently Connor could not avoid his company. Fitch caught up and blocked his path, pulling the protective kerchief down to his chin so Connor could see his mad sooty grin. Together they surveyed the devastated village lying beneath a solid ceiling of smoke, its homes and barns sprawled over the blackened ground like ash skeletons. The fiery heat had melted any frozen stretches of dried grass into muck. Other than a few soldiers kicking through the smoking ash, Connor could see no sign of life.

"A right mess," Fitch mused. "I suppose it'll be us what cleans it up."

"I assume so," Connor said. "We created the mess, after all."

Fitch chuckled. "Bring back the women, make 'em clean it."

Connor glanced at him. "You are an unpleasant man, Fitch."

"Per'aps, sir. Only thinkin' of the best way to get things done, I am. I s'pose the officers won't be lifting a hand when it comes to cleanup."

Connor's gaze skimmed over the spot where Amélie and her family had once lived. Looking at the remains made him ill. He wasn't sure he could go anywhere near them. Fortunately, Fitch was right; cleanup was not a task for the officers.

"Speak with Winslow about my getting reinstalled, 'ave you?"

"There's no talk of that, Fitch, and you know it. You're fortunate to still have a position here at all, considering your crime."

"Oh, aye? That's rich, comin' from you."

Connor closed his eyes, craving peace. Or perhaps a well-aimed bolt of lightning.

"I seen ye with her, I did. With that French slut."

His eyes opened slowly, and he resisted the urge to look toward the harbour, toward Amélie.

"Don't s'pose ye had clearance to be messin' about with her, didja?" His face pushed closer to Connor's, almost completely filling his line of vision. "Good thing she's gone now, aye? Guess you'll have to hunt up one of them injun squaws. They'd be willing, I'd bet, with a pretty lad the likes of you. Show them our welcomin' English customs, aye? Tell you what, you bring me back one and we'll forget all about what I saw."

"You have a strange way of speaking with your betters, Corporal Fitch," Connor said, his expression carefully blank. Then he strode away, giving Fitch nothing more.

He could not allow the vindictive arse to see the fear raised by his underhanded threat. Nothing and no one could come between Connor and Winslow at this time. He must have his hands and eyes on Winslow's correspondence—his window onto Amélie's future—for as long as possible. He would have to be very careful; Fitch could not be permitted to interfere.

SEVENTEEN

November 1755

Amélie and her family had been on that stagnant ship for weeks. When the wind carried the stink to the tents, the soldiers covered their noses and mouths, grimacing with displeasure. The people in the transports had no choice. They breathed in the rank air and ate what stale rations they were given while the army awaited orders. Connor had been unable to get to the ships, and the torture of seeing them in the distance, achingly close yet impossibly far away, was too much on some days.

By now Amélie would have given up on him, would believe his promises had been nothing more than words.

He had feared the same himself until recently. At last the paperwork he'd been waiting for arrived on his desk: the listing of which Grand Pré Acadians were imprisoned in which ships. The initial boarding had been massive confusion, and the soldiers on the docks had discarded the original lists in favour of expediency. At least they had written down names as the people had been loaded. Connor scoured the pages until he found Amélie's family, but he could find only the women. Shuffling through the other papers, he eventually found the rest of the Beauliveaus, on two other ships. The women were aboard the *Pembroke*, Charles was on the *Elizabeth*, and Mathieu was on the *Hobson* with Claire's fiancé, Guillaume.

Connor couldn't simply pluck Amélie's family members from the various ships, but at least he could do something about their separation. When the timing seemed right, he approached the colonel.

"Sir," he tried, "I have a question regarding the shipments of families."

Winslow looked up, distracted as usual. He was a fair enough man, but he had a great many worries on his mind. Connor had been witness to many of his eloquently written concerns.

"What is it?"

"These lists, sir, they indicate some of the families have been separated despite your best efforts to keep them together."

The lines of Winslow's brows drew together and he nodded. "Yes. Well, I suppose we cannot get it all right. We've done what we could."

"Could we not shuffle some to different ships, sir? Allow the families to be together in this trying time?"

Winslow rested his brow in one hand and sighed heavily. "Sergeant Mac . . . Mac . . ." The hand that wasn't propping up his face lifted helplessly.

"MacDonnell, sir."

"Sergeant MacDonnell. No. We will not be using our limited resources in that capacity. The family members will have to re-unite at the end of their journey."

"But not all ships are going to the same place, sir."

Winslow's eyes rolled up at Connor from beneath heavy brows. "I am aware of this."

"Sir, I understand you are dealing with much more import-ant issues. Would you permit me to work on this project myself?

I could coordinate which family members should be moved to which—"

"Unnecessary added work, Sergeant."

"I'd be happy to do it, sir."

"No. Thank you, Sergeant. That will be all."

The dismissal was clear. Winslow's attention returned to his work, and Connor bit back his disappointment as he stepped outside. The dismissal was a bitter blow, and it left him feeling more helpless than ever. There should have been no problem with allowing Connor to rearrange the prisoners, but the colonel had plainly had enough. Constant complaints from commanders of other Acadian settlements and the day-to-day concerns of managing this one all added up to a load of responsibilities Winslow was not willing to delegate.

November had long since settled over the land, and the dry chill spoke of impending snow. Departure would happen in a matter of days. The influx of letters, organization of provisions, bustle around the docks—all of it was increasing hourly. His own duties—as usual—were aggravatingly minimal. Feeling rebellious, he left the little field of tents and strode down the hill toward the docks.

The decks were much busier than the fort. Soldiers carried large sacks over the gangplank, making way when others rolled kegs across. In contrast to the soldiers by the churchyard, most of these men were more focused on the job at hand than on making idle conversation. After so long spent doing little more than writing letters, Connor craved action. Shouts rang out from farther down the dock, catching his attention, and he saw someone had dropped a sack. Precious flour rose in a choking white cloud, and the man at fault hung his head, nodding and accepting the rebukes of the men around him. Connor was tempted to head over and break up the scene. He wanted to lift the next sack himself in illustration of what needed to be done, but a man wearing a uniform such as his would not be permitted to do such a thing.

An idea struck him unexpectedly, like a spark from a flint. He blinked, needing to organize his thoughts. No, he could not join those men; however, as an officer he might possibly be able to do something else.

Two days later, Connor stood at attention in the doorway of Winslow's office, trying not to fidget. Outside the church window the ships bobbed in the distance, stark against the early December snow. They sat noticeably lower in the water than they had the week before, since almost everything had been loaded in preparation for departure. The ships' motion was an urgent reminder to Connor that he had no time left. If nothing went wrong, the colonel would order the ships' captains to lift anchor *today*.

The commander was leaning back in his chair, enjoying a glass of port and chuckling about something with another officer who had recently arrived. Considering all the other activities currently under way, Connor couldn't imagine their conversation being anything other than wasted time. If he didn't interrupt, Amélie and her family would be gone from his life within hours.

When at last Winslow had turned his angular face toward him, Connor cleared his throat and lifted his chin.

Winslow sighed and sipped his port. "Was there something you needed, Sergeant?"

Connor fought the urge to rush forward and thrust a sheet of paper under the man's nose. He must pretend his request was the farthest thing from urgent.

"Sir, if you recall, I put in a request that I be permitted to travel to North Carolina aboard the *Pembroke*. I've family there I'd like to visit." Technically not a lie. It would be interesting to meet his cousins at long last, if they were still there. "I require your letter, if you'd be so kind."

The colonel lifted an eyebrow. "Family?"

"Two cousins. Soldiers as well," he threw in for good measure.

Winslow tapped his knuckle on the desk. "The *Pembroke*, you say? Leaves today, does it not?"

"It does, sir."

"Well then. You'll be in a hurry, I expect."

"Yes, sir."

He frowned slightly. "You've done an exemplary job for me, Sergeant. I should hate to lose you."

"You'd not lose me, sir. I'd be back before the spring."

Winslow nodded thoughtfully. "I will be less in need of a translator once all these people are gone." He chuckled to himself. "I suppose this time I must write the missive myself, not ask you to do it on my behalf."

"Thank you, sir."

"The captain's name?"

"Milton, sir."

The colonel dipped his quill in the inkwell on the corner of his desk, set the tip on the paper, and began to write.

DEAR CAPTAIN MILTON of the PEMBROKE,

The Bearer, Sergeant MacDonnell has been with me. He Chuses to Go to North Carolina to visit his Family and has Requested he take the Pembroke. I Therefore beg to Favour you would Embarke him for that Collony upon your ship. What Indulgence you Show him Shall reckon it as a Favour done to yours Most Sincerely. Excuse haste.

COLONEL J. WINSLOW

He waited a few seconds for the ink to dry, then handed the paper to Connor, smiling. "I wish you a safe and pleasant journey, and I look forward to your return."

Connor's fingers had just closed around the door handle when Winslow called his name again.

He froze. "Sir?"

"I have made note of your outstanding service in your file."

"Thank you, sir." Relieved, Connor bowed; then he strode from the building, shrugging into his long black cloak as he went. The impulse to leap over the steps and sprint to the docks was strong, but a sergeant didn't run. A sergeant didn't raise unwanted questions. He ducked covertly into his tent to retrieve what things he had then he headed toward the harbour.

"An odd place to see you, sir."

"Corporal Fitch!" Connor stopped short. "You startled me."

"Where are you headed, sir?"

"My business is my own, Corporal."

Fitch's eyebrows rose. "Well now. Sounds like a right mystery to me."

"Does it?" An apathetic shrug was Fitch's response, but Connor saw the eager glint in his eye. "What do you want, Corporal?"

"Most o' the work is done for now, sir." He winked. "Cattle's already been shipped, as it were. So when I saw you headin' this way, moving quick-like, I thought I might be of assistance, since I've nought else to do." His eyes went to the ships. "If you've a mind to visit the ships before they're gone, I'd go with you."

"Thank you, no. I am keeping my own company today. Good day to you."

He moved away, but Fitch stepped in front of him. "I've nought else to do, as I say." He scowled, scratching the side of his head. "Say, you wouldn't be thinkin' of visiting that mademoiselle, would you? Because I don't think the commander would think much of that. On the other hand, I'd be willing to bet he'd be interested in that kind of information, should it be true."

Connor stiffened. "Your suggestion is insolent and unfounded. As it happens, I am indeed on my way to the ships—not, however, to speak with any of the prisoners." He narrowed his eyes. "I would suggest you head back to camp and find business of your own to attend to. Good day."

It was thanks to the winter air that Connor did not have perspiration to mop from his brow as he descended the hill. Fitch, he knew by now, hated him. Hated Connor's promotion above him, hated Connor's favour with Winslow, hated that the other men liked Connor. And Connor was positive Fitch hated the fact that the mademoiselle to whom he was undoubtedly referring actually *wanted* to be with Connor.

Or at least he hoped she still did.

EIGHTEEN

The downward slope was perilous, the snow pounded into ice by many boots. Connor glanced back once, needing to assure himself he was alone; then he headed quickly on, focused on the voyage ahead. Despite the thickening stink wafting toward him, he smiled with anticipation.

By the time he reached the ship, the crew appeared just about ready to set sail. From the looks of it, Connor couldn't have put off his meeting with Winslow by even an hour.

Over two hundred prisoners filled the *Pembroke*'s hold, and another seven men made up her crew. The passengers were locked below, so he couldn't see them from the docks. He didn't know if the list had been accurate, if the soldiers had recorded the right people on the right ships. Was Amélie even here?

A scruffy-looking man stood at the base of the gangplank, and Connor paused to speak with him. "Are you sailing aboard this ship?"

The sailor scowled, blinking wearily at him. His round, bald head was partially covered by a winter cap, but at its base Connor could see dirty brown skin, heavily spattered with indiscriminate freckles. It looked as though someone had shaken a blackened paintbrush at him.

"I am not."

Connor glanced up the walkway, unsure of where he should go to present his paperwork. "Do you know the captain of this ship?"

"Aye," he said, opening his mouth wide enough for Connor to see that most of his teeth were gone. Those remaining were grey-black and turned at odd angles. He twisted to the side and jabbed a thumb toward the ship. "Cap'n Milton be there."

Captain Milton was easy to pick out from the crowd on deck, since he stood in the midst like a flagpole, directing the others. Unlike the crew, he was dressed neatly in a pressed white shirt and navy waistcoat over fitted black pants. He wore the expression of a man perpetually unimpressed.

"MacDonnell," he muttered, reading the paper. He squinted at Connor, assessing him, so Connor stood a little taller. Milton's face didn't change. "Been a-ship before?"

"Aye, sir."

"You can handle rigging?"

"Aye." No need to tell him his only experience had been on much smaller boats than this.

"Good. We're a small crew. Four hours on, four hours off. Put your back into what's left of the cargo. We'll be gone once that's done."

The icy boards of the dock were worn in distinct pathways by the sailors' activity, but it appeared the heavy work had been completed. Most of what the captain referred to was rations, with which Connor was well acquainted. He'd included the orders in his own paperwork. For each period of seven days, each passenger had been allotted two pounds of bread and one pound of salt beef. The crew—which numbered eight now that Connor had joined them—would receive a little more. The *Pembroke* was a large snow of a hundred and thirty-nine tons, and she would sail alongside six other merchant ships, all of them filled to the brim with Acadians. Like them, the *Pembroke* carried provisions estimated to last four and a half months. Unfortunately, by Connor's reckonings, Winslow had packed at least sixty too many passengers on board each ship. He could only hope they would reach their destination before the supplies either ran out or rotted.

When voices rose from the docks below, he set down the crate he was carrying and leaned over the side to see what was happening. A fairly large crowd was making its way toward the *Pembroke*, but it took a moment before he could discern the reason for the noise. When he did, a satisfied smile spread across his face. A week before, he'd quietly written an addendum at the bottom of one of Winslow's memos, wording it blandly enough that it got past the colonel without his taking notice. This little procession being led from the *Elizabeth* to Connor's gangplank was a direct result of that addendum.

The hands of the older male Acadians were shackled behind them. They stumbled between their guards, weak and almost blinded by the sun. Seeing the light of day and walking the length of the docks would—despite the freezing temperatures and the clanging irons—be a gift from God to these men, who had gone too long without space to move, fresh air to breathe. Connor glanced quickly toward the single mast of the *Hobson*, waiting. Wee Mathieu and Claire's Guillaume should be along soon.

As ordered, the prisoners stopped before a young soldier who had hastily set up a desk at the bottom of the *Pembroke*'s gangway; he was assigned to write down names before any prisoners could board. Connor listened intently, waiting for one name in particular.

"Joseph Guilbeau," the soldier droned, scribbling on the page.

"Next! Denis Petit-tot. Is that how you spell it?" He showed his paper to the prisoner, who merely shrugged. For the most part, these men couldn't read. "Right then. Move along. Next! Charles Belliveau. Good. Charles Dugas . . ."

Charles Belliveau. Amélie's father was a sturdy man, but his recent incarceration had had an effect. His thick golden hair had gone dark for lack of washing, and he wore a three-month beard to match. Despite his weakened state, Belliveau walked confidently onto the deck, standing as straight as a man in his position could. He was thin, his once-strong muscles wasted from the ordeal aboard the other ship, but his eyes still burned with contempt.

All at once Belliveau stopped in his tracks and stared at the mainmast, looking stunned. After a second, outrage flashed in his eyes, and Connor was transported back to the day when Amélie had baited the guard to take up arms against her. He could easily see where her fiery temper came from. Despite the line of men waiting behind him, Belliveau didn't move a muscle. He never even lifted his chin, but his eyes took their time, winding slowly up the mast. They paused in places as if to seek some sort of confirmation, then moved on. An odd sort of satisfaction seemed to settle over him, and it showed itself in a weak smile. Then, as if a shutter slammed closed, he shook his head, his lips tight. A guard nudged Belliveau from behind, urging him along, and the prisoner slowly turned. The murderous look in his eyes would have given Connor pause, and he was oddly pleased to see the soldier take a half step back.

In his own time, Belliveau faced the bow, his movements deliberate. He gave the mast one last look; then he shuffled toward the hatch along with the other men, the heavy metal around his wrists clanging rhythmically with every step. When they reached the open door in the deck, the prisoners held out their hands to have their irons unlocked, and the heavy shackles tumbled into a pile at the guard's feet. One by one, the men descended into the hold, and their slouched shapes were lost in the darkness. The sailors who had paused in their work to stare at their new cargo returned to their stations, and work continued as before.

From out of the darkness flew the voices of women and children, filling the air like finches in the trees, and Connor listened hard.

"Papa!" He heard through the boards of the deck. "Papa!"

"Papa! Ici!"

"Papa!"

"Ah! Mes chéries!" The men's voices cracked with emotion as they realized why they'd been moved to this ship, and warmth filled Connor's chest. Charles Belliveau was not the only father who had been missed. At least he had been able to give the families this small kindness.

"Mes enfants!"

One choked male voice cut through the others. "Oh, merci Dieu! Sylvie, ma chérie! Claire! Amélie! Ma petite Giselle! Comment vous m'avez manqué!"

Connor smiled. *She was here.*

He looked back over the side, expecting to see Mathieu and Guillaume's group being marched toward them, but no one else was coming. Then he saw why, and his heart sank. During the noisy confusion of the prisoner transfer, the *Hobson* had cast off. She was setting out to sea within the convoy of twenty ships, her sails billowing as she rode a strong wind.

NINETEEN

It was important that Amélie not see him. At least not until he'd come up with some sort of plan, some explanation that might help her understand. He didn't think she'd reveal who he was— she would be concerned for her own reputation if not for his— but he had to be careful.

But he could not resist watching her. The first time he saw her, Connor's resolve to stay away almost melted completely. She looked so small, so forlorn. Her clothing and face were filthy, and strands of her lovely brown hair hung beneath her soiled bonnet. Hunger and exhaustion glazed her eyes, and the line of her jaw stood out in sharp relief. He wondered when she had last slept. Had she been eating her meagre meals, or had she deprived herself and shared them with the others?

Occasionally father and daughter came on deck together, but often they came separately, accompanying the more infirm. Echoing her father's strength, Amélie often supported her mother. He memorized the rough order of the visits to the deck as best he could, but he still looked over every time the hatch creaked open. He regretted the times he didn't see her, when he was sleeping in his bunk or eating, but he'd needed what moments of rest he could get. As one of only eight in the crew, he was working harder than he ever had.

The first week had been the worst for them all. The trapped farmers—most of whom had never set foot on anything larger than a small fishing boat—got their first taste of cutting through some ocean swells and crashing over others. Retching punctuated the constant sobbing, and wails of misery filtered through the hatch along with the stench. To make matters worse, the much-needed breaks on the deck reduced most prisoners to convulsive shivers, since the December days were formidably icy whether the wind was high or not. At least the cold gales blew steadily and they had no rain, keeping the captain in relatively good spirits. Then one afternoon the sky hardened and the black sea rolled with froth, warning of an approaching storm.

"Batten down the hatches!" the captain hollered over the rising wind. "Use deadlights as well. She's a big one."

At first Connor wondered if the captain had misread what was coming. The weather moving steadily toward them seemed so solid, he wondered if it was simply a thick fog. Then again, fog would have brought dead winds, and all the ship's sails suddenly began to jerk at their ropes. As the threat drew closer, Connor was able to make out a hint of what the low-hanging clouds held, and he realized fog would have been a blessing. He'd never thought about snowstorms at sea.

"Caldwell!" Captain Milton roared.

The first mate staggered against the wind toward him. "Sir!"

"Lock the hatch. No more walks until this blows over."

"Aye, sir."

The walls and floor of the ship shuddered at the next blast, and the *Pembroke* rolled eagerly up one side of a huge swell Connor could swear hadn't been there seconds ago. Before he'd set his balance, she dove down the other side, splashing like a breeching whale. He grabbed a rope, trying to ignore the panicked screams cutting through the howling of the storm from below, but the sea twisted again, and the rope slithered through his fingers. Desperate, he gripped the rail with two hands, willing his feet to stay where they were though his stomach rolled with the sea.

"Brace yourselves!" Milton bellowed, and the echo of his first mate's voice was sucked into the storm.

Snow blew in horizontally, a wall of ten thousand needles aiming for Connor's face and at the hand he used for a shield. As he tucked his chin under his coat, a wave shot the bow straight up, plunging the stern into a valley of froth, and the slush-covered deck slipped from under him. Connor crashed flat onto his back, slammed his head into the boards, then was tossed down the deck toward the abyss. Instinctively, he flipped onto his belly, grasping at ropes and fixtures, managing to hook onto the bottom of the mast as his knee jammed against a post.

The planks holding the ship together moaned in near surrender as the ocean battered the hull, and he easily imagined the whole craft twisting, snapping, pitching him into the frigid ocean depths. The ship's bow dove again, dumping a torrent of frozen water over the deck, and Connor held on for his life. He had no idea where the rest of the crew was. If he squinted, he could see the vague outline of the mast, then a terrifying view of the foamy waves below, but nothing more. The cabin was the safest place to be, but he didn't trust his feet to get him there. If he let go, he could easily vanish into the roiling blackness, and no one would see him go. He gritted his teeth and pressed his body against the deck, praying both he and the ship would outlast the tempest.

At last the blizzard dwindled, but it was a few minutes more before Connor could convince himself to stand. Eventually he clutched the rail for balance and rose carefully, trying to still the vibrations trembling through him. His stomach lurched and his head pounded, but he thought if he breathed deeply enough, he could manage to not be sick. In the next moment the sun emerged, peeking out from behind the clouds for the first time since they'd been afloat. The golden light felt like a blessing, and he held his face up to it in gratitude.

The sailors emerged slowly from their refuges, casting critical eyes over the deck. Connor was relieved to count seven men. No one had died. Not on this deck, anyway.

"Check the prisoners," ordered the captain, and two of the crew members went to open the hatch.

The weeping was desperate, and prayers seeped through the hatch. Connor was distinctly aware of the cries of little children, and he turned away in shame.

"We need help," came a woman's exhausted, broken English. "A young girl fall. I think the arm break."

"We need water!"

A man roared in vehement French, "Someone must clean the floor. We cannot live like this!"

"I'll go," Connor said, but the captain put up a hand.

"No, no, Sergeant. That is not a job for you. First mate! Send the surgeon for the lass. And let's get the hold pumped out."

"I don't mind going," Connor tried again.

"The ship needs your hands, lad. Set to it."

The storm had stripped the ship of its double-lashed awnings and torn the trysails clean out of the gaskets; rails had splintered. Connor slid his hand along one, testing its stability and finding it lacking. It was a miracle they were still afloat. If they were to sail another day, most of the craft would require repair and cleanup.

Connor squinted through the sunlight, marvelling at the

welcome calmness of the sea. It was as if a great beast had feasted and now sprawled before them, sated.

In the next breath, all the blood drained from his head.

"Captain? Where are the other ships?"

TWENTY

For a day and a half they floated without a breeze. The lull gave the crew time to make needed repairs, and the appearance of the sun raised their spirits. Unfortunately, its light barely touched the entrance to the hold. Protests and screams for mercy had faded to the occasional defeated sob.

They never saw the other ships again. Not even the frigate, which meant the *Pembroke* was unprotected. They searched the surface of the water for fragments, for splintered boards or floating barrels, but there was nothing. Connor prayed that meant the others had only sailed off course, not been destroyed. Since they had no evidence either way, the captain said nothing about it and ordered the rest of the crew to do the same. No one informed the prisoners they were alone. They didn't seem to notice the difference when they came on deck; they were simply grateful for the short, glorious intervals when they could breathe the air.

Connor noticed. Every time he looked out over the empty sea, he was torn by an agonizing sense of both grief . . . and hope. With the disappearance of the other ships had come the solution for which he had been searching. The plan involved a significant personal sacrifice, however. He deliberated over that, trying to find some way out, but in the end he had no other choice.

He would speak with Amélie tonight, and his anticipation rose as dusk approached. He knew where she would walk, where she would pause to breathe in the night air. He also knew approximately where the other sailors would be when all this was going on, and he wanted his meeting with her to be far from them.

The sun rested on the horizon, casting one last yearning look upon the world before departing, and Connor watched its crimson light bleed into the sea. *Red sky at night . . .* The morning should bring a fine day of sailing, with clear skies and steady wind. The prisoners enjoying their brief half hour on deck stood silently at the rail, watching the same sunset. What did it mean to them? In the beginning of this journey the sight had induced tears, had coaxed the prisoners to hold one another tightly . . . seeking what? Comfort? Hope? Other than sorrow, grief, and each other, that was all they had left.

Four little ones had come out on deck with their mother and grandmother this time. The elderly woman looked feeble, and her white fingers gripped the rail, though Connor knew they must be numb from the cold. He wondered how old she was—probably twenty years younger than she looked. This journey was sucking the life out of everyone.

Connor usually had little liking for this time of day, but he was glad to see this sunset, for tonight would be significant. He watched the backs of the prisoners, now making slow, painful progress toward the hatch, and nerves skittered through his chest. Next it would be Amélie's turn. He would have less than a precious half hour to spend with her, and he needed every moment of that time to convince her he had not abandoned her.

"Move along," one of the sailors ordered. Smith was his name, Connor recalled. Smith's usual partner at supper was Adams. They were strong-enough lads, he knew, since he'd seen them hauling in sails, but they weren't the smartest. None of them were all that bright. He hoped that would work to his advantage when it came to carrying out his plan.

The Acadian mother stopped at the hatch and glared at Smith, mutely demanding he give her a hand onto the ladder. It was, after all, a dangerous and slippery descent. Especially for an undernourished, sickly woman who had barely stood on her own for the past twenty-four hours. Smith blinked at her, obviously not understanding, then his eyes widened with apology. Connor was pleased to see him take her hand and elbow and ease her down.

A few moments after the little group of six had disappeared below deck, Connor watched Amélie climb out of the hold. The storm had taken its toll; her bright blue eyes had faded into the pallid grey of her face. She clung to Smith's arm for balance, then shrugged it off, not giving the sailor even a hint of gratitude. How long had it been since she had actually smiled?

She and her sister Claire were the first of the six to appear, their white bonnets like faded beacons in the dusk. Amélie turned back to check on her younger sister, who climbed up ahead of their mother. Two other children emerged after them. With eyes round as owls' the group shuffled down the deck, heading in his direction. Amélie and Claire came last, shepherding the children ahead of them.

The night was clear, and moonlight fell over the sparkling water like a thin layer of snow. Connor waited in the frosted shadows until Amélie was close enough that he could almost touch her, and he realized he was holding his breath. Suddenly, approaching her seemed the most difficult part. But he could put it off no longer.

"Mademoiselle Belliveau," he murmured from the shadows.

Both sisters spun toward him, startled. In the dim light of the lantern emotions flickered like flames across Amélie's face.

"Sergeant MacDonnell."

He put one finger over his lips and bowed politely at her sister.

Amélie regarded him with suspicion. Then she nodded to Claire. "Please. Give us a few moments to speak alone."

"You know him?"

"Did you forget? He cut our firewood."

Her sister's expression was unforgiving. "I recall. He cut it because he had already taken our axe."

"He cut it because I asked him for the axe, and he did not wish us to freeze."

"You spoke with him? On your own? That was reckless."

"Perhaps," Amélie allowed. "But we were warm, were we not? And now I would like to speak with him again. Alone."

When she looked at Connor, Claire's eyes flashed with contempt. The poor woman was not even aware of how deeply the army deserved her spite. She did not know the *Hobson* no longer floated alongside them, carrying her fiancé.

Eventually Claire turned away, leaving Connor alone with Amélie. They stared at each other, clouds of their breath filling the space between them.

"I . . . I didn't know you were on this ship," Amélie whispered, pulling her shawl tight around her shoulders.

"I know. I'm sorry for that."

She blinked, and any tenderness he'd seen at first vanished behind the deep, hard anger in her eyes. Still, she did not look away. She took a measured breath, shuddering with cold and held his gaze.

"You're sorry? For what, in particular?"

"For a great many things, including tonight. I didn't mean to startle you by appearing like this, but I had to let you know I was here." Connor jerked his head toward the nearest sailor. "They cannot know we are acquainted."

"No?" Her nostrils flared, and her chin quivered beneath her chattering teeth. "Are you—the much-respected, powerful sergeant of the British army—ashamed to be seen with a filthy Acadian like me?"

Her inflection was as raw as the night, and though it was deserved, it still hurt.

"Ashamed? Never. But if they knew, it would make things . . . uncomfortable. For us both."

She crossed her arms. "I'm already as uncomfortable as I can get."

"I can help."

"What are you talking about?"

One of the other sailors glanced at Connor, so he ignored Amélie's resistance and took her elbow, guiding her away from curious ears. He didn't know if the sailors could speak French, but he wasn't taking chances.

"How could you possibly help?" she whispered. "Why would you want to?"

"You know why."

She shook her head, twisting at his heart.

"You do, Amélie."

"I know nothing. I thought I knew, but I was wrong."

Every fibre in his being longed to reach out, to fold her into his embrace until she believed, until she looked at him as she had before. If he'd been anywhere else, he might have been able to do that. Not here, though. Not on this ship where he and the rest of the army had trapped her.

Water lapped at the side of the ship, a soft rhythmic rocking, and the ship groaned at the suggestion of wind, but there were no other sounds. Even the crew and cargo seemed quiet for once.

"I thought you'd left me."

"I was never gone. I was here, watching over you. I have been waiting for the right time to speak to you, and that is tonight."

"Why? What is so special about tonight?"

The wariness in her voice pained him, but he understood it. She believed he'd lied to her before, so why should she trust him now? He had to be careful. If he said too much, she'd think him mad; he didn't want to frighten her off.

Before she could protest, he removed his heavy black cloak and wrapped it around her. "You know I have never agreed with what is happening to your people," he reminded her, tugging the thick edges of the material together to seal in the warmth of his own body. She was dwarfed by the cloak, her skin paler than ever within its black embrace. "Not with any of it. But, Amélie, I am a soldier. I have a duty. I'm also an honest man with a conscience. Long ago I was convinced this mission was wrong, and I told you that. I also said I would do what I could to keep you safe."

She looked down, away from him, her fingers clenching the edges of the cloak. He could practically read her mind. *Words, Connor. Those are just words.* On impulse, he took her hands into his own warm ones.

Her eyes widened. Despite the comfort he offered, she pulled away. "Don't."

He spoke gently, as if to a cornered animal. "I understand you're angry, Amélie, and I deserve all the anger you have. I know you don't trust me. I haven't been able to help any of you, and for that I'm truly sorry. But now I have a plan," he said carefully. "And I need your help."

She grimaced. "What are you talking about? It's too late to help us, Sergeant. Too late for everything."

"No, it isn't. I think I have finally found a way to help you."

She stared at him, then her eyes darted over his shoulder. He glanced about, but no one was near.

"Can any of the men sail?" he asked.

"What?"

"Could your men sail a ship?"

She thought about it, then nodded. "Papa has repaired ships and sailed them as well. Most of the others have sailed fishing crafts. Why?"

He had been hoping for exactly that answer. "I need to speak with your father. Do you think you could convince him to speak with me?"

But Amélie's expression had hardened again. "What is this? More treachery?"

Connor had purposefully positioned them so they were downwind. The message could not be intercepted, and yet he leaned closer. "There are only eight crewmen on this ship, Amélie, including me. There are two hundred and thirty of you, though many are either very young or very old."

"And most of those are sick," she said. Despite his cloak, she shivered openly now.

"Aye, but still." He needed her to understand. Most of all, he needed her to believe in him. "Amélie, it would not be difficult for the strongest of you to take charge of this ship."

She opened her mouth to speak, her expression confused, and he hardened himself to the next part of the conversation. It nearly killed him, knowing it would fall to him to tell her the awful truth.

"Understand this, Amélie. Other than the captain, six sailors, and me, there is no one to stop the Acadians here on the *Pembroke*." He paused, knowing her heart was about to break all over again. "All the other ships were lost in the storm, including the frigate. There is no one left to fight you."

She did not move. She stared at him, but her eyes had gone blank. Then grief pulled tight across the pale planes of her face, and he imagined she saw again the panic-stricken expression of her little brother as he'd been led away so long before.

"All?" The word was barely audible.

"I cannot say for certain they were destroyed. All I know is we have seen neither hide nor hair of any of them since the storm."

Amélie staggered to one side, but he caught her and pulled her against him. She gasped and pushed him away.

"Mathieu and Guillaume were on one of those ships," she managed. "Maybe they got away. Maybe the storm pushed them off course and they're fine."

He remembered the murderous rage of the storm, how the wind had sliced like razors at his numbed fingers, how the salt water had roared up over the sides and burned his skin despite the snow. He'd been sure none of them would survive. But how could he deny her this one feeble hope?

"Aye. That could have happened."

"That's what happened. They're fine," she said, trying to convince them both. "I will see them again. God could not have—"

The words stopped but her lips moved in prayer.

"I need to speak with your father. Will he talk to me?"

The line of her throat moved as she swallowed, tried to breathe. Could she see him as a man, not a soldier? Would she trust him that far? He doubted he could have done it in her position. He could only pray she was stronger than he.

Her gaze softened. "If we take over this ship, what happens to you?"

The unexpected question was more than he could have hoped for. "We would become your prisoners."

"If the English knew you were speaking to me this way, they would hang you."

He nodded.

The moonlight dimmed, muted by a stray cloud. She tucked the cloak more tightly around herself, watching him the entire time. Her lips were chapped, her cheeks as well, and yet a tiny flame of hope had come to life in her eyes. He was transfixed by that little spark, by her strength. He couldn't have looked away if a gun had gone off.

"We would no longer be your prisoners?"

"You were never my prisoner, Amélie, and no. Eight men cannot stand against two hundred. If my plan works, you would be no one's prisoner. You would take possession of the ship and go wherever you want."

"Home?"

"Except there. Your home is gone."

She hesitated. "What if your plan does not work?"

"You cannot end up much worse than you are right now, can you?"

"Why?" she asked slowly. "Why would you do this? It makes no sense."

"It does to me."

"I don't want you punished, Connor."

At the sound of his name, the world came alive for him again. "If I am caught, it is no one's fault but my own," he assured her. He tugged the cloak, pulling it more snugly around her, and this time he kept hold of it. "Even then, it would be worth it to see you and your family go free."

Amélie pressed her cold fingertips against the back of Connor's hand. "I will speak with my father." He felt her need to believe stretch between them, as tangible as any rope. Desperate hope shone in the intensity of her stare. "And I will tell him I trust you."

Slowly, Connor turned his hand over so their fingers intertwined. She took a deep breath, watching him. Did she feel the same strength as he did when they touched?

"I know how valuable that trust is," he said, "and I will show you I am worthy of it."

She tightened her fingers around his. "I may be stupid and gullible and naive, but I believe you."

She hadn't thought far enough ahead, he could tell. Caught up in the idea of being free of this hell, she was not seeing what must follow. But Connor's heart was already broken. If all went as he planned, this would be the last time they'd ever speak to one another.

"Amélie, should fate separate us, I want you to have something of mine."

"What? Why would you say such a thing?"

"Your life is not as it was, nor is mine. We do not know where God will send either of us."

He lifted the chain from around his neck and slid a small silver ring from its links. His mother had given it to him as a child, saying it was a charm to keep him safe, and he believed it had. Now Amélie needed that protection more than he.

"Take this, Amélie. Think of me."

Her eyes were on the little ring, her lips parted in surprise. Then she looked up at him. "I cannot accept this."

"Please," he said. "It was a gift from my mother. I want you to have it."

When she did not move, he took her hand and slipped it over her cold finger. It was a perfect fit, as if it had been made for her.

She stared at her finger, then back at at him. "I do not intend to be separated from you again, but if you insist on giving me this kind of gift, then I shall give one to you as well."

Before he could object, she had lifted a beaded necklace over her head and ran her thumbs fondly over the beads. When she held the necklace out for him, he didn't take it, so she held it higher, opening the loop wide. He leaned forward, bowing slightly so she could reach, and she placed it carefully over his head.

"Do not forget me." Her whisper was warm on his ear.

Taking advantage of that moment was wrong of him, he was sure, but nothing could have stopped him from kissing her, from drawing her body against his. She kissed him softly at first, but her passion quickly built, rising urgently from so many disappointments, so much grief. Her need for comfort, for reassurance, for any kind of hope was so dire it broke his heart, and he held her close, giving all he could. When at last they drew apart, she touched her lips with two fingers and stared at him with a sort of fascination. It occurred to him that she might never have kissed a man before this moment.

"I could never forget you. Never in a million years," he said softly, suddenly realizing it was the truth. *So this is love.* He tucked the necklace inside his shirt, savouring the feel of it against his chest. "Thank you."

"Be careful, Connor," she whispered. "I could not bear to lose you as well."

Amélie

TWENTY-ONE

Maman slept with her head in my lap. I had already assured her I was not in need of rest, and it was true. Certainly my body craved it, but my mind and heart were filled with such joy, I could not have surrendered to sleep. To see Connor again, to feel the warmth of his body through his cloak, to know he had not abandoned me, and to kiss the lips I'd watched for so long . . .

But how could I linger on that moment? Just as he had given my heart wings, he had torn my life apart with his news of the other ships. To preserve my mother's fragile health, I kept the inconceivable message to myself, but the knowledge threatened to engulf me, as the sea had surely engulfed my brother. I tried to force my memories to return to happier times—Mathieu's laughter, his enthusiasm when he told stories around the supper table, Papa putting his broad hand on my little brother's head and roughing up the blond curls—but my mind betrayed me. It led me back to the last time I'd seen him, marching toward the docks. None of us could have imagined he was actually marching toward his death. To think of him drowning, plunging into the frozen Atlantic . . . Oh, I could not. The pain was too much. Who had been there to hear his last words? To hold him tight?

And what of Claire, whose heart and soul were always with Guillaume? How would she live her life knowing his was over?

But my traitorous mind took me back to Connor. He had spoken of escape. He had brought light to the nightmare, and I clung to that hope with everything I had.

Connor. What had I done, kissing the enemy? Worse, I craved more! Connor was Winslow's translator, believed by many of my people to be the worst of the English, since he understood our language and had still sold us out. I had believed the same thing. But I did not see him that way anymore. He had explained to me so many times that he had a duty to fulfil, that he had no choice but to follow orders . . . and yet now I knew he planned to defy those orders and endanger himself so he could set us free.

The hatch opened, letting in a brief moment of moonlight as Papa descended the ladder, and I sat straighter at sight of him. Though he was barely visible, I knew it was he. Our eyes had been forced to adjust to living in darkness, and I had been watching the hatch ever since he had ascended a half hour before. From the set of his shoulders, I knew he had spoken with Connor.

"This man . . ." He groaned with effort, settling onto the moist floor beside me. I felt it as well: the stiffening of my limbs and joints. If we did not get out of this prison soon, I feared we would all be crippled.

I kept my expression blank. Papa must not know my thrill at speaking his name out loud. "Sergeant MacDonnell?"

"Yes. The Scotsman. He has a good idea. But can we trust him? I know you do, but . . . he has a pretty face. That doesn't mean the rest of us should believe what he says."

My fingers curled over the silver ring. "What do we have to

lose, Papa? If we do as he suggests, what can they do other than throw us in the hold and ship us off to somewhere?"

"This is true. It cannot get much worse, can it?" He took a deep breath. "What do you know of him?"

"I know he is a good man in an impossible position. He cut our firewood, Papa, when we were cold. I went to ask for our axe, and he gave it to me, but not before he had cut us enough wood for more than a month." I could have told him that I'd stayed out in the cold, watching him, talking with him, and that he'd carried the wood inside and built up a roaring fire for us, but I didn't think Papa would like to know another man was in his house while he was imprisoned elsewhere.

I took a chance. "And he told me to make sure my brothers stayed in hiding. He said they were safer wherever they were than they would be if they were captured for trying to escape."

He stared straight ahead, taking my words into consideration. Then he slapped his hands on his knees and turned to me. My heart leapt at the anticipation shining in his smile. I had not seen him wear that expression in far too long.

"I'll speak with the others."

"Will you tell me what is happening?"

He nodded. "You need to know, and the sergeant asked me to explain it to you."

He squinted toward Maman, trying to see if she was asleep or not. I knew he didn't want her to get excited about anything or to worry. She didn't seem herself lately. We both feared she was falling ill, like so many of the others.

Papa tucked his knees under his chin. "I am trusting your friend based on what you say. He appears to be a brave man, a little reckless as well." He glanced at me. "I am not certain your friendship with him would be considered appropriate—"

"Please do not tell Maman."

"That is what I thought. As your father I should tell you this is a mistake, but my little girl is a young woman now, with a mind of her own. And our world is changing. No matter what uniform this man wears, if he can keep you safe, I cannot order you away from him. I only ask that you be careful. A wounded heart is slow to heal."

"Yes, Papa."

He sighed. "I am to pull together a dozen of our strongest men, and in the morning I will assemble them in two groups to go up for the walks. When the first group is ready to return, the sailor will open the hatch and the next group will be ready to come out."

I nodded, envisioning the scene.

"Your Sergeant MacDonnell will create a diversion. There will already be six of us on deck, with the hatch open and six more to come, and the rest to follow if we need. There are only eight men to control us all, and one of them is the Scot. They will not be able to stand against so many."

"What about guns? Are the sailors not armed?"

"MacDonnell has said the sailors are chiefly unarmed. Even if they happen to have guns, eight weapons cannot do much harm against two hundred people." He hesitated. "There is danger in everything we do. Some of our own may be injured or killed in a fight like this, but it would be for the greater good. I would gladly give my life if I knew it would allow the others to live their own."

So simple. So terrifyingly simple. My heart soared. We would take the ship and despite what Connor had said to me, we could sail back home—

"We are near New York now, and when we are in control, we shall sail to Saint John Harbour," Papa said. "MacDonnell told me he has learned there are other Acadians there, and we would be welcome."

"But Papa! Why not—"

"This soldier of yours is wise. He has warned me we cannot return to Grand Pré. The English have burned everything, and they will throw us into prison."

He set a comforting hand against my cheek, and I was surprised by the touch of his palm. Normally my father's hands were coarse with calluses, but those had faded with lack of work, and the smoothness of his skin reminded me that he had been imprisoned for even longer than I had.

"We will find a way from here," he promised, "but we cannot go home."

How I longed for the fields, for the circling gulls, for the battling hummingbirds who would return in the warmth of *siwkw*. I even missed the snow and the shrieking, punishing wind as it piled in drifts against our doors and windows. During the most wicked of winter storms, we had all been safe inside, huddled before the fire, singing songs or telling stories. I loved my home, my life, my world.

But of course even if we could go back and rebuild, we would never be the same again.

"Papa?" I whispered. "Did he . . . did he tell you of the other ships?"

In the darkness I could not see the grief which stole his response. Tears surged to my eyes, but I blinked them away, knowing they would only make things worse. It was more difficult to control my emotions now that he knew the terrible truth, for it meant I was no longer alone with it. I longed to share my grief with him and to let him burden me as well, but I swallowed it back. Now was not the time.

Papa leaned in to kiss my brow. He struggled to his feet, and the sound he made was that of a much older man.

"I know about Henri, Papa," I said quietly. "I saw him with Mali and the others. I told my sisters."

He paused. "Is he well?"

"He and Mali looked very pleased with the situation."

Papa chuckled lightly. "I believe that."

"He said you arranged for him to be there," I added.

"Young men can get themselves into trouble when they are antagonized, and your brother is not meek."

"He will fight with the Mi'kmaq if he has to, Papa."

"If my son is to fight, he should not have to do it as a prisoner in his own home."

"Where is André?"

"Ah. You did not find him, my little huntress? He did not want to go to the Mi'kmaq. He believed he had a responsibility elsewhere."

This was news to me. "What does that mean?"

Papa had always been proud of his children. He told us constantly that we were smart and kind and polite, and courageous as well. When he spoke of André, his pride was obvious. His eldest son was so like him in looks, thoughts, and beliefs. André had grown into a man about whom he was very pleased.

Now he squatted back down beside me, wanting to keep his words between us. "André has gone to the French, Amélie."

I opened my mouth to speak but snapped it shut. I could not imagine my brother in a uniform. "A soldier? André is a *soldier*?"

"Not the French army, but the resistance. He is with a number of young men his age, and a large number of Mi'kmaq as well."

"But how . . . ?"

"I have friends you do not know, ma chérie. In many places," He smiled. "They will take good care of your brother."

I thought of André and of Henri, and my heart felt lighter, knowing they were out there. Neither of them would have fared well in this hell.

"Oh, Mathieu . . . ," Papa whispered. He dropped his face into his hands and breathed deeply, saying nothing. I knew he prayed for the son he could no longer protect. After a moment he raised his head and looked at me, remnants of unshed tears shining in his eyes.

"Are you all right, Papa?" I ventured.

The sorrow in his expression was unbearable, and I longed to take it from him, to take us both back to a place where pain did not rule every moment of every day. If only I could be a child again, running through the fields or the water or the forest, giggling as my brothers tried to find me. Oh, to be the little girl who tumbled like a boy down a hill then came to Papa, crying about a bloody knee. To sit on his lap and listen to stories told in his deep, soothing voice. To know that when I was tucked in at night, when the fire was banked and my parents had pulled up their own blankets, I was safe. I was home.

"I will be, Amélie. Everything will be all right eventually," he said, but his assurance fell flat. "And your handsome sergeant has given me hope when I needed it most."

He rose again and walked away. Though my eyes had adjusted as well as possible to this place, it wasn't long before his lurching figure disappeared from my view. He had gone to put Connor's plan into place, and I thought I knew whom he would speak with about it. The men he chose had to be strong, and they had to be trustworthy. They must be men he knew would step up to the challenge without fear, and they must be able to hold their tongues until morning so as not to raise any suspicions. How I longed for my brothers!

I leaned back against the wall of the ship and closed my eyes, wondering if I'd be able to sleep. The news, both horrible and hopeful, had drained me. Every muscle ached with exhaustion, and I felt sure my thoughts would race, preventing slumber of any kind. But when I opened my eyes again, Papa slept nearby, Maman cradled in his arms. It was comforting to see them like this, and I closed my eyes again.

TWENTY-TWO

I awoke to sounds to which I had become accustomed: the whining of dozens of children begging for food, the weak, hushed assurances of parents who could offer nothing. Occasionally I might hear a guarded laugh. Our existence in this pit had become a sad, pointless routine.

"Good morning," Maman said, smiling at me. Even in the dark I could see the dark lines under her eyes were vivid this morning, like bruises against her pale skin. "Sleep well?"

A sunbeam snuck through the boards of the deck over our head and lit the hold. People struggled to their feet to stretch, balancing against the rocking of the boat.

I smiled back at her and shook my head. "Did you?"

"No. But it seemed a good question to ask on such a morning."

That reminded me suddenly that this *was* a specific morning, unlike all the others. "Where is Papa?"

She lifted her chin slightly but her weary gaze rested on me. "He went up for a walk with some of the other men this morning. I didn't mind. I said I would go later, with you."

I barely heard her. It was already happening, and I had almost missed it! Across the hold, six men had grouped together at the base of the ladder. A few more had gathered around them.

"How long have they been gone?" I asked.

Maman's eyes had closed again. "They will be back soon."

With one hand on the slippery wall of the ship, I edged over and crouched by Claire. She lay on one side with her eyes closed, but I could tell she was awake.

"Claire!" I whispered.

Her eyes blinked open. She hadn't spoken to me since I'd begged for private conversation with Connor the night before. Now she was too curious to regard me with the scorn I knew she felt.

"What is going on, Amélie? Something is happening."

I didn't want anyone to overhear, but it was difficult to keep my voice down. In truth, I wanted to sing!

"Papa and the others are about to take over the ship!"

She sat up. "*What?*"

I explained the plan—neglecting to mention the fact that we were now the only ship—and watched a smile bloom on her weary face. Just as quickly, her excitement faded. "The sailors are armed, are they not?"

I waved a hand, dismissing her worries. "Pah. They don't expect anything. We have been stupid animals this whole time, doing nothing to arouse their suspicion. Why would they be prepared this morning? No, they will have no idea. Think of it, Claire! Soon we will all breathe the air whenever we want!"

"I hope Papa is careful."

"He will be fine."

The hatch creaked open, and my sister and I gripped each other's arms. When sunlight shone down on the six waiting men, they stood taller, puffing their chests with a pride they still felt despite everything. Hands flexed into fists then relaxed, and I imagined the men's hearts hammered like woodpeckers' beaks. How I admired them for their bravery. What I would give to climb up there with them, to set us all free!

But what of Connor? At least he would be ready. He had put all this into motion, so I felt certain Papa would keep him safe.

Monsieur Guilbeau was the first man to put his hands on the ladder, and despite the thrill of the moment he managed to maintain a grim expression. He began to climb, his eyes on the open hatchway; then he could not contain himself a moment longer. He grinned down at the others, and a few fists were silently thrust toward the sky.

"Sergeant?" A sailor spoke sharply above us, his voice carrying down the hatch. "Step back, would you? Those men need to—"

It was beginning! I leaned forward, intent on the sounds above me.

Connor's indignant reply came back, though I couldn't make out his words at first. I pictured him, drawn up tall in his long black cloak, his chin lifted with authority.

"—speak to me like that," I finally heard. He spoke more slowly than I'd heard him speak before, every syllable deliberate, and I understood he was stretching out the moment, ensuring the Acadian men were prepared and in position. "Can you not see this uniform, lad? You'll show respect, you will, and I'll bloody well move when I'm ready. These prisoners can wait"—I heard him snarl—"as can you."

The sailor didn't sound impressed. "Pardon my saying so, *Sergeant*, but I—"

Our ceiling, black and shiny with slime, shuddered under the weight of a sudden crash, and the men at the base of the ladder rushed up on cue. Behind them hustled more men, each as eager and determined as the one before. The women and children below hushed, straining to hear as violence erupted above us. The ship resonated with pounding boots and yelling men, and down below we all held our breath.

I heard English protests and garbled threats, but more than that I heard French voices raised with triumph. I heard Papa over them all, though he sounded different, and I knew why. For twenty years, he had lived a quiet, proper life as a farmer and shipbuilder. He had worked hard and gone to church. He had been a strong, loving father, and he had been a leader among our people. But now, finally released from our stagnant prison and given the opportunity to fight for his life and ours, he had slipped back to his younger days, those days when *right* and *good* became confused, and decisions were made in the moment.

Would the battle be short and straightforward? Would the sailors put up a fight despite being outnumbered? God help us all if it went wrong, if blood was shed. Claire's nails bit into my skin, and I'm sure mine did the same to hers. I listened hard, but all we could do was wait.

To our relief, the scuffle didn't last long. Soon Papa appeared at the top of the ladder. Moving slowly, he climbed down, and when he turned, I could see he was smiling broadly, though blood from his nose ran over his lips and into the filthy linen of his shirt.

"Charles!" cried Maman. "You're hurt!"

She started to struggle to her feet, but Claire held out a calming hand. "Wait, Maman. He is fine. Listen to what he has to say."

"Mesdames et messieurs," Papa said, his strong voice ringing clearly through the hold, "this morning the Acadians have revolted against our English captors. Against our brave men, they had no choice but to surrender and give us the ship."

The reaction was delayed as the truth sunk in. What did this mean? What would happen now? The chatter began as whispers and grew to exclamations and noisy questions.

Papa put up his hands, and everyone fell quiet again. "We shall sail to Saint John Harbour. I welcome everyone to come to the upper deck when you feel well enough. You, my friends, are no longer prisoners."

My chest filled with pride. We had done it. Even more prideful of me was knowing that I had something to do with this thrilling change in our fate. I raced with the others toward the ladder, impatient to see Connor, and when I emerged through the hatchway the sun's rays tasted sweeter than maple syrup. All around me people laughed and embraced. It had been too long since I had heard laughter.

Papa held a happy but weeping Maman in his arms, and he smiled when I walked up to him.

"Where are the prisoners?" I asked.

His reply was only for me. "Your Scotsman is an honourable man," he said appreciatively. "The captain and his men are secured in the bow, and do not worry. No one was badly hurt. Just a little blood and some bruised pride." In reply to my unasked question, he said, "You can look, but I do not think it would be wise to speak with him."

"Why not? Surely there is no danger now."

"I am sorry, ma chérie. But it was he who convinced me that if it became known you were acquainted, he would be blamed when the English return to their own kind. To them he would be a traitor. They would punish him. They could even hang him for treason."

"But I mean to express my gratitude."

Papa shook his head, and my throat closed. This could not be happening. Connor had made it possible for us to be together, and now . . .

Should fate separate us, he had said. So he had known it would end this way all along.

"Does this mean I cannot even say thank you?"

Papa didn't say, but his tight expression told me I was right. I must never speak with Connor again.

TWENTY-THREE

The ship no longer controlled Papa. He stood at the helm, tall and powerful and in full command. Charles Belliveau was in his element behind the wheel, and though he was much too modest to say so, I imagined he was proud to be the new captain of this ship.

"Amélie!" he called. "Come here. See what I see."

I stood by my father and looked beyond our former prison, letting the ocean become something exciting and new again, not the abyss of loss it had been until now. Even Maman had roused herself, though it took great effort. Her illness had worsened, but with Papa's help she climbed the ladder and managed to stay upright for a while. I stood at her side, providing extra support.

"Coming about!" Papa bellowed, and the call was echoed down the deck. Maman stepped out of his way, and he turned the wheel back in the direction from where we had come. The sail spun into position and the wind came alive, whipping around us and filling the huge square sails as if it were on our side. The gales rushed through Papa's golden curls, and his cheeks flushed a victorious red.

"Would you like to hear a story, ma chérie?"

I would do anything to hear Papa laugh again. "Of course, Papa. Does it have a happy ending?"

"Oh, yes. A funny one," Maman replied, gazing up at Papa with adoring eyes.

"Do you know, Amélie," said Papa, "that I already know a little about this ship?"

We all knew a little about this ship. It was old and terrible. But Papa was grinning, so I asked, "What do you mean?"

"Not long ago, the army came to me. They told me they had a ship with a broken mast. After I had made a new mast for them, they said they would not pay for it."

"What? That's criminal!"

He shrugged. "It wasn't a problem. I told them that was fine. I would cut the mast into firewood."

I could imagine him standing up to them, bold and unafraid, and the idea both thrilled and frightened me. "Papa!"

"Oh yes, Amélie. I told them that, and I would have done it. But you know what happened then? A funny thing. They paid me exactly what I asked for, and not a penny less." He looked up at the bulging sails, obviously proud. "I made this mast."

I followed his gaze. "*This* one?"

"The Lord works in mysterious ways, ma chérie!"

Once we were on our way back north, all the Acadians moved from the hold to the more hospitable lower deck. We were grateful for what small comforts we had, like sleeping in shared hammocks instead of on the slippery wood floor of the hold. We ate better and we slept better, though no one could claim to be happy with the situation. Still, no one was forcing us to do anything, and the air we breathed was clean and fresh.

Although life had improved, many had fallen ill since we'd been on board, and their condition declined a little more each day. Families clustered around loved ones who were stricken, quietly encouraging them to sip water, to swallow bits of food, but most were too weak. Many suffered feverish hallucinations, ranting and recognizing no one. We thanked God none had died, but I did not think we could celebrate even that small miracle for much longer.

The captives had been dropped into our dismal former living area. I tried not to think of Connor's discomfort and hoped his wounds would heal cleanly, but when I asked if I could check on them, Papa shook his head.

One night, after he had passed the wheel to the next man in charge, he pulled me aside. "We are leaving the English prisoners on shore tomorrow."

I couldn't speak. The ring on my finger seemed suddenly too tight.

"They will be fine, Amélie. Their injuries are healing, they are fed, and they will be landing at an English port. They will find their way back."

"I want to go with him," I whispered, tears filling my eyes.

"No good could come of that. I am sorry, ma chérie. Truly I am. He was a brave man to do what he did, but now it is time for you to forget about him. He would want to know you are all right, that you can start again without him, because he must do the same. Our lives are changing every day, and we must do what we can to make them the best they can be. The Lord will guide him home, and he will guide you as well."

I had thought I was lonely before. Now it was as if I were completely empty.

In the morning the prisoners were brought up on deck. Their hands were bound in front of them, chained by the shackles my father and the other men had once worn. Their attention was focused on the deck before them. All but the most ill of us lined up to watch them go, and most—though not all—of the Acadians took the opportunity to spit angry farewells. I stood with my back to the rail, trying to keep my emotions at bay as the men trudged past us in a silent, sullen procession.

I could not go to him, could not say a word. I longed to reach for him, to bring comfort of some kind. His eyes were cast down; the dark waves of his hair had come unbound and now tumbled over his face. The skin around one eye was a deep purple-red, and patches of dried blood stained his shirt. Evidently he had put up a fight, wanting the others to believe he was oblivious to our plan rather than its creator. Either that or one of our men had let out his frustration on him. In any case, he had done what he had set out to do.

Finally, *finally* Connor glanced at me, and anguish twisted through me. I forced back tears, but I could do nothing about my faltering expression. Connor made no attempt to speak to me, and I did as my father had bid me: I said nothing. But I watched like a hawk as they lowered him into the ship's tender, where it waited on the frosty water, saw him take his place on a bench and struggle to tuck his cloak around himself—the same cloak he had wrapped around me, wanting to keep me warm.

My misery was such that I could not move, and it became so much worse when he looked up at me. I was sure everyone would notice the terrible expressions of loss on both our faces, but I could not look away. I wanted to remember everything about him, every line of his face, every strand of his hair. Finally I lifted my fingers in a suggestion of a wave, certain that I was saying farewell to any dream of love in my life. In reply, he uncurled all ten fingers as if he were stretching against the shackles and opened his palms to me. When he moved, the collar of his shirt fell slightly open, and I saw the white beads of my necklace. More than my heart was going with him, but Mali would understand. My fingers went to the small silver ring I wore, and I rubbed it with my thumb, wishing I could reach him somehow through the pressure of my fingers, infusing my affection into its dull surface.

Papa said the harbour where we left them was in Maine. All I remembered of it was the icy fog. Connor and I watched each other through its veil until he disappeared, and the rhythmic splash of oars carried clearly to me after he was gone from view. I stood at the rail a long time after that, waiting for the tender to return. Then we pulled up anchor and Papa turned the ship back toward the sea.

Once we were sailing and the danger of discovery was past, I dropped my facade, letting tears course down my cheeks and drop onto the rail. He was as safe as he could be at this tumultuous time, I knew, and because of his sacrifice, hundreds of us were free. By abandoning him, we had done what had to be done. Our English captors were gone; the deck filled with the familiar sound of French conversation. Yet I felt entirely alone in this crowd of family and friends. The ocean seemed a vast, endless stretch of nothingness.

So low did I sink that I had trouble rousing any sense of excitement when someone spotted land. On the day we were finally to disembark, Papa informed me it was January 8, 1756, exactly one month since we'd first set sail aboard the *Pembroke*. The month of Punamujuiku's had arrived, bringing with it the frost fish moon. It seemed we had been gone much longer than that.

We sailed up the Bay of Fundy to the mouth of Saint John Harbour, having met not one other ship along our journey. Connor had told Papa there were other Acadians here, but what would we find? I scanned the bleak shoreline, hoping to see another person, but the banks were empty. Would there be shelter in this frozen port? Comfort, even? I hardly dared to hope.

To the cheers of those on board, we floated toward the shore and dropped anchor in the freezing water on the south side of the waterway. The harbour was narrow and too shallow for our huge ship, so the tender made many trips, transporting us all to the rocky beach. The little boat had to go right up on shore—the water was very cold, and we were so weak we would not fare well if we got wet. Many of those stepping off lost their balance after having been a-sea for so long, and those who had already been on dry land for a few minutes tried to catch them. Papa remained on the *Pembroke*, managing the disembarking, and he sent us on ahead. Maman was so weak when we arrived, I practically lifted her out.

"Come, Maman," Claire said, helping me. "We will find you a place to lie down. It may not be warm, but at least it will be still."

But our options were few. We set up camp on the north bank of the Saint John River, wary of being spotted by any passing ships. I believed this concern was unfounded, since there was no sign anyone had ever walked this grim coast before. We were entirely alone. If there were any other Acadians, they were not here. Winter gales cut across the sea and over the frozen land, and we huddled together for warmth. Disappointment returned, making me bitter. I had allowed myself to hope, and once again my dreams had not come true.

We unloaded all the weaponry and stores which the English had set aside on the ship, so once we had staggered farther inland and established meagre shelters among the scraggly trees and boulders, we did what we could to improve our situation. Despite our limited mobility, the denseness of the forest, and the crippling cold, we eventually became organized enough to hunt and fish. We lit small fires for warmth and cooking but always took care to keep them hidden. Papa reminded me that the Englishmen we had left behind—as if I could ever forget!—would reluctantly admit to their compatriots about how they had lost the *Pembroke* to us. No one had any doubt the army would soon scour the coastlines looking for us, and we could not afford to be caught again. Though it was difficult to believe, I imagined our punishment for escape would be worse than the dire situation we had left behind.

My heart was still in turmoil over Connor. I grieved for what might have been, and I longed for a friend—someone I could trust as I had always trusted Mali. In a weak moment I opened my heart to Claire. As I had feared, my sister was more aghast than sympathetic.

"An English soldier? For shame, Amélie!"

"But he's not English," I explained. "He's Scottish. And he's the one who helped Papa take over the ship."

She only shook her head. "I cannot imagine what might have made you think it would be all right to kiss a British man. Do not tell Maman unless you mean to break her heart."

I said nothing, though I did think Maman might have understood better than Claire. I should not have expected any sympathy, I realized. Claire did not know what I knew: that the *Hobson* had been lost; however, she did grieve the absence of Guillaume in her life. She did not understand the true extent of her loss, and I was too much of a coward to tell her. I thought she might find strength in the hope that they might meet again in another land, no matter how fruitless that hope might be.

When winter storms blasted through our little settlement, it became obvious we'd need to move. Illness was rampant now. As a whole, we were too weak to journey into the unknown, so a group of men was selected and given the responsibility to scout out a new and better location. Since Papa had already assumed a leadership role, he was one of the chosen. He was loath to go, for Maman was suffering from a clinging, sticky fever. When she coughed, her body shuddered with a dry, hacking motion, and her breathing was laboured. I tried to give her water or tea, but her throat was so sore she could barely swallow. Had we been at home, I would have been able to ease her pain by boiling the petals of water roses with honey, but I had no access to any of these things anymore.

Papa spent a few minutes alone with her before he left, but he could not look either Claire or me in the eye afterward. "Take care of her," he'd said hoarsely. "I will be back for you all as soon as I can."

Once he was gone, Maman worsened dramatically. She shook her head at our persistent request that she drink tea, saying she'd had enough. "Truly, I cannot drink another drop."

Claire looked as tired as our mother and almost as pale. "Maman, your skin is hot. You know you would do the same for us."

"I am feeling much better," she assured us.

Claire, Giselle, and I took turns, but we could do nothing to lower the fever besides wipe a cold, wet cloth over Maman's pallid face and neck. She dwindled; then she fell into a delirium. Her tongue laboured over words that made no sense, and by the next day we barely understood anything she said. We kept waiting for the fever to break, for the light to return to her eyes, but it never did.

Then Claire fell ill beside her. I forbade Giselle to come near either of them. So far neither she nor I had been affected, but I didn't want to gamble on her health. My body begged for sleep as I mopped the two dear brows, holding hands, whispering encouragement deep into the night.

In the morning, Maman no longer suffered. I had fallen asleep accidentally, toppling to my side with exhaustion, and when I awoke she lay still as stone. Guilt washed over me, as powerful as any ocean swell, though there was nothing I could have done to change what had happened. I stared at her colourless profile, wondering if she'd laboured for air at the end. Would I have heard her gasping? If I hadn't been selfishly rewarding my fruitless efforts by sleeping, my fingers would have wrapped around hers when her heart finally ceased to beat. Would she even have known I was there? Despising myself, I curled over her, whispering "Maman! Maman!" in case she might still hear, sobbing as quietly as I could until I could barely breathe.

"Amélie," Claire whispered.

I smeared the tears off my face with the heel of my hand, trying to be inconspicuous. I didn't want my ailing sister to suffer. She needed to believe in her own returning health, not see the nearness of death. Yet when I looked at her, she had the same glazed stare our mother had worn the day before.

"I'm sorry, Claire. I thought you were asleep. I should have been more quiet. I—"

"I want to go with Maman."

"Don't speak that way," I begged her. "You must be strong. You are young and have so much to live for."

"You are wrong, little sister. I am weak to the marrow of my bones. I could not summon the strength to fight this illness even if I should want to."

"What do you mean, even if you should want to? Of course you want to fight and live!"

"I do not. I want to go home, but we have no home. I miss Guillaume every second, and I will never see him again." She drew in a wheezing breath and coughed, her slight frame jerking with the impact. "Amélie, I do not have the spirit of adventure you have always had. I do not want to start again in a new land."

"But I need you, Claire. Don't leave me."

"Amélie. I want to apologize."

Her manner was calm, and that frightened me the most. It was as if these awful words she now uttered had been considered deeply.

"There is nothing to apologize for."

"Yet I am sorry. I treated you like a child. I'm sorry I said those things about your soldier." Another cough seized and shook her. She held out a trembling hand, and I took it in my own. "I envied you . . . your forbidden passion. I am sorry he is gone."

I couldn't find words, so I let my tears answer for me.

A sort of peace settled over Claire's features. "You will survive this, Amélie."

"No, Claire. Do not give up."

I felt a light pressure on my fingers as she tried to squeeze my hand, and she closed her eyes. "I promise I shall watch over you."

Then she fell asleep. I set her hand on her stomach and backed away, feeling lost. Hours later, she was gone as well, leaving Giselle and me alone. We clung together and rocked ourselves to sleep with sobs. When Papa returned, we would break his heart.

TWENTY-FOUR

February 1756

"A ship!"

The fog was thick, muffling the cry of alarm, but it woke me from my restless sleep. I roused myself, forcing my eyes open despite the endless exhaustion. I was hungry, and my head was splitting. Squinting hard, I spotted the red, blue, and white colours of the French flag seeping through the grey, draped from the stern of the approaching ship, and my heart gave a little leap. As the ship cleared the fog, nearing our own anchored ship, half a dozen navy blue coats appeared. They stood by the rail, waving at our men standing guard on the beach. Who could this be? More like us? Or were we to be rescued by the soldiers in blue?

God, let them have brought food, I prayed.

If only Papa were here. He would have approached the ship, spoken to the men, found out if they could help us. But he had not yet returned from the scouting mission; I had not yet told him that our family of eight was now reduced to three, not including the two brothers I prayed still survived in the forest.

"Bonjour!" called the captain of the ship.

"Bonjour!" replied one of our men, walking toward the water.

"We are come from Louisbourg," they said. "We are looking

for a pilot to help us navigate farther up the harbour. Can you help us?"

Young François Landry strode to the water's edge and volunteered, always happy to help. He somewhat sheepishly apologized, saying he didn't know a lot about the area, but he promised he would do what he could. Pleased, the newcomers sent a boat for him and took him on board.

As his feet touched their deck, his friendly smile turned to an expression of confusion. We watched in horror as the captain suddenly hoisted the English ensign over the French one, and the beautiful blue coats were tossed to the floor. I heard a command. Then—incredibly—a cannon was fired. The percussive noise shook the ground beneath my feet, nearly bowling me over. Never in my life had I heard such a sound! Rocks blasted into the air, and our men ran screaming back toward the woods to take cover.

"It's a trap!"

Panicked, I chased Giselle into the forest, and in that moment a small group of men burst from the trees, all of them bearing rifles, muskets, and pistols.

"Papa!" I cried. "You're back!"

He stopped beside me and pressed a rifle into my hands, and I was suddenly very glad he had insisted I learn how to use one. Had it only been one summer since he'd taken me to the open field and shown me how to load and fire? It felt like another lifetime. Giselle did not know how, so I ordered her to stay burrowed under a shrub.

"Follow me!" yelled Papa.

I joined the makeshift army and ran toward our ship. When we were close enough, he ordered us all to stop and kneel. We prepared our rifles and waited for him to roar, "Fire!"

I pulled the trigger along with the others, and noise and smoke exploded from the beach. Regardless of how many of us hit our mark, the effect was exactly what we needed it to be. The English had obviously not been expecting any kind of fight from us, for when the smoke cleared, we could tell orders were being shouted for the ship to turn around. They did not know what kind of defence we had—for all they knew we might even have the cannon from aboard the *Pembroke*, though of course we did not!—and they could not navigate their ship in these shallow waters.

Temporarily deafened by our blasts, I walked toward the water with the others, watching the English turn away. Then I froze, and my mouth dropped open. I stared in horror at a familiar face.

The wicked Corporal Fitch stood at the stern of the ship, and he had spotted me as well. I saw the shock in his own expression, watched his attitude change quickly from disbelief to awareness, then finally fury. I knew he was not a smart man, but he was not entirely stupid. In that moment I felt sure he put everything together. He recognized me, and he would have seen that Connor and I were friends.

"Your brave sergeant will hang for this!" he shouted, and the words cut through the wool in my ears.

He turned from the rail and marched purposefully toward the captain. I stared at his receding back, feeling more helpless than I'd ever felt. Connor would have no idea Fitch was coming to denounce him, and I had no doubt the British army would punish their traitor. Connor had committed treason in order to save my life, but there was absolutely nothing I could do to save his.

Papa stood beside me. "I am sorry, ma chérie. Your sergeant is a good man. A noble man. But he is also a soldier. By law, he should have let us all remain under British rule."

"He knew what they were doing to us was wrong. He helped us because he couldn't stand it anymore. You should understand, Papa. He was doing the right thing!"

"You and I know that, Amélie, and God knows that. A heart can be a very powerful guide, but it can also lead to trouble."

"He will *hang* for me!"

He wiggled one finger, scolding me gently. "You have very little faith in your courageous soldier, Amélie. I am surprised at you. MacDonnell is resourceful. If he is caught, he will not go easily. And they will have to find him first. Remember, this is a very big land." He kissed my forehead. "Be strong. He needs you to believe in him."

A fresh wave of grief swept over me, a reminder that I had a terrible truth to tell him. "Papa, I—"

"Papa?" Giselle had crept out of her hiding place and now pointed at the people standing on the beach, still watching the shrinking ship. "They are afraid. You need to lead them, and I . . . I have an idea," she said meekly, surprising us both.

"Do you, ma fleur?" Papa smiled.

Perhaps she had interrupted me on purpose, or perhaps not, but I was grateful for the delay. Papa had to be told about Maman and Claire, but a few minutes would change nothing, and it was heartening to see Giselle step forward for a change. She started shyly, telling us her thoughts; we nodded and encouraged her as she explained.

"What a wise young lady you are," Papa told her. "Just like your Maman."

Maman. The word landed like a stone in my belly. How was I going to tell him she was gone? I opened my mouth to speak, but he was already walking away, his mind on Giselle's plan.

He stood before the rest of our people, his arms folded over his chest, looking as he had the first day after we'd taken the *Pembroke*: strong and brave and dependable. He was a born leader, my papa. His eyes passed over the others, silently counting to be sure no one had been hurt, and I found myself doing the same. Miraculously, no one had fallen. Before he could speak, a wail rose from down the beach. Suzette Landry, her mother, and her sisters were kneeling in a miserable, swaying pile of skirts and bonnets. That's when I recalled that Suzette's husband, François, was the pilot who had disappeared along with the English.

"That ship is gone," Papa said, "and with it our noble friend, François Landry. We grieve with you, dear Suzette." He paused a moment as the crowd muttered their sympathies. "But that ship—" He turned and jabbed his finger in the direction the British ship had just taken. "It will report its findings. They found us because they saw the *Pembroke*. Others will come, eager to take both us and our ship." He gave Giselle a small, secret smile before he faced the others again and shared her idea. "I believe we must say farewell to our transport."

A few people frowned, and I imagined they had dreamed of sailing it away, far from this place. But Papa and Giselle were right. The British would always be looking for it.

"Eh bien. After we have removed what useful things may still be inside, we shall burn it."

My horrible news would have to wait. All the supplies had already been unloaded and brought to our shelters, but we rowed the tender back to the ship to be sure we'd left nothing of use. When all was done, some of the younger men stayed behind to accomplish the challenge of setting the *Pembroke* alight. The rest of us returned to the stony beach and bowed our heads, saying prayers of thanks for our deliverance to this place. When it did catch, Giselle squeezed my hand. Papa stood behind us, a hand on each of our shoulders, and we stared at the fire, mesmerized. Eventually its intensity weakened, the inferno dying down to a strong, crackling blaze, and more smoke clogged the air. We turned away.

Finally, we were alone. I could wait no longer. Oh, how my heart ached. How could I tell him we were all he had left?

My throat closed, and his name came out in a sob. "Papa."

His eyes searched mine; then they filled with tears. I wouldn't have to tell him after all.

"Where is Claire?" he managed.

"Gone," I whispered.

I had never seen my father cry before that moment. It was the most terrible thing I'd ever seen. He sat quite suddenly, unable to stand, and Giselle and I knelt on either side of him.

"Sylvie," he whispered hoarsely to my mother, wherever she was. "Que ferais-je sans toi?" His hands clenched then opened into claws, and he brought them to the sides of his head as if to hold it together. "Que ferai-je sans toi?" *What will I do without you?*

The shoulders I had seen bear so much weight now shook with sobs.

"I am sorry, Papa," I said, over and over. "I am sorry."

"Oh, Amélie." The pain in his eyes almost destroyed me. "It is I who am sorry. I should have been here with you." He reached to pull us against his chest. "I shall never leave you again."

I held on tightly, but I didn't want to hear him promise anything; it seemed to me that all promises did was break hearts.

A loud crack split the air, and I turned back toward the fire. A rope hanging over the side of the ship had burned through and snapped, sending a long, thin line of flames skyward. Smoke billowed into the sky like bubbling tar, dropping ashes onto the beach. I was close enough that curious tendrils of heat tickled my face, bringing comfort to such a cold day, but before long the fire shoved at me with a weight too hot to bear, and I turned away, my eyes burning.

Without another word, we trudged back toward our pitiful

accommodations, all of us miserable. Other than what was left of my family, the horrible, stinking ship which now roared with fire had been the last connection we had to home.

Giselle and I each took one of Papa's hands, and we led him past our little settlement to the mounds of rocks which sheltered the bodies of our loved ones. Theirs were not the only new graves. After the final stones had been placed, Giselle and I had bound two sticks together, marking both graves with a cross, then our friends had come to say prayers with us and send Maman's and Claire's souls to God.

Papa stood and stared, and I saw a beaten man.

"Papa," Giselle eventually said, "we must be strong for them. They would want us to be."

But Papa was not ready. He shook his head slowly, his eyes on the graves. "I am not strong, ma petite."

"You will be," she assured him gently. "We need you."

TWENTY-FIVE

When Papa returned to us an hour later, the whites of his eyes were red from crying, but he had washed his face and slicked his hair back, bracing himself. His strength was coming back one breath at a time.

By now, some of the others had started a massive bonfire near our homes. It didn't matter if anyone saw it, I imagined, since the burning *Pembroke* would already have alerted anyone to our presence. Tonight was a night to remember those who had passed, and perhaps to celebrate our small victory over the English ship. For whatever reason, it was comforting to gather like this with our friends. We could almost pretend we were still at home for a little while.

"We had success on our scouting journey," Papa told Giselle and me, settling on a log with us. "I brought someone back with me, and I asked him to come and see us tonight. He should be here soon."

"Oh?"

"They call him Boishébert. He is from a nearby village which already houses about two hundred Acadians. They are settled farther inland, where it is safer, and he has invited us to join them."

I nodded, willing myself to hope.

"I think you will find him interesting."

"In a good way?" I asked. Something about his expression made me wonder.

He smiled in welcome and got to his feet. "Ah, here he comes."

A man approached, hand outstretched. I stared not only at the formality of the stranger's gesture but also at his immaculate clothing. Beneath his tricorne he wore a white wig, and that accoutrement here, in this rough place, struck me as almost ridiculous. I supposed he aimed to impress upon us all that he was a man in control, a man of some circumstance, but the effort seemed unnecessary.

"Bonjour, Charles," said Boishébert.

They clenched their right hands together, and Boishébert covered them both with his left. I stood beside Papa, but the man gave me little more than a nod. A number of other men had come with the stranger, and they reminded me of my Mi'kmaq family. I looked over their faces, searching for a familiar one.

Papa leaned toward me and whispered in my ear, "They're Maliseet. Cousins of the Mi'kmaq, sort of."

I regarded the visitors with fresh eyes, curious to know if they spoke the same language as the Mi'kmaq. A couple of them glanced at me, met my gaze with the guileless expression I knew well, and something inside me calmed.

Papa was still standing, and I could see he meant to address the group. His expression was tight with grief, but he was moving forward as he must, as our father, and as our leader.

"May I have your attention, my friends?"

He held out a hand, gesturing to our group, then apologized to Boishébert. "Please forgive my friends and family if we stare. We have been here about a month, and you are the first souls we have seen."

"That is why I have come," the man declared to them all. "My name is Charles Deschamps de Boishébert," the man said, "and I represent our Acadian village on Beaubears Island on the Miramichi River." He cleared his throat and made a poor attempt to look humble. "We call it Camp de l'Espérance, but some call it Boishébert's Camp."

I was not the only one to lean closer, hearing this wondrous news. Our shared hopes were whispered through the crowd: *A village of Acadians? Surely there will be food! Maybe even homes protected from the freezing tempests! Perhaps we may be safe at last!*

Boishébert nodded, appearing to enjoy the sounds of interest. "And we would like to welcome you all to our humble home, since we understand you are looking to settle in more permanent quarters."

⟩

After a brief, unanimous vote, our whole group left with Boishébert and the Maliseet. His village's fleet of boats transported us up the Bay of Fundy and into the Petitcodiac River, going as far as we could. I was disappointed to note that the coastline changed little; the terrain remained bleak and rocky, but I kept my hopes up. When we could sail no farther, we trekked across the land for four days until we reached another waiting ship moored at Cocagne Bay. Along the way I listened to Boishébert speak with Papa. He said in confidence that he had been promised provisions but none had been sent. He reluctantly admitted that he feared the coming months, since there was already a shortage in the village.

"Already?" Papa frowned. "Why take us in if you are already suffering?"

Boishébert put his hand on Papa's shoulder. "Because we are

Acadians, oui? We help each other. And there is strength in numbers, my friend. We are stronger together."

To my delight, I discovered the Maliseet travelling with us did indeed speak Mi'kmawi'simk. Of course they were strangers, so our conversations could not be the same, but I was comforted by the soft, round syllables. I begged them to tell me what they knew of the Grand Pré region and its people, but they had little news. The system of communication among the Mi'kmaq was well developed, with messengers keeping everyone as up-to-date as possible, and the Maliseet were the same. Unfortunately, news had been sparse of late because of the danger of travelling anywhere near the British.

"If the people did not go to the boats," one man told me, "they were taken away. Some went to the jails in Halifax; many were killed."

My mind went immediately to André, but he shook his head. "I have not heard of any real trouble with the French resistance."

"What of the Mi'kmaq?"

"Our brothers and sisters of the forest are safe. They know how to avoid these English pond scum. Many have moved to safer camps, though some fight because they feel they must."

He knew no more than that, so I had to be satisfied. I could not ask about eight English sailors making their way to l'Acadie, but the question sat heavy on my tongue. Every day I wondered about Connor, envisioned him on board a ship, returning without me to my old home. I could only pray he was safe. But when I thought of him, I also thought of Fitch, remembered the terrible threat he had shouted. The dark voice in my heart hoped that Fitch's ship might sink, that he might not live to see his hateful threat fulfilled.

The ship eventually sailed down the Miramichi River, and the closer we got to Camp de l'Espérance, the more our excitement grew. Boishébert had said there were houses, and all we could think of was warmth and comfort and food.

When at last we put down anchor, the few people who came to greet us smiled and waved, but their cheery welcome seemed forced. The truth, when we saw it, was more than just a little disheartening. Conditions were worse at the camp than Boishébert had said, and the settlement was far from what we'd hoped it might be. Many of the Acadians already living there were ill, some gravely. The familiar build of their log houses was relatively sturdy, but fitting all of us in was difficult. I wasn't concerned; our people had always helped each other build homes, and with the wealth of pine all around, we'd have no trouble finding supplies. I hoped we would start soon, because despite the friendliness of our hosts, I felt certain we would all weary of each other in such close quarters. After all, our coming had swollen their little village to double what it had been.

Early spring was on its way, and the wet land underfoot was littered with millions of White Pine needles. At night we huddled near weak fires, trying to convince ourselves we were sated by the scant food. The Maliseet occasionally brought in meat, which was quickly devoured. Giselle and I went into the woods and set snares for muskrats, otters, and martens, but game was difficult to find. At one point we wandered along the river and discovered a beaver dam, which was a rare opportunity. The animals were usually hidden at this time of year, but when we found them, they were easy prey, since they could be caught when they came to their breathing holes in the ice. Still, it wasn't enough. If it hadn't been for the weak run of fish, we would surely have starved. I knew Papa felt as I did: this was hardly an improvement from the frozen banks of Saint John Harbour.

"Why did they bring us here?" I whispered to him one night.

"We must do what we can, Amélie." He shook his head. "This

is not what we had hoped for, but it is what we have. It is up to you to create your life out of what you have been given."

I planted my wise father's words in my heart, and they began to grow.

The Mi'kmaq believe Kisu'lk created the world so our spirits can live here as humans and heal through our experiences. They say our lives are shaped by the spirit world so we can accomplish what we are meant to do. Everyone we meet and everything we do is for a greater purpose. Mali's mother had told me that once we found the path we were intended to walk, everything we needed— though not necessarily what we might want—would come to us.

What was my purpose? It seemed suddenly so important for me to know the answer. It had been a while since I had done any true thinking; I had simply been reacting. As a child, I had been carried by my family and friends; then I had let the British push me. What if I dared to walk forward on my own?

Outside the ramshackle house we shared with eight other people, the full moon shone on fresh snow. Ice crystals sparkled a greeting to the stars, inviting me to join them, so I wrapped a blanket around my shoulders and stepped into the bright winter night. Quiet as the stars themselves, I waded into the forest, listening for the answer I needed.

Life had dropped me in this terrible place, and all my body wanted to do was lie still. And yet a small part of me dared to believe I could find the courage to fight back. The easiest thing to do would be to fail, to resign myself to dying here along with so many others. The challenge was to look ahead, to stand up to death. I had never been one to flinch from a dare, and the realization that I was allowing myself to give in made me angry. *You must be strong*, Papa had said. *You are special.*

I did not know which path I was meant to follow, but seeing my footprints in the moonlight reminded me I was already on one. I must not rely on others to find my direction for me, though their guidance might be of help.

I decided my first duty had to be caring for Giselle, for she had declined until she was a shadow of herself. She slept with her back pressed against me, and during the day she was constantly underfoot or following closely behind. She grieved and was afraid. I needed to divert her. I went in search of other girls her age and found more of the same: starving, confused, and anxious young people either orphaned or left without siblings. Without our farms or dikes to tend, we had no real chores. Boredom stretched the hours, creating more time in which to wallow in despair.

In the morning Giselle and I walked to the little church to speak with l'Abbé Le Guerne. As always, he was warm and welcoming as he ushered us inside. When I asked if there was anyone in the village who might be able to teach, if only to draw people's minds from our circumstances, he smiled broadly and said he knew just the man for the job. Within a few days, the church began opening its doors for a few hours each day, and Monsieur Pitre taught lessons to anyone who might be interested, whether child or adult. Even Giselle brightened briefly whenever I asked what she'd learned that day.

The lessons could do nothing to help with our hunger, though. The village had outgrown itself. The river could no longer provide what we needed, and it showed in the dragging feet and skeletal faces all around me. One time I saw a man chewing on his moccasin, and when I asked what he was doing, he explained that it had originally come from a deer, and he was sure he would find more meat inside the skin if he kept chewing.

I had not sunk to that level; however, I had adjusted. The small pieces of stale bread I occasionally received hurt my bleeding gums, but they were something. One day I bit into a crust but dropped it with disgust when I spotted two pale maggots within. I squatted by the morsel, watching the maggots take their fill, and wished it could be that easy for me. Back at our farm, I'd laughed at the antics of our chickens when they begged for a piece of earthworm. The hens were healthy, and they were always happy to devour little creatures just like these maggots. Eventually, we had eaten our chickens—the same ones who had eaten the worms. Intrigued, I picked up the bread and took a wriggling maggot between my fingers, imagining how the chickens would react if they saw it. They'd think I'd found a treasure.

It is meat, I told myself, *nothing more*. I placed it back onto the bread where it calmed its squirming, then I took a bite. The maggot was gone when I looked again, and I had not tasted a thing. I ate the rest of the bread, and after that I barely thought about the little white worms.

A long time ago, in another lifetime, Connor had warned me that one day I would have to change my way of living. I'd been sure he exaggerated, and I had shrugged off his warning. But his earnest expression hadn't changed. *You must adapt*, he'd said.

I finally understood.

TWENTY-SIX

June 1756

Week after week more Acadians arrived either singly or in groups, escaping from wherever they had been taken. Partway through June, five families arrived from South Carolina. The governor of that colony had made it clear he wanted nothing to do with forcing the expelled Acadians to stay; he'd been relieved to see them go. The group had arrived by boat, and we were well acquainted with the travails of that kind of journey. They had brought mothers and fathers and children to our crowded village, but they had not brought any food.

One night a group of us went outside to sit around a fire and enjoy the comfort of fellowship, since it was the first night in a while that rain wasn't falling. It was a glorious, starry night, and the magical twinkling of fireflies in the woods made the stories seem all the more fantastic. I was intrigued by two of the refugees from South Carolina: a pair of rough-looking men travelling with seven others, all of whom were full of stories. The older one I estimated to be about fifteen years older than Papa. His name was Alexandre Broussard. The other man, Victor, was his nephew. Alexandre was one of six brothers, all of whom had been at Fort Beauséjour at Chignecto. They had fought alongside the French militia when the fort was first attacked by British and New England soldiers. I knew nothing about this battle, so I asked Papa.

"Ah, ma petite, that is a sad story because it was the beginning of all this." He looked very tired. "Almost a year ago—it was June, I believe—the British decided they wanted Chignecto. Our friend Winslow was one of the leaders, of course. When the English attacked the fort, the French discovered they were too few," he said grimly. "They called for the Acadians to help."

"But the Acadians were neutral, weren't they? They couldn't fight."

"That was the agreement we signed, but many of the Acadians went anyway, to defend our friends. When the British eventually took the fort, they discovered the Acadians hidden with the French. Governor Lawrence was furious, for by doing that they had broken the agreement. He did not trust any of us after that. He assumed we would all turn against the English."

My eyes went to Alexandre and Victor, calmly telling their stories around the fire. "So," I said, speaking quietly enough that only Papa could hear, "the Acadians who went to fight are the reason the English sent us away and burned our homes?"

"I do not think it is fair to blame them. They were most likely the final straw on the donkey's back, but the English never would have let us stay. We speak French, oui? That makes us French in their eyes; they know nothing of being Acadian. To them we are all the same."

Alexandre was laughing at someone's comment. "We were not good fighters at all," he exclaimed. "We were always better with hoes than with muskets!"

"I like to think we have improved since then, Uncle," Victor objected. He was young and strong, his handsome features not at all disturbed by the scar which cut across his right cheek, under his eye.

The smile on Alexandre's angular face faded. "Think what you like. We are farmers, you and I."

Should I hate Alexandre for being one of many who had ignited the powder keg? Why had he fought at Chignecto? He was Acadian. He should not have been there. But thinking of this brave farmer turned fighter made me think of André. Like Alexandre, my quiet, noble brother had chosen the path of challenging the most powerful army in the world. I could not see André as being anything other than righteous, so I decided I could not judge the Broussards.

Alexandre and Victor were wonderful storytellers, helping us temporarily forget our miseries. They were as expressive with their hands as they were with their faces and words. When Victor looked across the fire and caught my eye, I was caught off guard by the intimacy of his smile. I was surprised at how good his admiration made me feel.

"I was never so happy as the moment I saw my brother Joseph escaping," Alexandre told us, shaking his head. "I was done for, since I was already shackled and had been left with a group of other prisoners. But Joseph, he was out of their reach, and he saluted me before he disappeared."

"Your brother is Joseph Broussard, the Beausoleil?" exclaimed Pierre Gourdeau, one of the men with whom we had travelled on the *Pembroke*.

Alexandre's smile was broad. "Yes. I hear my brother is a legend."

"He is indeed!" Pierre said, impressed. "He keeps the English chasing their tails even now."

"He was always quick. And lucky. What have you heard about him?"

Pierre was pleased he had the answers Alexandre sought. "After that battle, he went home to his wife and children at Petitcodiac."

"Ah. That is good to hear."

"They did not stay there, for it was not safe. Instead they hid from the British patrols by living in the forests north of their home."

Alexandre's brow lifted. "Is that so? Yes, I can imagine where they went. Smart. Very smart."

Pierre went on to describe tales of Joseph's antics, much to his brother's satisfaction. As he spoke I learned about this man they called Beausoleil. They said he lived with others like himself and battled alongside Mi'kmaq fighters, attacking the British from hidden bases. There were tales of ambush and sabotage, of raids and of quick, decisive skirmishes. Beausoleil and his men did not always emerge the victors, but they kept the British busy, as Pierre had said.

"That is not all!" another man added. "Beausoleil has become a privateer as well!"

"What? My brother is a pirate?" Alexandre said, throwing back his head and laughing at the thought. "Now I know you are telling tall tales. A privateer?"

Victor laughed with his uncle. "My uncle Joseph is a terrible sailor!"

"Maybe he has learned since you knew him," replied the first man. "Now he sails the Bay of Fundy, terrorizing British ships and creating havoc with their shipments."

Alexandre shook his head with wonder. "Such wonderful news! Thank you all. I still cannot imagine him on a ship—not by choice, anyway. But maybe he does not hate them as much as I do now, since he did not have to suffer as we did."

Victor rubbed his wrists and grimaced. "I can still feel those chains we wore on the *Syren*. My ankles bear the scars."

His uncle nodded, sober once more. "That was a terrible time."

"I do not miss those guards and their hateful glares. They never gave us a moment's peace. What did they think we would do? Swim to shore with chains dragging us down?"

Alexandre agreed. "It is hard to believe they thought we were dangerous at that point. But still, they did." He regarded us over the fire, his eyes sparking orange with the flames. "By November we had reached Charleston, and they held us in close confinement outside of the city, on Sullivan's Island. Even there we were shackled."

Victor gave his uncle a smile. "Then they made the mistake of putting us in the workhouse in Charleston."

Alexandre's smile was much like Victor's, which made me think of Claire. She and I had been told we looked almost like twins since our smiles were so similar. The memory threatened to loosen the tight hold I had on my grief. Fortunately, Alexandre's story distracted me.

"Yes, that was a mistake," he said. "We escaped, but then we ran into something almost as terrible."

"Remember the swamps, Uncle?"

"How could I forget?" He grimaced at the memory. "The water wriggled with snakes. At least they were more interested in smaller creatures than us."

"Some were not so friendly," Victor reminded him. He met my eyes again, and his expression reminded me of when my brothers had teased me, looking for a reaction. "They hid among curtains of weeds and curled beneath bushes, waiting to dart out and kill a man."

"I heard you can eat snakes," someone said.

Alexandre nodded. "We did eat some, though it was difficult to catch them. Their meat wasn't bad. Almost like chicken."

Perhaps we could add snakes to our hunting list, I thought.

"How did you get all the way up here?" someone asked.

Alexandre chuckled. "South Carolina did not want us. They put us on an old ship and waved farewell. She was falling apart, so we beached her in Virginia. We had to pool all our money so we could buy another ship, but this only lasted to Maryland."

"I thought we would never get here," Victor said, smiling. "We worked on that ship for two months, then we finally sailed back here."

We had been trapped in our own worries for so long, it was a welcome distraction to hear stories of others, as well as tales of the battles raging on our behalf. Papa seemed interested as well. It had been a long time since I'd seen any twinkle of curiosity in his eye—not since we'd taken over the *Pembroke*, actually—and I saw it that night.

"What are your plans now?" he asked.

Victor shrugged. "You have too many people in this village already. You do not need two more hungry men eating your food. We plan to continue to Shediac, to try and find our families."

"I hope to find my brother as well. If I can help him in his efforts, I will," Alexandre added.

"When will you leave?"

I leaned forward, keenly aware of Papa's line of thinking, for he and I had discussed our own plans for departure not more than two nights previously. We could stay here no longer; another winter would kill us all. With no food to sustain us, and with influenza running rampant through the crowded houses, we were better off in the forest on our own. Most of the other refugees lacked the energy to leave their new home despite its condition. They had had enough of running. I understood their fear as well as their desire to establish roots, but I could not stay here.

When Papa had spoken recently with Boishébert, he had encouraged us to leave. In kind but definite words he said he could not guarantee our safety if we stayed. There was simply nothing he could do. He suggested we travel to Quebec, saying many other Acadians had already headed that way, having taken the Saint-Jean portage route to Rivière-du-Loup on the lower Saint Lawrence.

When the conversation moved away from the Broussards, Alexandre scrutinized Papa through the flickering firelight. "We will leave soon. Are you interested in travelling with us?"

My heart leapt at the opportunity. I had no doubt any trek would be dangerous, but with their guidance it need not be impossible.

Papa looked at me, seeking my approval, then back at them. "I think we are very interested."

And so we made plans to travel once again. As excited as I was to leave the place, I could not go quite yet. The evening before we departed, I told Papa I would be back in an hour, then I left him and Giselle in the sad little village. When I was alone I sat beneath the sky as I had before, seeking reassurance from the stars. The moon was no longer full, the sky no longer clear. I stared at the wispy clouds overhead and thought of my dear sister. When I left here, I would be leaving her and Maman forever.

"Can you see me, Claire?" I whispered.

The night's silence was broken only by the soft hoot of an owl. The creature sounded far away.

I wiped the back of my hand across my nose, sniffing. "I miss you." I almost lost control of my emotions, but it was important that I finish, so I took a deep, bracing breath. "I hope you have found Guillaume, for I am sure he is looking for you. And Maman, and Mathieu . . ." I had to pause a moment before continuing. "We are going to Quebec, Claire. I can only pray it is better than here."

The night was darker now, the clouds gathering thickly around the moon. I could see shadows in the snow; were they hidden threats or promises?

"I am afraid," I admitted. My voice sounded small even to me. "Our paths were so clear before, but now I feel as though I'm fumbling in the dark. Please, Claire. Help me find the right way."

So many lifetimes had passed in such a little span. The first was when we had been herded onto the ship. In the shadows of my memory lurked Grand Pré: the meadows, the trees, the ocean, the laughter. The next lifetime was taken from us a few months ago, when Claire and Maman had died. And what about the lifetime I could have had with Connor? That was plainly gone. How could it be possible to grieve so bitterly over something I had never experienced?

"I hope you cannot hear me, Connor," I said softly, "because I do not wish to speak to your spirit. I want to believe you are still alive. But if . . . if the Lord has chosen to take you to heaven, I pray you will seek out Claire and Maman and my dear little brother. And Guillaume. Find comfort with them, for I am sure they would have loved you, given the chance. And—"

Panic fluttered like tiny wings in my chest, but I fought it back. My voice dropped to a whisper. "If you are there, if you are among the angels, then I beg you. Please. Keep me safe."

PART TWO

Beginning Again

PART TWO

Me'tekw

TWENTY-SEVEN

The tip of Me'tekw's paddle flung a string of droplets across the top of the water, then dove beneath to retrieve more. A hint of sun peered through the fog, and the little jewels glimmered in greeting before melting back into the river. Me'tekw's existence twisted like the weeds over which he floated, instinctively seeking the sun but rooted in the dark. He no longer saw the gems he drew to the surface, paid no attention to the simple conversations of birds as they fluttered through branches and swooped to admire their reflections in the water. He no longer cared.

Marguerite was gone, and their child as well. Me'tekw's still, unbreathing son had lain in his hands, hot with her blood but cold within. He had drawn back the baby's translucent eyelids, gazed at the death inside the shell, then handed the tiny body to the women.

He was not so quick to give Marguerite away. In death she was as beautiful as she had been in sleep, though her skin was paler than during those sweet, sweet nights, and when he brushed his fingertips across her brow, she did not wake and reward him with that smile she gave only to him. Blood had dried and caked in a swipe across one cheek, and he wondered how it had gotten there.

Her fingers? His? The blood was hers, though, and he leaned in to kiss her there. He kissed her lips too and silently whispered something he hoped her spirit still heard.

Inside their wigwam her quillwork lay unfinished on the floor. A terrible waste. Marguerite had small hands, but such elegant, quick fingers, such a beautiful talent. Now this shirt she had been making for him would be finished by another pair of hands, worn by another man. Me'tekw would never wear it. To feel her spirit in the fibres and know her to be flying free without him would be too much.

He sank onto their bed and lowered his face to the place where her head had rested a few hours before. They had made love, hastening the birth, and he had burrowed his nose into her thick hair, breathing in her musk as she moaned. He regretted now that she had been lying on her side, facing the wall of their home, since he had missed the ethereal expression of rapture when it had swept through her for the final time. How were they to know she would never face him again that way? At least she had rolled to her back after, her belly huge, and smiled into his eyes.

Now when he inhaled her scent again, pain ripped through him like a physical thing, and he shoved his face into the furs, roaring soundlessly with loss.

When his sobs slowed, he waded into the forest and dropped to his knees, giving in to his roiling belly. Afterward he stood up, tasting bile, waiting for his head to slow its rhythmic pounding. Marguerite would have pressed her fingers over his temples, moved them around his head and neck, eased the pain. No one else could do that, and he didn't want anyone to try. He would suffer. After everything his wife had experienced, this was nothing.

The wigwam was already strange to him when he returned. He rolled shirts together with his weapons and packed them in a fur sack, then cast his eyes over the space one more time. She sat there, she teased him there, she cried there, she worked there. She loved him in all those places. Someone else could have this home now, for Me'tekw had no need for any of it. He would not fill it with sons and daughters. He would not fill it with any more memories.

He stepped into the dark forest, and he never looked back.

Rain tapped on his shelter, reluctantly slowing after the early morning downpour. The air swelled with the ripe aroma of sodden leaves, and he inhaled deeply, letting the peace of the moment fill all the empty spaces in his lungs and mind. Withdrawing his legs from his blanket, he slid them onto the wet carpet of leaves and watched the drops splatter on his skin before it snaked down the sides of his legs. The sensation tickled, but he didn't smile. He had been here for a full moon now, and nothing had made him smile. Nothing had taken her face from his mind, her touch from his memory.

Marguerite had been like an otter with her playful spirit, like a lynx in the bold, direct way she could meet a challenge. Me'tekw had never thought himself good enough for her, but she had wanted him. She heard him when no one else could. She gave him a voice for the first time in his life. The miracle of her love was proof the Creator had finally seen him, for Kisu'lk had given Me'tekw a gift greater than any other.

She had meant more to him than anything on earth. He'd made love to her whenever she looked at him that way. When she realized she was going to have their baby, she couldn't have been happier, and he loved that he'd given her that joy.

But becoming a family meant he would have to share her, and Me'tekw had never wanted to do that. So in the beginning, he had secretly hoped the baby growing in her womb would die. That selfish whisper had grown louder with time, becoming part of his prayers. *There are always consequences*, she had told him, though she had no idea what he'd prayed. He'd never suspected, never dreamed the Creator would heed his prayer and punish him in this terrible way. Me'tekw would have shared her with a thousand infants if only she could be alive still, sitting next to him, threading her fingers through his.

What lesson was he supposed to learn through this? How was he to grow when his heart wanted to cease pumping altogether?

Their deaths were his fault. He knew that truth to the core of his being. Kisu'lk was punishing him and rightly so.

And more than Marguerite's death plagued him. Now that he was alone, he had time to remember that. He had been so filled with his own happiness, he had neglected the vow he had made to Charles Belliveau so many years before, promising to watch over him and his family. While Me'tekw had revelled in his own life, Charles and his family had been taken by the redcoats and sent far away. Their home had been burned to the ground.

Me'tekw slid forward until he sat under the slow trickle of raindrops falling from leaves overhead. The water cooled his eyes when he lifted his face toward the forest ceiling, and he kept them open as long as he could, praying, begging for guidance, all the time knowing he was unworthy. He stayed that way, his lips soundlessly forming penitent words as rain mixed with his tears. Water slid down his cheeks, rolled onto his shoulders and chest, meandered down his body, and Me'tekw forced himself to feel nothing at all.

He still didn't move when the quiet pattering of the rain was interrupted by a soft huffing noise. The damp, heavy odour of an animal reached him, and Me'tekw slowly lowered his chin. As he'd expected, the traveler was a black bear, its small eyes focused on the flourishing blueberry bushes all around him. From his infancy, Me'tekw had been taught the strengths and powers belonging to Kisu'lk's animal world, and at the sight of the great beast standing only a few feet upwind, his heart soared with gratitude. The animal's appearance was clearly a message from the Creator, and of all the spirit guides, Me'tekw couldn't have hoped for better. Bear brought healing and renewal, two things Me'tekw needed the most.

"*Kwe, muwin*," he greeted the bear, knowing that even though the words sounded only in his mind, the animal would hear.

The bear snuffled and threw up its massive head, alerted to a possible threat. When its curious stare landed on him, Me'tekw apologized for interrupting its foraging. He told the animal it was an honour to be visited by such a powerful spirit, and he wished it good hunting. He didn't move when the bear took a step toward him, then another. After a few more grunting breaths, it seemed to tire of the man. It rose to its hind legs, reaching for loftier berries, and Me'tekw discovered the bear was a female. She was also pregnant, and tears of joy came to his eyes, making everything clear.

Kisu'lk had a purpose for every living being, though that purpose was rarely made clear. Me'tekw's spirit was on a journey, but he had gotten lost in the maze of living. All this misfortune was Me'tekw's doing, he knew. He was responsible, and he accepted the entire weight on his shoulders. But now the bear had shown him what to do, how to make it all right for Marguerite's memory.

To create a future, he must fulfill a vow he had made over twenty years ago.

Amélie

TWENTY-EIGHT

We did not leave Camp de l'Espérance until near the end of August, and I was restless every day leading up to our departure. With every new journey we had less to carry. Giselle, Papa, and I gratefully accepted moccasins from the neighbouring Maliseet, but that was all. This time we left with little more than the clothes on our backs.

The late-summer air changed swiftly from hot to cold then back again, forcing us to either carry our heavy wool cloaks or wrap them tightly around our bodies. Papa seemed never to mind the extra weight when Giselle asked him to carry hers, and though I longed for her to pull her own weight, I understood. Once she had been a vivacious, spoiled little girl. Now she was a sad young woman, reduced in every way by the horror of the past year. She ate little and spoke less. If Papa or I managed lift her spirits even temporarily, it was a reason to celebrate.

Whenever possible we stuck to the shoreline, since the breeze there cleared away most of the stinging insects. Alexandre and Victor were skilled guides, but if it hadn't been for the Maliseet, I doubted we would have found our way. Still, I felt safe with the two Acadians, and I learned valuable lessons. Victor collected a number of bones from the riverbank, then he put his hands over mine and showed me how to make strong knives out of them by sharpening the edges against rocks. He taught me how to use a knife to cut under the bark of a birch to scrape out a bit of sap, which we could eat. When we found rapids, the men hunted along the still edges until they spotted black sturgeon gliding slug-gishly through the water. They caught the fish with forked spears, and any we didn't eat right there were strung up by the fire to dry so we could take the meat with us.

"Shall I show you how to make tea?" Victor asked one night.

"How can you make tea? We have no pot."

"Certainly we do."

His idea of a pot was a large boulder by the riverbed. Time had worn a dip in its surface, and rainwater filled the hole. Using a couple of blades as a shovel, he plucked a stone out of the fire and dropped it into the water. Almost immediately, it came to a boil.

"That is amazing," I said, staring at it. "I never thought of doing that."

He puffed his chest out and grinned down at me. "Impressed?

I had to laugh. "Yes. I am impressed."

A pine tree stood beside us, and he plucked a small handful of needles, which he cut into small pieces and dropped into the water.

"We'll leave this for a few minutes," he said, pulling two cups from his pack, "then you and I can enjoy a cup of tea."

While we weren't armed well enough to take in any large game, we followed the tracks of larger animals—such as moose— to the side of a calm lake. We tied hangman's nooses from spruce roots and hung them across the paths of smaller animals, effec-tively snaring a few rabbits and squirrels. Fortunately, I never saw the snakes they had spoken about back at l'Espérance.

At night we built small fires, not wanting to be detected by any passing soldiers—though we neither saw nor heard any—and on clear, happier nights we sang quiet Acadian songs and told stories. We slept in lean-tos built of saplings, covered by overlapped birch bark to keep out the rain. Our beds were soft, fragrant cushions of balsam, the branches set out in such a way that we faced the fire for warmth. But on the nights when the wolves sang, I lay quietly under my cloak, unable to sleep.

"I will keep the fire high," Victor assured me. He sat a few feet away, feeding the fire until the entire camp flickered with an orange glow. "You do not need to worry about them."

"But you will need to sleep. What then?"

He tugged the top of my coat higher over my shoulders. "I will protect you, Amélie. Go to sleep now."

Victor was attentive to me, and his advances became more obvious to everyone by the day. I was sorry I could not return his feelings. He was handsome and brave, and his stories were witty, but my heart still ached for Connor. Papa watched, gauging my reactions. When it became apparent I held no particular affection for Victor other than friendship, Papa began to step subtly between us.

We travelled on foot and in canoes we borrowed from friendly Maliseet. With every exhausting mile I prayed our destination would be worth it. Practically every step was difficult, and we began to wonder how many more we could take. Our moccasins served us well, but between the wetness and the cold, we suffered greatly from blisters. Giselle became miserable with them, and though I had hoped we could continue on despite the pain, we were forced to rest for a few days here and there so our wounds could heal.

Many days and many demanding portages later, we arrived in Quebec City. We were not the first Acadians to stumble in, half starved and hopeful; I was told over a thousand of our people already lived in the city. Sadly, they looked to be faring no better than we had back in Boishébert's village. With no other options available, Papa, Giselle, and I were put in a cramped house we shared with another, much larger family, and we huddled close together to ward off cold nights. Everyone was starving, everyone was sick. At night I was constantly jarred awake by someone's hacking cough or worse. One woman suffered terribly from pain in her ears, but I was unable to help. At home I would have applied the juice of salty onions to the source to give her some reprieve, but since we had none, her daughter was reduced to the old method of blowing smoke into her ear. It did little good from what I could see.

"Papa," I said after the first night, "we were living better in the forest. Can we not return to the woods?"

He shook his head. "Let us give this a chance."

Alexandre and Victor left for Shediac as soon as they could, saying they needed to find their families and join the ongoing fight against the British. I was sorry to see them go; I had enjoyed their company. A part of me longed to follow them.

Quebec City had been blasted by the war, which had gained strength while we'd been gone. The British forces were close, and their ships blocked any French support attempting to come from the sea. As a result, the city was suffering and greatly underfed. We quietly ate small offerings of cod, but I could not force myself to eat the awful grey meat they set in front of us. I didn't even know what animal it had come from, but the look and the smell were terrible. On those nights I heard more retching than coughing, and I was relieved that I'd chosen to go hungry.

Not everyone settled into despair without a fight. When meals were distributed, disagreements often broke out: people accused others of taking too much or stealing. One night I was cornered by two men who did exactly that. I protested, saying I had eaten my share and no more, but one seemed determined to search my person for bits of stale bread. I shrieked and pushed his hands away, and Papa was there in a moment, shoving them back. That was the night he agreed with me, saying we needed to find a place to live outside the city.

The next morning he set out, promising to return the same day. When he did, he brought a familiar face with him. I stood in welcome as he and Victor walked into the house.

"I thought you were gone!" I exclaimed, fighting the urge to throw my arms around Victor's neck. I hadn't realized how much I'd missed him.

"Soon," Victor said, smiling warmly. "Very soon."

"Victor has found us another place to live," Papa said. "For now, anyway."

"Yes, I think I can get you out of here, if you don't mind living in the woods. It's a small cabin, about a day's hike from here."

"I don't mind at all!" I cried, but Papa put his finger to his lips, warning me to be quiet. Everyone in this awful place would want to live somewhere else, so for Victor to offer us this prize was a great thing. "When? When can we leave?" I whispered.

"Go and get your sister," said Papa.

"It's an abandoned trapper's cabin," Victor explained as we walked through the forest the next day. "It isn't much, but it is four walls with fresh water nearby. I am sure you will be able to do something with it."

As long as we were away from the ill, starving crowds, I was happy. When we finally arrived, we stepped out of the trees, our bodies shaking with hunger, and stopped short at the sight of a dilapidated building.

"How did you come by this?" Papa asked, staring at it.

"The Maliseet told me about it. The trapper died last winter."

Giselle looked dubiously at the door, hanging off one remaining hinge. "Is he still in there?"

Victor laughed. "No. They took him away when they found him."

It was difficult to envision living in this place. The roof drooped, weighted down by moss, and the timbers were half rotted. The forest had crept to the door and almost taken possession, though a section close by the cabin remained relatively clear of growth. Perhaps the trapper had attempted a garden. Beyond the yard I could hear the bubbling of a stream, and my mouth watered at the thought of a cool drink.

"The fellow left all his traps inside," Victor said, "so you should be all right for eating."

I was surprised by my disappointment. "You're leaving after all?"

"With regret, Amélie." He took a breath. "I know I speak boldly, but time is short. I must say what is on my mind." He swallowed, his Adam's apple rising and falling behind his beard. "You cannot be unaware of my affection at this stage in our journey."

I tried to avoid his gaze.

He nodded. "You do not feel as I do."

He was a patient man, good, strong, loyal, and brave. And he cared for me. Why could I not consider him as more than a friend? But my hand went to Connor's ring, and my fingers tightened around the cool metal.

"I'm sorry, Victor."

"I understand. I do. If you felt otherwise, if you could see yourself with me, I would be happier, but we cannot force affection on one another. Still, I want you to be safe, you and your family. This house will be of some help, I hope."

Papa clasped both Victor's hands in his. "Thank you, my friend. I am in your debt."

"We must all do what we can for each other."

He released Papa's hand and stepped away. "Farewell, Charles. Farewell, ladies." His eyes paused a moment longer on me, then he turned and strode into the woods.

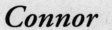

Connor

TWENTY-NINE

As a British sergeant, Connor had no choice but to return to the fort at Grand Pré; however, since war had extended to the sea, he would have to make the journey on foot. Before he left, he decided to dispose of his bright red coat. He could masquerade as a Frenchman, if need be, along the way. The decision was a good one, for French travelers offered informative conversation. When he told them he was going to l'Acadie, they advised him against it. The British had taken control of the area and were holding fast, they said.

"Travel with us," one militiaman suggested. "We are stronger if there are more of us, and you look like you can fight."

"I thank you, but I cannot. My home is in Chignecto, and I must see what is left of her."

He never mentioned Grand Pré, for stories travelled as rapidly as birds here. His best ploy was to travel in secrecy whenever possible, stay on his own. The journey would go more quickly that way as well. On occasion he was forced to share food and transport with other travelers, and at times he enjoyed the company.

Questions always came. "You were on the boats?"

"Yes." It was easy to fill his voice with loathing, since even as a sailor he had seen what hell those boats were.

"What do you remember?"

"I do not wish to speak of it," was his response, and no one asked any more after that.

One night a Mi'kmaq hunter appeared silently from the forest and stood by Connor's fire, gesturing toward it. He was perhaps twenty years Connor's senior, his face scarred heavily by small-pox. Connor invited the man to share its warmth, and the two ate well, exchanging the stranger's dried venison and Connor's dried fish. Strangely, the conversation was one-sided. Evidently the hunter could not speak. At first Connor wondered if his din-ing companion was deaf as well, but he appeared to be paying close attention to both Connor's words and the surrounding for-est, though his only responses were facial expressions. Eventually Connor stopped speaking as well.

The following morning the hunter gestured for Connor to follow, pointing to a fish Connor had set out to dry the day before and indicating an even larger one farther down the shore. As they trekked along the river's edge, the way became rockier, the water faster as it built toward rapids. The farther they went, the more erratic the shoreline became, interrupted by rocks and increasing numbers of fallen trees, and the noise of the river became over-whelming. The men were obliged to climb over the debris, using it as bridges when possible. Eventually Connor would not have been able to hear the other man even if he'd been able to speak—but he did hear the snap of rotten timber as it gave way under the hunter's moccasins.

For a moment the man was lost to him, sucked under the frothing white water. Connor scanned the surface, but it was a few seconds before the sleek black head appeared again, bobbing briefly above the water several feet ahead. His face rolled to the open air, his mouth open, every muscle slack.

Connor dropped the sack he'd been carrying and ran downstream, needing to get ahead of the racing current. There was no clear pathway, just scattered rocks and brush, but he had no time to worry about his footing. Once in a while the hunter's face appeared, his limp body shoved closer to the river's edge, toward Connor. Downriver Connor spotted an outcrop of boulders that formed a slick yet promising pathway into the water. He tore off his heavy cloak, left it on the shore, and splashed into the freezing river. His eyes stayed on the body moving rapidly in his direction, bumping off rocks as it came; he hoped it would continue on its present path, but at the last moment the Mi'kmaq hunter jolted away, forcing Connor to go in deeper after him.

Bracing his hand on the last boulder as long as possible, he waded to the centre of the rapids, fighting the current's constant jerking and tugging on his legs. At last he reached out, trapping the man's arm as he was about to drift past, but he was almost dragged down by the dead weight.

"Don't you dare," he roared, not knowing if the order was directed at the current, the silent man, or himself.

He leaned as far over as he could and snaked his arms under the man's frigid underarms, then he began the treacherous backward walk to the shore. The unconscious hunter had been beaten by the rocks, and one arm bled freely. He showed no sign of life as Connor dragged his body onto dry ground and squatted beside him. He cleared the tangled strands of hair from the man's face, then rolled him to one side and pounded between his shoulder blades, the thud of Connor's joined fists like a drumbeat on the cold, wet skin. Suddenly the body jerked and water gushed from his mouth, followed by such a hacking and gasping that Connor feared he might cough himself to death. After the convulsions eased, the soaked hunter lay still, but soon he began to vibrate with shock and cold.

Connor reached for the cloak he had dropped on the ground and laid it over the shaking man. "You're all right," he said quietly.

The dark eyes swam into focus then closed. Leaving him to rest, Connor gathered what he needed and lit a roaring fire to warm them both. The hunter awoke an hour or so later, weak and battered but able to struggle into a sitting position. He seemed whole: no broken bones, and the bleeding had stopped. Still, he was in no condition to continue on that day.

Bruises darkened the man's skin overnight, but the Mi'kmaq hunter was ready to go in the morning. He was moving a little stiffly as they continued their journey.

Days later they met two Acadian men travelling all the way from South Carolina to Nova Scotia. One, named Victor, was about Connor's age. He was travelling with his uncle Alexandre. Connor introduced himself as Pierre Guilbeau—remembering a surname from the rosters that had once passed across his desk— and said what he could about his Mi'kmaq companion. He could only hope these two were not well acquainted with any Guilbeaus. Both the Acadians had seen battle and months of harrowing travel, and their stories were engaging. Connor was content to spend a few nights around the campfire with them, and his Mi'kmaq companion seemed satisfied as well, for he had not gone his separate way yet. The Acadians had not only seen conflict, fighting alongside the French militia during the battle over Fort Beauséjour at Chignecto, but had been victims of the expulsion as well. When Connor asked how they had escaped, they explained that their reluctant hosts in South Carolina had wanted nothing to do with Acadians.

"We left most of the others on the way to Saint John when they wearied of the journey. Now we travel alone, my nephew and

I. We have not met many others of late," Alexandre said. Of the two, he did most of the talking. "At first I thought we would have trouble with the British, but they must be busy somewhere else. I have not seen even one in the past two weeks."

Connor's mouth went dry. Was the man testing him?

"They would be easy to find, Uncle. Even just one on foot is as loud as four horses crashing through the brush."

Both men laughed, and Connor joined in. To his relief, neither eyed him with suspicion.

"The Mi'kmaq keep us safe," Victor said. "They hate the English as much as we do."

The silent hunter gave a shadow of a smile.

Connor did not contribute much to the conversation lest he inadvertently say something that could reveal him for what he was, but he encouraged the men to say more.

"I am glad to meet men such as you," he said at one point. "Like me, you are not defeated despite all you have suffered."

"Many men and women feel as we do," Alexandre said, "but they are not always able to do anything about it." He stared into the fire, then shoved a stick into its heart. Sparks shot out like gunfire, but Connor leaned closer to the heat. The night was crisp. "This has been a cruel, cruel winter. We have met a great number of people who will not survive it."

"People are dying because they can find no food," Victor muttered, "and what they are eating is rotten."

"There is no place for them to go," Alexandre agreed. "We do what we can, but it is not much. Victor helped a small family recently, but those opportunities are rare."

"It was generous of you to concern yourself with strangers when you, yourselves, are suffering," Connor noted.

Alexandre nodded. "We must all do what we can. That is what men of God do."

"And not all of them remain strangers for long," Victor said, shifting on the log. "We have even learned about our own families' fates through the stories of strangers."

"And we have made many friends along this voyage," Alexandre said. "My nephew even thought he had found a wife, but it was not to be."

"Ah? I'm sorry you were disappointed," Connor said.

Victor shrugged. "She loves another, so I understand."

"Did she say that?"

"No, but she wore his ring." His gaze dropped to his own hands, and he spoke with regret. "She turned it constantly on her finger. For a while I had hoped—selfishly, I know—he had died so she might be more open to my attentions, but it was not to be."

"And now you must stop moping, nephew. Find another."

Victor nodded. "This is not the right time to fall in love anyway."

The three stared at the fire, their minds elsewhere; then Victor looked at his uncle again. "She was something special, wasn't she? She was not afraid of anything, that girl. If I could have married sweet Amélie, I would be much happier right now."

Connor blinked, suddenly alert. There must be thousands of Amélies in the world. Surely he didn't mean—

Alexandre chuckled. "Charles would not allow you near his daughter. You know that. He watched her like a hawk."

"Where did you meet this girl?" Connor asked, fighting to keep his tone steady.

"She was near Saint John with a group from Grand Pré. At Camp de l'Espérance," Alexandre said. "She and her father and little sister came with us to Quebec."

Connor stared at him, grateful his face was shadowed. It was too incredible. These men had been with Amélie! She was alive and so close!

"But Quebec City was in a bad way," Alexandre continued. "Victor heard of a cabin an hour outside the city and brought them to it. He left them there."

"It was the best I could do," Victor added.

"Do you know the family name of the three people you helped?"

"Belliveau," Alexandre said. "Why?"

"I just . . ."

He hesitated, not wanting to sound eager. He noticed the silent Mi'kmaq beside him had leaned forward, looking as surprised as Connor felt. He had to be careful. Anything he volunteered could be misinterpreted. But he had to know.

He shrugged. "When you said Amélie and Charles, I wondered if I knew them."

"But you said you are from Chignecto, yes?"

"Yes," began the lie. "Although my wife was from Grand Pré."

"Ah. Je m'excuse. I did not know. She . . . ?"

"Was taken."

The men exchanged a sympathetic glance and did not pry further.

"We are leaving tomorrow," Alexandre said, breaking the silence. "We go to Chignecto. Will you travel with us?"

He tried to think of a reason to refuse, but in the end he had no choice but to go in order to keep his secret. Now that he had a vague idea of where she was, he planned to return later for Amélie.

On the first day the four men were met by a larger group of Frenchmen, Mi'kmaq, and Acadian fighters. It was something of a shock for Connor to see the blue-trimmed, white uniforms of the French army up close, but he did what he could to hide his apprehension. Alexandre and Victor appeared overjoyed to see the others, and it became apparent that they knew each other from before. Since they were friends, they seemed to trust Connor, and they exchanged news freely. Connor sat quietly in the background, listening, but he heard nothing that would have been a secret anyway.

Suddenly a sharp blow crashed into the base of his head, shooting lightning through his vision, and he crumpled to the ground. Through the roaring in his head he heard Victor come to his aid, heard Alexandre's startled exclamation. Voices were raised in accusation and denial.

But nothing they said could save him, he knew.

"He is an English soldier and a liar, you fools," he heard. "I know this man."

He *knew* him? Connor pressed his palms against the forest floor and struggled to turn his body so he could squint up at his accuser. A furious Acadian glared down at him, rage pulsing from familiar blue eyes: André Belliveau, Amélie's oldest brother, the one who had left the family so he could fight with the French. The one who had once dragged him under a shrub and demanded a promise.

"Wait!" Connor's voice was choked with pain. "I have news! Your family—"

André Belliveau's hard black boot swung up, striking Connor square in the stomach, nearly lifting him off the ground. He curled instinctively into a ball, all the air gone from his lungs. In the next instant, Connor's hair was yanked back and his nose punched. His vision swam with the impact, rolling waves of black beneath hazy smears of colour. The urge to vomit was strong, but there was no time for that. André knelt beside him and pulled his hair back again, setting the ground spinning beneath him.

He stared into Connor's eyes with a terrible hatred. "No more lies, Sergeant MacDonnell," he hissed in a slow, deliberate English. His lips trembled with anger.

Blood drained from Connor's nose, sliding over his teeth.

Based on the Acadian's expression, he thought it possible that he was about to die. André was not finished. He dragged his captive toward a boulder a few feet away, grunting with the effort, then he seized Connor's head in his hands. Once again, he squatted in front of Connor, his bloodshot eyes delivering the message before he even spoke.

"For my family."

Connor squeezed his eyes shut just before his head was slammed into the rock face.

André

THIRTY

André Belliveau paced before the wigwam, his moccasins having already beaten a dark path across its entrance. He had kept his determined vigil for hours.

What was he to do with MacDonnell? He and the other fighters had come all this way, had farther still to go. He couldn't spare the men to send the Englishman back to their headquarters, but he certainly couldn't just let the two-faced, lying criminal go free. Perhaps he had only to wait. The brief beating had laid the man out flat. It would be a while before he could fight back. If he chose to try, perhaps André would slit his throat and leave him here to bleed among the hungry creatures of the forest.

Seeing the British soldier had been a shock. Catching sight of him in the midst of André's friends and fellow fighters had angered him beyond what he could have expected. He remembered that face well. A lifetime ago the man had made him a promise. The next time André had seen MacDonnell, the Scot had been standing beside Winslow on that horrible morning, stoic and proud as he sent Papa, Mathieu, Guillaume, and the other men to the boats. Ever since that day, André had witnessed the inhumanity of which the British were capable, and he had connected

MacDonnell with all of it. He had wept when he saw his dear maman carrying food to the ships day after day, but there was nothing he could have done. They were so few, and the English seemed to multiply by the day, as had their weapons and resolve. Certainly the freedom fighters kept the army busy, but there was nothing the Acadians could do to halt the bulk of this disaster.

They should not have trusted the English to have hearts. He should not have trusted MacDonnell.

He was aware that his emotions were taking control, and he struggled to think beyond them. Throughout his life, Papa had shown him how important it was to resist giving in to the animal within, to rise above nature and think logically.

"There may be times when killing is the only choice," Papa had said when André confessed long before that he wanted to do exactly that to the soldiers. "But those times are few. Killing, my son, inevitably leads to more trouble. A good man knows this."

André had never imagined himself to be a killer. Observing his father's penitent, bowed head in church, André believed he was forever tortured by the guilt of killing those two men many years before. Like his father, André was strong. Like his mother, he was practical. Killing, he had understood, could only be a last resort.

But life had changed. Having watched his family be stolen away, he had joined the fight. He had grieved over far too many slain friends both Acadian and Mi'kmaq, and their deaths had infused his life with the need for revenge. Still, he had never killed a man, had hoped he would not have to. Now he wasn't sure he could. To look in a man's eye and end his life seemed . . . daunting—even if that man was MacDonnell.

Perhaps there was another option. The man lying behind him was more than an ordinary soldier. He was one of Winslow's important men, though heaven only knew why he had been wandering these woods as he had. Was he a threat? Would Winslow pay to have him returned? If so, what was he worth?

On the other hand, God had practically handed the man to André. Was this a message? A sign he should kill him?

He stopped pacing, leaned down through the wigwam door, and peered into the darkness. The beaten soldier lay by the fire, his senseless, bruised face lit by the flames. André's hand went to his hip and slid his knife from the sheath on his belt. *It would be easy.* With his eyes on the unconscious prisoner, he ran the blade against the callused skin of his thumb, trying to think clearly. *So easy.*

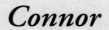

Connor

THIRTY-ONE

Connor lay on his back like a starfish, unable to move. His eyes were swollen shut. At one point someone had come and tended to him—he felt a difference after the tightness of the dried blood was cleaned from his face—but they could do nothing for the pitchfork of pain that dug into his brain. He couldn't breathe through his nose, and his lip was split. If he inhaled too deeply, he felt as if he were being stabbed, so he imagined André's boot had broken a rib.

The wigwam flap swept back, letting in the suggestion of sunlight. He forced his eyes open a crack, wary of the next attack, but was relieved to see it was only a young woman carrying a bowl of water. She knelt at his side and had slid one cool hand behind his neck before he could object. When she urged him up so he could drink, he gasped at the pain of movement, sucking air through his teeth. She didn't stop, didn't offer sympathy, simply angled the bowl high enough that she could pour the water between his lips. He sputtered, shooting agony through his chest. She kept pouring, so he kept swallowing, though much of the water dribbled over his lips and down his chin. He didn't mind. It was soothing. When the bowl was empty, she placed his head back on the ground and left. He was too weak and beaten to contemplate escape, so he drifted back to sleep.

Sometime later, the woman returned. This time she carried a bowl of stew as well. The light was different outside the wigwam, and he realized it was raining. How long had he been lying here?

"Why am I still alive?"

Her distaste was obvious in the tight set of her mouth. "Because we have not killed you."

Surprisingly, when the corners of his mouth curled upward, it didn't hurt too much. "And I thank you for that. Why not?"

One eyebrow flicked up, but her overall expression didn't change. At first he thought she wouldn't say anything, but then she exhaled slowly through her nose.

"We're trading you. They say you are worth two Frenchmen." Her shrewd gaze wandered over his injuries, at least the visible ones. "I am not sure why. You might have been worth something before, but you do not look good now."

"Who?" he asked, suddenly anxious. His mind had gone immediately to ten years before, when he'd been sold to the highest bidder. *Please God, don't let me be traded as a slave.* "Who is trading for me?"

"Winslow," she said. She dropped the bowl of food before him and got to her feet. "Tomorrow."

She was reaching for the flap when he spoke again. "Thank you."

Her hand stopped, and she turned. "I have no reason to hate you, soldier. You are a child of Mother Earth, no different from me. But André hates you, which is interesting. He does not hate easily. You must have done something very bad."

Perhaps it was the curiosity in her voice; perhaps it was the overwhelming misery he felt. Whatever it was, Connor wasn't strong enough to hold back the wave of regret that washed over him in that moment, remembering the terrified Acadians he had helped destroy. Remembering Amélie. Remembering the vow he had once made.

"Yes," he said. "I did."

"And are you sorry for it?"

"With all my heart."

She looked thoughtful. "You should sit up and try to walk. You will have a long walk tomorrow."

He took the woman's advice and carefully raised himself to a seated position. He had to wait a bit before going any further, since the ground was swaying, but the food she'd brought was warm, and he discovered he was ravenous. After he finished the stew, he wiped the thin bannock over what was left, savouring every bit. He felt stronger, and his head ached a little less, so he felt able to think about what she'd said. She'd brought good news, for sure. At least Winslow had decided he was still of value. Connor was certain things would not have ended well for him had he been forced to remain here.

The next morning he got to his feet and tried in vain to assure himself that the agony radiating from the side of his face was only temporary; it felt as if half his skull were missing. His entire body felt bruised, but when he tried to pinpoint the source of the worst pain, he narrowed it down to his head, his gut, and the back of his neck. Mostly his head. If only it could be removed and replaced, he'd be a much happier man.

Wary of sudden movements, he shuffled through the door flap and stood a moment, letting his eyes become accustomed to the dreary light. The sun had risen, but overall the day was grey. A light mist tingled over his skin, barely more than a fog. Connor took a couple of tentative steps and raised his face to the sky, and the chill was soothing.

"So. You live," a familiar voice stated flatly.

Ten feet away, André leaned against the trunk of an oak tree, whittling a branch to a fine point. At sight of him, Connor's heart leapt to his throat, but other than the quick widening of his eyes, he didn't react. André wasn't looking at him. He had removed his coat and now wore only navy trousers and a loose linen shirt. Waves of golden hair hung to his collar. Surely he couldn't mean to inflict more pain. The woman had said he was a good man, that he didn't anger easily.

"Yes. Thank you for that."

André's blue eyes slid from his work to his captive. "You weren't worth killing."

They stared at each other, and Connor's eyes dropped first.

"What does it feel like to break a promise?" André asked. "I have never done that."

Connor thought hard about that. "Never?"

"Never."

"I don't think that's true."

One blond eyebrow lifted quizzically, and in that expression Connor saw Amélie, clear as day.

"You promised to hunt me down and kill me. And yet here I stand."

André nodded slowly, giving a hint of a smile. "I stand corrected. It is never too late, of course. But today I return you to your miserable commander. If it were me being returned to that man, I would consider it a sentence almost worse than death."

⌒

Later that morning, Connor was assigned a stone-faced Mi'kmaq companion as a guide to the site where he would be traded. The warrior spoke little more than had Connor's earlier Mi'kmaq companion. It was a long, painful trek, but Connor did not complain.

He was walking toward life—not a long, drawn-out death—after all. After about an hour they stopped at the foot of a hill lined by spruce and waited in the mist. Some while later they were alerted by a crashing through the brush.

"English," the warrior muttered with disgust.

Two Frenchmen entered the clearing first, both of them struggling with their balance since their hands were tied. The Mi'kmaq looked unimpressed but stood to welcome them. Behind them was a British soldier.

Fitch. He strode over and slapped Connor on his shoulder. "You've looked better, you 'ave. Bit of trouble with the locals?"

"Good day, Corporal," Connor managed, offering a tight smile.

"Bet you're surprised to see me, aye?"

"You could say that."

"We'll get you all settled in back with your own soon enough." A shadow darkened his expression; then the glint was back. "Winslow's eager to see you, he is."

"I look forward to seeing him as well," Connor lied.

Fitch stood with his legs apart, arms crossed importantly over his red coat. "Right. We're good then. Let's go. Farewell for now, lads." He shoved the bound captives toward their waiting guide. "Next time I see you filthy French frogs, I'll shoot you." Looking toward Connor, he gestured with one hand toward the path. "After you, Sergeant MacDonnell. You're the sergeant, after all."

The forest was less dense here, making following the path easier, and it seemed to frustrate Fitch that Connor couldn't walk quickly. But the pounding in Connor's head hadn't eased, and sometimes when the path dipped, Connor took a step that went farther than he'd planned. He fought dizziness by insisting they pause at any river crossing, where he gulped the glacial water and splashed his face, breathing deeply.

"We'll make camp here," Connor informed Fitch late that

afternoon. The spot seemed perfect in more ways than one. First, it was near the river and offered shelter in the way of a shallow cave. Second, Connor didn't feel he could take another step.

"What, 'ere?" Fitch sneered. "You've no stamina anymore, Sergeant. Made you into a bit of a nancy, did they?"

It didn't matter what he said. Connor was—as Fitch had reminded him many times—the senior officer, and this was where he was going to sleep.

"Come on!" Fitch whined, walking a few more paces. "We can make it afore nightfall if we keep on."

Recent rain had dampened most of the wood in the area, but Connor spotted a fallen tree which had sheltered a few twigs from the weather. He set to work building a fire.

Fitch watched him work. "I'd rather keep going," he muttered.

"So you've made clear." Connor fed a spark to a handful of dry moss, then dipped a piece of birch bark into the growing flame. "You seem in a hurry. I'm surprised. I'd have thought you'd welcome the opportunity to sit by a fire one more night and not return to active duty."

Fitch wandered closer, surrendering to the inevitable. "Think you know me, do you?"

There seemed no real response to that other than a shrug, but yes, Connor knew exactly who Fitch was. He was a shallow, jealous man with few scruples. Since he could never move back up the military ladder as a result of his dishonourable conduct, he made himself feel important by belittling others.

"You don't," Fitch insisted, squatting by the fire.

Connor sighed, drained by the man and the day and the constant, pulsing pain in his head. "If you say so."

The fire was rising, crackling cheerfully. Connor held his hands toward it, enjoying the delicious warmth, then slipped off his boots and laid his soaked stockings on the ground nearby.

Perhaps in the morning they would be dry. When the weather was warmer, he promised himself, he would treat his blistered feet by going barefoot more often. He was aware of Fitch watching everything he did, hostility radiating off him as tangibly as the heat from the fire, suggesting his rage was unpredictable. Considering the condition Connor was already in, he decided the safest thing he could do was say nothing.

Evidently that was not enough for Fitch. He sprang to his feet and began to pace. "You might be a sergeant, but you're not half the man I am."

"True enough," Connor said, on alert.

"You think you've outdone me, Scottish pig, but ye haven't."

This new reference to Connor's nationality was a shock, and his hackles rose in reaction. "I have no such thoughts, *Englishman*," he retorted. "In fact I don't think of you at all unless you are with me, talking my ear off."

"That's not true!" Fitch hissed, leaning toward Connor's face.

"It is."

"Get up and march, soldier!" Fitch snapped.

Exhaustion was set aside, replaced by irritation. Must he spend his entire life dealing with this ass? "If you're in such a hurry to get back to the rum in your tent, go on your own. I'll follow in the morning."

Fitch's eyes flashed with anger. He kicked at the fire, pelting Connor with burning twigs. Despite his pain, Connor leapt to his feet.

"You'd kick fire at me, wee man?" he said through gritted teeth. "What would possess you to do that? Stand down, Corporal! I've no idea what has you in such a state, but you'll quit it now. We will stay here the night, and I'll hear no more about it."

They glared at each other, breathing hard, until Connor turned away. It wasn't worth fighting over this. He started to walk back to his place by the fire but stopped abruptly, struck by a sharp pain in his back. He dropped to his knees, hand at his side, then turned it palm side up. His hand was slick with blood. The wound didn't feel deep, but it burned.

He looked at Fitch with disbelief. The man clutched a bloodied knife in his shaking hand, and he shuffled from foot to foot, appearing uncertain. He looked more like a simple thug than a soldier.

"Now who's in charge?" he nonetheless demanded. "You'll do as I say, you will!"

Connor dared himself to laugh, looking away again. Taking his eyes off Fitch was a gamble since the man might still kill him; he was already unstable, yet it seemed what Fitch truly craved was confirmation he had won. Connor could not give him that.

Moving carefully so as not to jar the fresh wound, Connor slipped out of his coat and pulled his shirt over his head. He shivered as he wrapped the material around his torso, tying the sleeves tightly at his side so the bleeding might stop. He wished he could see the damn thing. And he wished people would stop attacking him from behind. Once the makeshift tourniquet was secure, he huddled back into his coat and settled in front of the fire as if nothing had happened.

The burning twigs Fitch had kicked at him before had all died out, leaving tiny lines of smoke behind, so Connor tossed them back into the fire.

"Idiot. I cannot walk now, so we are obliged to stay here a while longer," Connor calmly informed him. "You stabbed me in the back like the coward you are, and now I must heal. You did not think that through, did you?"

Fitch's nostrils flared with anger. "At least now you cannot escape."

"I had no plans to escape. I am a sergeant in the British army, and unlike you, I know my place."

"Ha! Do you indeed! I say you do not!"

"What are you saying now?"

"Only that I know about you."

This was going nowhere. Connor shook his head and stared back at the fire.

"You're a traitor!" Fitch roared. "You were on that French ship what got away. And I know who else was on it, don't I? Didn't I just find that ship, then see your dolly on the beach after?"

"What?"

"Never thought I'd see her again, and she looked surprised to see me as well. But she knew who I was, and she knew I would come for you."

Blood rushed into Connor's cheeks.

"She was mighty glad to see me. Welcomed me to her bed, she did."

The image sickened Connor, though he knew Fitch was lying.

"I had thought you'd be on that beach as well," Fitch mused. "Then I caught wind of this prisoner exchange, found out it was you. I made sure Colonel Winslow sent me to fetch you." His smile was back, as greasy as it had been in Grand Pré when he'd spoken of wanting to hunt down the Acadian girls. "I told him what I'd seen. Told him you were responsible for letting all them French folk go free. Told him you should hang for it. Guess what your little friend said? He agreed wit' me, he did."

Connor stared at him. The bastard had done it; he'd managed to catch Connor when no one else had. What was worse, Fitch was right: Connor's actions labelled him a traitor, and he'd hang. The realization settled solidly in his gut and spread through his body as he staggered to his feet. The wound in his back radiated through him, jagged and burning, cutting through all the other pain, but fury drove him forward. Fitch watched with horrified fascination as Connor took two steps toward him, then punched him hard across his jaw. Fitch landed on his back with an exclamation of shock, his nose and lip bleeding, and sidled away like a crab as Connor came after him again. When his back came up against the trunk of a long-dead tree, he scrambled to his feet and jabbed at Connor with his knife again.

"I'll see you hang!" he shouted.

Using the back of his hand, Connor brushed the weapon to the side, spinning Fitch with the motion. Fitch's free hand gripped one of the dead tree's branches and it broke off in his hand, providing him with a second weapon. He swept the sharp branch across Connor's face, and when Connor belatedly raised his hands in defence, Fitch stabbed the splintered end into the fresh wound on his back. Agony shot through Connor, and he collapsed. In the next second Fitch had leapt on top of him, brandishing his knife again. He brought it down hard, stabbing into Connor's shoulder, then he yanked it out and raised it over his head, ready to strike again. Connor tried to roll, tried to dislodge his stubborn attacker, but he was weakened by too many injuries, and the pain was too great. Fitch's twisted face was blood-smeared, his eyes manic, and Connor thought, *I'm going to die.*

In the next instant, Fitch jerked with surprise and his eyes went blank. The knife dropped harmlessly from his hand as gravity carried him forward and dumped him, lifeless, on top of Connor.

Staring down at Connor was the silent Mi'kmaq he had dragged from the river. Connor hadn't seen him since they'd come up against André. The hunter wiped the blade of his knife on his leggings, leaned down, and rolled Fitch onto the ground. Connor stared wordlessly up at him, bewildered, and the big man looked back, a smile stretching across his face. As a dark blanket of consciousness closed around Connor and his vision blurred, he realized it was the first time he'd seen the man smile.

THIRTY-TWO

He dreamed he stood on the ship, waves swaying beneath his feet. Near mid-deck he thought he spied grass poking up from between the boards, but when he got closer he realized they were fingers clawing through. He flung the hatch open and the hands burst out, scattering into the air like birds.

The water became the forest floor, and the gentle waves solidified, jarring him awake. Connor blinked, suddenly alert, and tried to make sense of his surroundings. After a moment he realized the Mi'kmaq hunter had fashioned a travois of sorts, and Connor was its passenger. He had been bundled under his own black cloak and tied securely, and judging from the care with which he was wrapped, he assumed the man had bound his injuries as well. The forest canopy bounced above him, the branches like random prison bars. He thought to ask where he was being dragged or how long they'd been travelling, but what answer could the mute have given him? He might as well have been on that rolling ship in his dream.

But something was wrong. The day was cool, yet sweat rolled off Connor's brow, and the stab wound in his shoulder throbbed with a sinister heat. Panic fluttered in his chest, but he forced himself to be calm. There was nothing he could do. He was either the man's captive or he was in his care; either way he was helpless to save himself. Lulled by the motion, he let himself melt into the rising heat of his body.

It was near dark by the time he awoke. Voices penetrated the fog in his head, setting off an alarm, and he struggled to understand the unfamiliar words. They seemed to be coming from far away, but faces loomed directly over him, their features confused by a dizzying array of stars. The travois was dragged inside a building, and when his eyes adjusted to the light, he made out the willow braces and birchbark walls, the woven baskets set around the edges; he was in another wigwam. The fear of becoming a slave roared up again, but when he struggled, trying to escape the bindings which kept him safe on the travois, an older woman set a hand on his chest and he stilled.

He was left alone in the sweltering heat, unable to think. Fever had spread through him like a wildfire, and his vision wavered when he managed to hold his eyes open for any length of time. The pressure of a cold, wet cloth on his forehead made him gasp, which made the young woman holding the cloth jump, but she quickly placed it back on his hot skin. Her touch was gentle, the water so cold it had to have come from heaven. He feared he might weep with relief, and the woman seemed to understand. She spoke softly, whispering and humming, treating him as if he were a child. When she brought water to his lips, he choked and coughed, then lifted his head despite its formidable weight and begged for more. Her slender fingers went to his chin, and she folded down the top of the cloak tucked around his neck. He had never known water could provide such pleasure. When his neck had been cleaned of dried blood and grime, she folded the cloak lower.

Then she stopped and pulled her hands away as if she'd been stung. What had he done? What had she seen? She whispered something to herself in the strange language of the Mi'kmaq; then her eyes rose from his chest to his face. He stared helplessly back.

"Where did you get this?" Her French was perfect. Now if only he could understand what she was asking about. When he didn't answer, she asked, "Do you speak French?"

He nodded, and the fever rose behind his eyes. Sleep beckoned, weighting his lids.

"Then tell me. Where did you get this?"

"Get what?"

She scowled. "This necklace."

Amélie. She had insisted he take it. He had kissed her . . . "A friend," he said.

"Who?"

"Why . . . why do you need to know?"

"Because I made it. I gave it to a friend to keep her safe. I need to know if she gave it to you or if you took it from her."

"She gave it to me. And I gave her my ring."

"Where is she?" she said urgently.

"I don't know." Should he tell her he would give his life to know if Amélie still lived?

She watched him. "On the same night I gave it to my best friend, my Acadian sister, she told me she had fallen in love. And she told me the name of that man. In return, I promised I would keep him in my prayers so he might be safe. I need to know your name."

He had heard that the eyes were the windows to the soul. If that were true, then this woman's soul was pleading for his answer to be the one she sought.

"My name is Connor MacDonnell," he said. "And the woman who gave me this necklace, the woman I love, is Amélie Belliveau."

Amélie

THIRTY-THREE

"Are you ready for a new adventure, ma chérie?"

Papa looked exhausted. His hair was long enough now that he had tied it roughly back, but in the late sun the blond curls were grizzled. It made me sad, seeing that. He was not old—barely past forty—but recent events had stolen any remnants of his youth. When I shrugged, he winked. "It could not be worse than what we've seen. Come. Let us see what we have inside."

The cabin door was reluctant, but eventually it gave way with a drawn-out creak. The musty smell of long-trapped air rushed out, making me sneeze. The trapper's little cabin reeked of abandonment. The remains of a long-dead fire, layered by dust and bird droppings, lay in the hearth. Other than a frail-looking table, a chair, and a rough cot, I saw nothing else. Any furs the trapper may have left had been claimed by the Maliseet. I longed to fling open the door and windows—I found a second one partially hidden behind a moth-eaten curtain—to replace the stagnant air with fresh, but we needed to retain heat until Papa could get a fire going.

Eventually the heat rose, warming the dank walls and bringing comfort to our bodies and souls. When night fell, the fire gave us light—and hope. Sitting before it on the rough floor, huddling with Giselle and Papa as we watched the flames, I thought we might truly survive this.

At last I had work with which I could occupy Giselle. The walls and both windows needed scrubbing, and the single cot was desperately in need of cleaning. In the morning, she set to the work with determination, making me proud. When Papa went to set snares, I sent her to the river with a bucket. When she did not come back right away, I went to investigate. The sun sparkled weakly through a break in the canopy of trees and twinkled off the water, showing me where to look. Giselle sat by the clear, cool stream, the bucket empty, scrubbing filth from her feet. She didn't look up when I joined her.

"I'm weary of being dirty," she said with a sigh.

"That must feel good."

"Take your moccasins off. Sit with me."

I was impatient to make the cabin a place where we could actually live, but I did as she suggested. When my toes dipped into the water, I gasped, then smiled with pleasure. For the first time in ages, my sister and I laughed together, and when I accidentally splashed her leg, she started to scrub it as well. The trees around us were thick as walls, the birds within their branches calm and vocal. I took off my coat and put it on the ground beside me, then started to untie my skirt.

"Let's clean ourselves off, then."

How long had it been since we'd been completely naked? She gave me the grin I remembered so fondly and accepted the challenge. We dropped our filthy clothing to the ground and waded into the water, shuddering with shock at the cold thrill of it, daring each other to dunk underneath. The dirt peeled away like stubborn birchbark, and when I eventually emerged, dripping wet, I felt lighter in every way. Giselle walked beside me, and

I tried not to react to the dreadful boniness of her body, at the way her arms looked more like tree limbs than those of a young woman. We had been away from home for well over a year, and her fifteen-year-old body resembled that of a sick boy. Her blond curls had long since lost their lustre.

She must have seen something similar, for she stepped closer and poked my ribs. "We need to fatten you up."

"It'll be better here. We won't have to rely on rotten meat or stale bread."

I shouldn't have mentioned the bread, for her mouth curved down. "I miss fresh bread. Remember how it smelled? How we could practically taste it from the garden when Maman set it out to cool?"

I wasn't sure that I wanted to remember. With regret we pulled our clothes back on, and I told her we would wash them someday.

"For now this will have to suffice," I said, plunging my bonnet into the water and cleaning what I could from it. She did the same, then we set them on our wet hair.

We filled the bucket and walked back to the cabin, picking up twigs and rotted chunks of wood for the fire as we walked. The cabin would never be our home, but we would do what we could with it until we could move somewhere better. In the first week we were there, Papa built another, wider bed, and we cut more branches for a mattress. Someday we would buy a real cot. We fished, we set snares, and when we felt safe enough, we made brief visits to the city to trade for what we could, including spare clothing. Autumn warmed the air and roused the mosquitoes, so we escaped them by going to the river or climbing a breezy hill nearby. When Papa went deeper into the forest, seeking larger game, we mended what clothing we had and tried to create new garments with the scraps of old ones. We were safe in our little home, and though we were much diminished in numbers, we were a family again. We did what we could, laughed when we could, and we breathed.

Still, memories of what had passed plagued my sleep. One rainy afternoon we stayed inside, and Giselle fell uncommonly quiet. She had been returning to herself of late, smiling, searching for humour in small things, but not on this day.

"Are you all right?" I asked, rubbing her cold hands in mine.

"Just tired. I have a terrible headache."

"You didn't eat. Maybe if you ate something your headache would go away."

"I'm not hungry. You should eat my share."

That night when she went to bed, she was so hot the air around her felt warm. In the morning she complained that the inside of her mouth hurt and swallowing was painful. I opened a window for light and peered in, and my heart sank.

Two weeks before, we'd gone to the city for milk. While we were there I'd heard the women in the city whispering of smallpox. From what they had said, the red welts which now covered my sister's tongue and gums were the first symptoms. Over the next few hours the inside of Giselle's mouth swelled, then her throat, making it almost impossible for her to swallow. Blisters rose on her brow and burst, spreading the hideous disease. By the second day her face, hands, feet, and practically every other part of her feverish body was covered in small white blisters. Though tiny in comparison, they reminded me of the blisters which had afflicted my hands and wrists one summer. The women of our village had said I'd caught them from milking the cows, that I had something called cowpox. They assured me the blisters would soon fade, and they had. I'd forgotten all about them until now.

As Giselle's blisters hardened into bead-like pox, Papa and I did what we could to cool her torturous rash with balms, dipping her poor hands and feet into buckets of water I fetched from the stream, trying to reach her tortured mind with songs.

Giselle hovered close to death, rose again with false, precarious health, then sank back into the fever's clutches. Smallpox struck Papa next. After that, dullness enveloped him along with the fever, swelling his skin with the same horrible blisters and smoothing his once-strong features into a mask of resignation.

The room became insufferable, and during the day I flung open the windows and gasped in clean forest air. I was not ill, had felt no effects at all, and I was determined to make use of my health by returning it to Giselle and Papa. When the nights came, I closed the shutters tightly to block out death and moved with determination through the dark house, my fingers sure over cups and pitcher as I poured what I could into my loved ones' mouths.

Papa rarely made a sound. I begged him to fight. He did not. Throughout his life he had fought too hard and for too long, and he hadn't the strength to wage war for the sake of his own life. I wanted to shake him, demand he return to me, but the fever kept sweeping in and carrying him off, its waves cresting and crashing like those which had carried us from our beloved home.

The women in the city had said the only cure could come from drinking water or praying hard, but they were wrong. Neither prayers nor water worked. Papa died first, and my little sister refused to let me move her from his side. Her confused wails melted into whimpers, and eventually into nothing at all. She lay helplessly beside Papa's body, gasping like a fish on land until she breathed no more.

Death had closed over the house like a fog over the sea, then evaporated as swiftly, taking the last two people I loved. Their eyes were closed, their faces serene after so much strife. Flies came alive with the day's warmth, and their bouncing celebration vibrated off the walls. At last the illness came for me, and having spent every moment caring for the others, I was too tired to fight back. My knees trembled, threatening to drop me where I stood, so I flung out a hand and braced myself against the wall. I was afraid that if I fell, I might never rise again. Exhaustion had taken root deep in my bones, and I felt it sprouting, its hungry vines winding greedily through my bloodstream.

I was so thirsty. I staggered outside, drawn by the song of the river, and cupped my hands in the water. It felt wonderful trickling down my throat, and I splashed it all over my face before gulping more down. Eventually I fell asleep. When I awoke, I felt the first of the blisters on my tongue.

THIRTY-FOUR

I was alone. That was the first sensation. The acknowledgement of still, unmoving air, the lack of shared breathing.

I could not recall stumbling back to the cabin, but that was where I had awoken. Somehow I had rolled myself in a blanket by the ashes of the fire, and I had succumbed again to sleep. Now my waking thoughts crept around the room in search of company but returned empty-handed. I could not look at the bed where the last of my family lay, but they watched over me. I heard them whisper, reminding me to breathe. To live.

The fever had come upon me, and ugly red dots rose on my skin. I pushed away the suffocating blanket, and while I could still lift my head, I surveyed my body. I thought I did not look as thickly coated with illness as the others had. Nevertheless, the floor beneath me became soaked with my sweat, the air ripe with vomit and diarrhea, since I could not rise to go outside. My insatiable thirst was more than a discomfort; I was losing so much fluid, I was in danger of dying a very dry death. But no one was left to bring me water, to help me drink. When a window of sanity opened a crack, I forced myself to scoop what was left in the bucket and pour it down my throat.

"God, if thou wouldst spare me . . . ," I whispered through cracked lips but then stopped, realizing I no longer cared if he did.

I couldn't move. Where once I had been strong, now I felt helpless as a newborn. Even opening my eyes seemed a daunting task. A breeze blew through the open door, wet and cool from a sweet autumn rainstorm, and I opened my mouth to drink it in.

Water. It dripped from leaves outside the cabin and sank into the earth. So close, so far. The rain had stopped and the day was done, dropping me into a dusk rich with the noise of crickets. I lay still a few minutes more, summoning the strength to roll to my side. If I did not, I would die. It was as simple as that. I groped toward the bucket, and the bliss that came from touching the murky wet wood spread through my fingers and up my arm. I dragged the bucket closer and tilted what I could into my mouth, but the water stopped at the back of my throat, blocked by the swollen tissues. A weak sort of panic trembled through me, until I remembered how long it had taken for Papa and Giselle to swallow anything. All I had to do was wait what felt like an eternity, and eventually a few drops found their way. I reached for more, but nothing remained. The final drops of water had soaked into the bucket's wood base just as my last hint of energy seeped away. I needed to rise and find life in the stream, but first I must sleep.

When I awoke, I lay in complete darkness. Even the crickets slept.

My thirst was too powerful to ignore. I visualized myself sitting up, then struggled to match the vision. My feet felt far away when they touched the floor, then completely foreign when I added my weight to them. Battling a weariness that had hardened deep within me, I rose and waited for balance. I dragged one foot ahead, then the other, my hand sliding along the wall. I forced my gaze forward as I shuffled toward the door, since I was unwilling to face what was left in the bed. I couldn't save them now. No one could.

The trees helped. They stood like a fence, catching the moonlight in their branches and using it to lead me through the night. Their sturdy trunks supported me, guided me to the water's edge, but the effort required from me was immense. Exhaustion rolled over my entire body, bringing with it another wave of nausea. Every muscle shook. My teeth chattered uncontrollably behind frozen lips, though the skin of my face burned.

What am I supposed to do now, Papa?

Suddenly lost, I clutched at the sturdy reassurance of a maple. Using the tree as a crutch, I sank to my knees in the damp, crackling leaves, praying for mercy. I lay down, gathering leaves around me like a blanket, then curled my body into a ball. Sleep came and lay beside me. She curved her dark assurances over me, and she stayed a long time.

At some point during my fevered slumber, a man appeared in my dream. He had no face, and he had no voice. He poured water through my lips and dripped it over my brow. I lay limply, offering no resistance as he wrapped me in a blanket and carried me to a small shelter cushioned with sweet balsam. I fell asleep, cradled within its branches.

I awoke to a roar like I'd never heard before. My eyes cracked open, and I became aware that the sky glowed an eerie golden red. A long, drawn-out *crack!* sliced through the air, sounding like a house beam splintering, and my heart rose to my throat. I could not ignore the terrifying noise, snapping and whooshing, reminding me of the terrible storm on the night when Mathieu had been lost.

I summoned what strength I could and rolled over to see through the open side of a lean-to. The sky, I found, was indeed on fire, the moon blocked from my view by towering black smoke. The raging source—my family's small cabin—blurred through my tears.

"Papa!" I whispered.

They were in there. The impossible thought came to me that I should run to them, drag their bodies from the ravaged walls, but even in my feverish state I knew I could not. All I could do was stare in disbelief at the inferno, asking myself how this could have happened. I had not lit a fire, not with the terrible heat of our fevers still thick in the air, and it was not raining, so there could have been no lightning strike.

My eyes caught movement between myself and the flames. The muscles in my arms shook when I pushed myself up, and the heat was such that I had to squint hard against it, but I could not peel my eyes from what I saw. The shadowy profile of a man stood before the fire, his arms raised toward the night sky, his face as well. His mouth opened and closed, but I heard no words, so I imagined they were swallowed by the terrible noise of the fire.

After a while, he turned from the house and faced me, his arms slowly lowering, smears of black soot heavy on his face. The fire lit the night so I could see he appeared to be Mi'kmaq. There was no threat in his stance, but I didn't move. For a moment, neither did he. Then he turned back toward the fire, and his arms lifted again as if in celebration or prayer.

I watched him until I could no longer support myself, then I lay down and closed my eyes. In the back of my mind I saw the haze of orange light hovering over Grand Pré as we boarded the ships, the glow of the terrible fires which had burned in our wake. I saw too the *Pembroke* burning, its rigging and dark wood panels devoured by the ravenous fire we had set. I remembered the broken people standing around me on the sand, uncertain whether to cheer or weep at the destruction. My delirious, wandering thoughts returned to the fickle sea, quietly catching sparks and embers from that fire. I thought of how she had opened her wide arms and carried us from our homes, how she had swallowed up my brother and so many others in one awful moment. Yet I had spent my whole life thanking God for water, for the life it had always given us: filling our fields so we could eat, filling our buckets so we could drink, cooling our skin, cleaning our bodies. But as easily as water gave, it took. Nothing and no one could ever be completely trusted.

Water rolled nearby. Too close. Panicked, I opened my eyes and found the reason. I lay on the floor of a birchbark canoe, wrapped in a blanket that stank of smoke. A few feet away, my saviour knelt on the floor, facing me as he paddled. His eyes, dark as the hair draped over the broad muscles of his chest, were trained on the shoreline, at ease one moment then alert as one of the forest creatures. His strength was a solid fact, powerful as the water he mastered, fluid as the river. He seemed unaware of me, as if he'd forgotten I lay curled at his feet.

I could feel the slight hesitation and gentle pulse in the boat's movements with each stroke of the paddle. The motion tempted me to fall back into that sweet slumber that had left me so unaware, but my mind had come awake. We had left the smoking ashes of the cabin and my family behind. And the illness had gone. My head felt clear, and my stomach no longer rolled. My body was drained from the battle, but I had won. I had survived the devil's disease.

Lying helplessly in the canoe of a stranger, I felt no fear, only gratitude. The stranger had nursed me back to health. I had only vague, hazy recollections of him feeding me and offering silent companionship, and I had no idea how long it had gone on.

"What is your name?" I asked in Mi'kmawi'simk. My voice sounded raw. Hoarse from disuse.

His lips drew tight, but he did not answer.

"I am Amélie Belliveau, from Grand Pré."

A shadow passed behind the dark eyes. He blinked once and the shadow was gone.

I tried to engage him in conversation again, but he wouldn't answer. I was confused by his silence. The Mi'kmaq with whom I had grown up were outgoing and friendly. This man was a mystery. And yet I still felt no fear. I knew nothing of him, but he was all I knew now.

A cross breeze blew by, not touching me on the floor of the canoe but plucking a few strands of the man's hair and dropping them back onto one naked shoulder. I saw no clouds; the sky stretched above him in an endless slate of grey. A bird sang, but I didn't recognize the melody. Where was I?

I closed my eyes, searching my memory for clues, then pushed the impressions away as soon as they rushed in. I remembered the heat raging within me as well as roaring in from the outside as I watched the cabin burn, and I wished I had no recollection of the bodies I'd left inside. Would there ever come a day when the nightmare wouldn't be the uppermost thought in my mind? It was difficult to imagine.

I tried to focus instead on the ripples washing against the sides of the canoe, dancing cheerfully against the bow. I needed to remember something good, something separate from the horror. Connor's smile came to me, the determined set of his jaw, the outline of his short beard after many days at sea. I even let my mind dwell on the bruised mess of his face after we had taken the *Pembroke* and left the sailors on shore. I heard clearly his silent farewell, and I recalled the acceptance in his eyes. He had done what he'd set out to do. He had wanted me to be free, and I was. But I could never go back to what I'd been before. I'd seen too much, experienced horrors and sorrow I never could have imagined. I could not return to my home in Grand Pré. Even the dikes that had made our lives possible were most likely in ruins, meaning the ocean would have reclaimed the fields.

Nothing was what it had been, including me.

The pace of the Mi'kmaq's paddle never slowed, but when I looked back up at him, he seemed to study my expression. I offered a tentative smile and his eyes lit with unexpected warmth. Just as quickly the moment passed, and he looked back into the distance, his thoughts as elusive as my own.

THIRTY-FIVE

I awoke to a dramatic purple sunrise over open water. My travelling companion showed little sign of wear other than a slight sagging of his shoulders, but it was apparent he had paddled without sleep. Moving carefully, I sat up and waited for my lightheadedness to pass so I could watch the approaching coastline. We floated silently into a small bay that looked like any other, and he steered us close to the rocky beach. Hopping into the water, he dragged the canoe onto the rocks and helped me out, supporting me as my legs got used to standing again. The ground swooped beneath me and I stumbled, but his grip on my arm tightened, keeping me upright. Looking up, I saw his calm expression had changed; he was tense, scouting the shoreline. Now that I stood close to him I could see he was not a young man. His hair was still thick, but hints of silver threaded among the black. Most likely he was in his forties, like Papa.

Why had he brought me here?

"I believe I can walk," I told him, hoping I was right.

Jagged white rocks shifted under my moccasins, causing me to stumble again, but my guide walked smoothly behind me. He caught me before I could fall, and when I started to wobble for the third time, he simply picked me up and set my feet on the grass. I spotted a well-defined trail on our left and wondered who had made it.

"There?" I asked.

He nodded, so I kept walking. I dared to trust him, dared to hope I would be safe at the end of this trail. After a while, the rich smell of smoke drifted toward us, bringing with it the feeling of comfort, not threat. A small camp came into view, and I heard voices; someone was cutting firewood.

"Amélie?"

I froze, my heart in my throat. "Henri!" I whispered, trembling anew. "Is it you?"

Impossibly, my brother was instantly by my side, holding me so tightly I thought I'd never breathe again. Our faces were wet with tears, and I stared at him in disbelief, my fingers on his stubbled brown cheek. While I'd been gone, Henri had become a man. I couldn't stop weeping. When my weakened body began to fail, he held me up. He touched my cheek with his finger, and I knew he had noticed the dried scars left behind by the pox.

"How you have suffered, little sister!"

Would I ever be able to tell him the depths of my sorrow? The idea was monumental, and I was afraid. To do so I would have to envision my family again, watch them slip away from me one by one.

"I am well," I insisted.

"I will believe you for now, but only if you will allow us to take care of you."

"I look forward to that!"

He grinned. "I know just the thing to help you recover. I have good news. André is fine. He fights with the Resistance, and we see him often. He was just here a couple of weeks ago. How he would love to have seen you!"

He could not have given me happier news. We hugged again, and I wished I could hold him forever. But even as I breathed in his scent and felt his arms around me, my mind warned me not to trust this moment. Happiness had been ripped from me so many times that I wondered how I could ever believe in it again.

"What about the others?" Henri asked, bringing me back.

How could I find the words? Moments before I had been so elated, my heart bursting for having found Henri. Now I must break his heart.

"We . . . we are all that is left."

My brother seemed to shrink a little. "All?" he whispered. "How?"

I closed my eyes, shaking my head. "I cannot speak of it. Not yet."

"But I need—"

I felt as if I hadn't slept in a hundred nights. When was the last time I'd closed my eyes and slept without dreams, unafraid?

"I know. It's just—"

"My poor little sister," he said, his expression drawn with sympathy. "You have seen too much. First you must rest."

"Oh, Henri. I am so weary of crying."

Very gently, he wiped a fresh tear from my cheek. "I have a surprise for you."

Suddenly recalling my guide, I spun around to introduce him and was startled to discover he was gone. I peered to either side of the trail but could see no sign of him.

"Where did he go? He saved my life."

"He won't have gone far." Henri wrapped an arm around my waist and helped me up the path.

Snuggled up against him like this, I could almost believe. I grinned up at him. "What is this surprise? Will you give me a hint?"

"I got married!"

"No!"

"Is my wife here?" he called out.

"Would my husband mind helping me with something?" came the reply.

My mouth dropped open at the familiar voice. "Mali?"

My best friend's face popped through the entry to a wigwam, and she burst into tears. "Amélie!"

Seeing her was almost more than I could bear.

"My heart sings to see you alive," she said, holding me close.

"As does mine. Oh, Mali. This is the happiest day of my life! And Henri told me something so wonderful I almost cannot believe it! You and he . . . ?"

"At last!" she said, laughing as he came up from behind and put his hands on her shoulders. He brushed the long braid off her back, leaned in, and kissed her neck. Of course they were married. They had been best friends since we were children. Before the English had sent us away, they'd begun stealing secret glances—of which I'd seen every one. This shouldn't have been a surprise to me, but still . . . it seemed incredible it should have happened while I was gone.

Henri glanced mischievously at me over his wife's shoulder. "There is something else—or rather, some*one* else. Wait here."

Mali's smile was contagious. It warmed my soul to share it with her.

"What is it?"

"Wait," she said, hugging me again.

Henri's eyes were shining when he returned. The tiny pink fists of a baby flailed happily beneath his chin, the rest of its body wrapped in a blanket in its father's protective arms. I thought I might collapse with joy. I stretched out my arms, aching to hold the bundle. When he placed her in my arms, I fell instantly in love.

"So beautiful," I cried, kissing the soft, round cheeks. The innocence in her wide brown eyes was absolute. She'd known nothing but love, had no concept of grief, and my heart raced to build a wall against any who might change that.

"Her name is Amélie."

My amazement gave way to longing. Unexpected loneliness swelled within me, and I hugged the baby tighter. "Hello, Amélie," I whispered.

The little cupid lips formed a perfect circle as I spoke. I could not look away.

"Maman and Papa would be so, so proud of you," I told my brother and his wife, my eyes still on their baby. "They would love her so much. If only—" I took a deep breath and finally looked at them again. "I am sorry. I have much to tell, but I am not yet strong enough."

Mali understood. She always had. "When you are ready, you can tell us."

"I told Henri the truth, and I will tell you," I said slowly. "We are the last of our family." I kissed the baby's brow again. "At least we have one more now."

We said nothing more; there was nothing to say.

In the next breath my Mi'kmaq guide appeared beside me, sliding from out behind the ferns that encircled the camp.

"Ah! I wondered if I would see you again," I said, smiling up at him.

Mali stepped back, obviously startled. "Amélie, is this a friend of yours?"

"I think so. He saved my life and brought me here. I don't know who he is, and he will not answer me when I ask."

"Well, *I* know who he is." She looked reverently at him. "Amélie, this is Me'tekw, the youngest son of our great chief. He will not speak because he cannot. He was born with no voice. He disappeared from our land many years ago, and for a long time no one had seen anything of him. I . . . We had thought he was gone from this world, until he came here unexpectedly two months ago."

Me'tekw. His eyes were on Mali's, looking like a doting uncle with his arms crossed over his expansive chest. He shifted his gaze to me, then looked back at her and nodded.

Her eyes widened. "I think I understand why he is here. My father told me a story a long time ago. May I tell her?" she asked Me'tekw.

He smiled.

"Your father and Me'tekw were friends, along with my parents. They hunted together, played together, did everything together. This was back when the British were here but they were not yet a threat. But then the British declared war on the Mi'kmaq by paying for scalps."

I nodded. I knew of that terrible time.

"One day, when Me'tekw was a young man, he went fishing near the British. He fell asleep in the sun, and they found him. When he could not answer their questions, they beat him until he was nearly dead. They shot him twice and threatened his village, but he still said nothing. They held him down and put a knife to his scalp," Mali said. "They said the scalp of the chief's son would bring a great reward."

I looked at Me'tekw, seeing an entirely different man from the one I had gotten to know in some small way. He had been my protector, my guide, my silent companion, and I'd never had any idea what suffering he had endured.

"Your father killed those soldiers," Mali said softly. "He saved Me'tekw's life."

I stared at Me'tekw, hearing my father's confession all over again. "And you saved mine." I touched his arm, and the baby I held gurgled softly. "Thank you."

He nodded once, gestured deeper into the woods, and disappeared again. Mali seemed to know exactly why.

"When he came here last time," Mali said, "he brought someone with him who needed help. Come. I need to show you something." Smiling, she took little Amélie from my arms, though I was reluctant to let her go. "I think you will want to have your hands free for this."

We walked back into the forest toward to the rhythmic echo of wood being chopped. All at once it stopped, and Me'tekw appeared. He walked toward us, and when he was about ten feet away, he stepped aside. A man stood behind him.

It was a face I'd thought I'd never see again.

"Amélie."

I don't remember the steps I took, running to him, but I will always remember the moment when Connor's arms went around me and his cheek pressed against mine. I couldn't breathe, couldn't speak. His quick breaths were warm on the side of my neck, and I knew he wept with me. When I drew back, needing to look at him, his eyes shone.

"Are you well?" I asked, not knowing what else to say. My hands skimmed over his arms and face, searching for proof of his health. He bore a new scar on one cheek, but I found no recent injuries.

"Very well." His hand pressed against my cheek, and his thumb stroked away a tear. "Oh, my beautiful Amélie. At this moment I am better than I've ever been."

Me'tekw stepped up beside Connor and eyed him closely, seeming to ask a question. Connor smiled as if he knew him well.

"Thank you, my friend. Our debt is more than paid. By bringing Amélie here, you have given me my life back."

Something happened to Me'tekw in that moment. The tension that had drawn his brow and flared his nostrils, the strain that had held his jaw tight, released.

"I'm sorry I couldn't save my father," I told him. "I know you loved him like a brother. He loved you as well."

His smile lit his eyes like a sunrise. A long sigh—the only sound I ever heard from him—erased any lingering doubts, and I understood at last. He could not have saved my father, but by taking care of me he had fulfilled his promise and more. What was left of my family was safely together again because of him. Me'tekw bowed slightly—humbly accepting absolution of some kind, I imagined. Then he turned and vanished into the woods, and I saw a lift to his steps that hadn't been there before.

THIRTY-SIX

After the initial excitement, after the thrill of embracing someone dear I'd thought long gone, after the impulsive looks of delight had faded to muted glances of apprehension, what was I to
do? I stood beside the man I had dreamed of for so long, held
hands with the one in whom I had placed all my trust . . . and
stared into the eyes of a stranger.

"You are tired," he recognized. "We have much to talk about,
you and I, but we can speak after you have rested."

"Sleep can wait."

We did not hold hands as we walked back to the shore where
Me'tekw and I had first landed, but we were side by side. When
his skin touched mine, I felt such a roaring in my chest that I
clutched my hands together, out of his reach. It was not that
I didn't want to touch him—I wanted that more than I dared
admit—but it was important that I think clearly. I must remember Papa's words and consult my conscience before diving head-
long into something so important. But when the rocks shifted
beneath me, I stumbled, and he caught me. I was undone by the
pressure of his hand on my arm, the arm he braced against my
waist. Confused by the swirling sensations, I practically ran the

rest of the way. By the time the ground levelled out, my heart had slowed, nearing its normal rhythm. Me'tekw's canoe was gone.

"I imagine he will return to be sure you are all right," Connor assured me.

"I wish I could have said goodbye."

"You said all he needed to hear. He saw what he needed to see." He turned from the water to face me, but I still saw its reflection in his eyes. "Have you?"

At his question, my arms tingled, my cheeks were on fire, and yet I could not speak. Fear seized me, its talons sharp and pressing. What was it that frightened me so terribly? After all I'd been through, why could I not simply accept the comfort he offered? For so long I'd been afraid of what was happening to me or to my family, living in the midst of terrifying circumstances beyond my control. This felt different. That's when I realized this new fear was for my future.

"I gave you up once before," Connor reminded me, "and I paid dearly for that decision. I have missed you every day since last we saw each other, and I prayed every night for your safekeeping." His throat moved, and he let out a long breath. "And yet, despite the pain of being separated from you, I'd do it again if I knew it would save your life."

He held out his hands, waiting. He asked for my heart, but what did I have to give him? Long ago, when I was a different person, it had belonged to him, and it had pulsed with love and hope. Since then my heart had come under fierce attack. Pieces had been chipped or gouged away. The shell was cracked, the foundation shaky. The unprotected kernel within had been diminished until it barely existed. Hardly a worthy gift to give to the man I loved. Yet still he asked.

If I gave him what was left, would it be enough? The fog that had wrapped around him on that terrible morning, whispering over his long black cloak and glowing in Mali's necklace, still existed between us. I was afraid to step through it.

"I died that day we left you," I whispered.

"You did not die, Amélie. You are right here. And so am I."

My throat swelled with apprehension, but I took the first step, laying my trembling fingers on his. They curled around mine and their warmth spread.

"There is nothing left of me," I tried to explain.

His gaze didn't waver. "I have loved you from the first time I saw you, Amélie. I will gladly take whatever you can give me. I can only imagine the pain you suffer, and I want to ease it." He squeezed my fingers. "Take my strength. Even when you are strong enough to stand on your own again, I want to stand with you."

"I am not the girl you fell in love with."

"Yes, you are, though you have grown. Now you are the woman I love."

"I missed you," I choked out.

With my declaration his shoulders relaxed, as if he had been holding his breath. "Never again, Amélie. You will never have cause to miss me again, nor I you."

I was barely aware of my own movement as I leaned closer. He pressed his lips to mine, and I kept my eyes closed even after the warmth of him was gone, needing to remember this sensation of pure happiness. If I did not, I was sure it would swirl away in the breeze and leave me, just as everything else in my life had.

"Open your eyes, Amélie," he said. "I'm still here."

⟵

André was not prepared for the scene he came upon when he visited our Mi'kmaq family. Since he stopped in to see them whenever he was nearby, he knew all about Mali and little Amélie. He did not know about me. When he walked into the camp one afternoon, calling out to Henri, I ducked out of the wigwam and flung my arms around his neck before he even recognized me.

"Amélie!" he cried. "You're alive! How did you—"

He froze, looking over my shoulder at a rustling in the bushes. He had always been alert, but war had quickened his reflexes. When I followed his gaze I saw Connor had returned to our camp from a hunt. He was staring back at André with obvious apprehension.

"André, you might not remember—" I began.

"What are you doing here?" André growled. "I thought I'd seen the last of you when I sent you off with that English weasel."

I didn't understand. "André! Please, I—"

Connor nodded, his expression wary. "I knew you would come eventually."

Henri returned at that moment, a couple of grouse hooked on his belt. I held up a hand and he stopped, regarding the stand-off with interest. He asked, "Do you know each other?"

Henri had never been able to stay out of a conversation, even if it had nothing to do with him. This time I welcomed his interference, since I was at a loss to explain the tension.

"You could say so," André said. "I recently did my best to kill him."

"That was your best?" Connor shook his head. "I doubt that. You didn't really try to kill me. You're not the kind of man to kill another without cause."

"You don't think I had cause?"

"No. As I tried to tell you at the time, I did not break my promise."

André glanced at me but did not move. "I may have acted prematurely," he allowed.

"Why would you try to kill him?" Henri asked for me.

"You know he's a British soldier, yes?" André asked, rounding on him. "You know he was Winslow's translator? Why would I *not* try to kill him?" He looked back at Connor. "I had a personal reason as well. He and I, we had an understanding, and I believed he had not held up his end."

"Which was?" Henri persisted.

"To look after our family." André's eyes were on me now. "After I left home, I saw him with Amélie, and I needed to know if he was the man she thought he was. If he was, I wanted to make sure he would take care of our family when I could not."

I smiled, hearing this. I had believed André had abandoned us in the beginning. Now I understood that even though he had left, he had still been watching over us.

"You did that?" I asked, looking between him and Connor. "You spoke with him?"

"Of course." André shrugged with reluctance.

"I will tell you all he did for us, André," I said. "How he risked his life for us." Connor threaded his fingers through mine, though he kept a wary eye on my brother. "For now, believe me when I tell you that you placed your trust in a worthy man. As have I."

My brother looked at our joined hands. "I think we have a lot to talk about. All of us."

"I hope someday you'll be able to see past the uniform you once saw on me," Connor said. Unhooking our fingers, he stepped toward André, hand outstretched. "I will not wear it again."

My brother still hesitated. "The army will wonder where you are."

Connor shook his head. "They believe me dead, I am sure. I did my duty, but I will not return. Your sister and I—"

"We plan to marry," I interrupted, thinking it might be easier for André to hear the news from my lips. A moment passed while André thought about my words. I understood his confusion, his concern, but I needed him to understand. His opinion meant the world to me, though it would not sway me.

"I could tell he loved you back in Grand Pré," André admitted softly. His expression relaxed a little, and he looked at Connor with fresh eyes. He finally accepted his handshake. "I owe you an apology. My gratitude as well."

"You owe me nothing," Connor assured him. "Amélie is fortunate to have such a devoted brother."

"One whom I missed very much!" I said, stepping between them so I could hug André again. He lifted my feet off the ground, and I felt the solid, reliable strength of him through his heavy coat.

"Oh, my baby sister. It feels so good to have you here, safe and happy. I thank God for it."

"So do I."

"Who's hungry?" Henri asked.

André set me back on my feet. "Welcome home, little sister."

"You as well, big brother."

That night by the fire, I sat between Connor and André. I would be lying if I said the two were great friends right away. I would also be lying if I said that our celebratory meal was filled only with laughter, because tears of grief also flowed that evening.

But from the depths of our sadness sprang hope for our future. Little Amélie snuggled safely in the arms of her parents when she wasn't being passed between her aunt and uncles. Connor held her close for a long time, and the pangs of longing I had felt before receded like the tide. Someday, if my prayers were answered, we would have children as well, filling some of the holes the last year had dug in my heart.

We would never return to l'Acadie—or to Nova Scotia, as it was now called. We would remain in Quebec, live off its wild and dangerous land. Quebec did not have red sand or generous dikes. It did not have the hundred houses and barns I had known as a child, with friendly plumes of white smoke rising from stone chimneys. It did not have my father's ship masts in the yard, nor did the air sparkle with Giselle's songs and giggles.

But it was beautiful, and it had land enough for us—land that would offer opportunities to our children and their children. In the morning, I would hear the songs of different birds or the whispering of rain on unfamiliar leaves, and it would come to me in this new land just as it had in the old one: the promise of another day.

Acknowledgments

We are forever a world in conflict. From battle-scarred continents to the peaceful little haven of Grand Pré, conquests have always existed; wars will always rage. We never know when we might be called upon to fight or flee, and we can never really be prepared.

We are forever a world seeking peace. Whether it is a global quest or one within ourselves, peace is often elusive or fleeting. When we need it most it tends to run, hiding and covering its eyes against ugly truths. Still, we cannot cease to search for it, to cherish it in our hearts if only for a while.

Between 1755 and 1762, over fifteen thousand peaceful, unsuspecting Acadian farmers and fishermen were ripped from their homes and sent to ports often unknown to them. Many of these men, women, and children never arrived at their assigned destination, and those who did quite often died soon after from illness or starvation. Some were more fortunate: they landed in new worlds and survived, even thrived. Others risked their lives to return to the land they had once called home.

I have been to Grand Pré, breathed the air these people once breathed, and I can tell you it is a beautiful place. It is a land of peace and quiet, a place where one can commune with history and nature, where one reluctantly learns to gently accept the history of atrocities, since there is no other choice. On a recent visit to the Grand-Pré National Historic Site, my husband and I followed our guide, Amy Antonick, who was the acting interpretation officer coordinator. The stories she told us were as fascinating as they were incredible; she was patient with my persistent questions both on the tour and in my follow-up emails. The place itself (featured at http://www.visitgrandpre.ca) is lovingly tended, with wonderful exhibits. If you are ever visiting Nova Scotia, I highly recommend a visit.

Europe and the United States have retained their history in part by re-creating it accessibly and abundantly in historical fiction; however, the more I read, the more I notice a shortage of similar interpretations of Canadian history. Recently I watched a wonderful TED Talk by Canadian journalist and author Chris Turner entitled "Why Canadian History Isn't as Boring as You Think It Is." He spoke about exactly that same concern, facetiously suggesting that conversation about Canadian history is often prefaced by "Welcome to Canada. Sorry we're boring." He is, of course, keen to impress upon his audience that Canada—our country and our past—is not the least bit dull. Our stories are just waiting to be written, and they need to be written so people will want to read and learn more. Often that means they require fictional reimagining, and that's where I come in. My goal, my passion is to breathe life back into Canadian history.

When I began working on *Promises to Keep*, I did not expect the reaction I received. While people nodded with enthusiasm at the focus on World War I and the Halifax Explosion in *Tides of Honour*, they positively beamed with anticipation at the idea of reading about the Acadian Expulsion of 1755. I was surprised by that; I had assumed the interest would be higher for the more recent time period. From that I learned to appreciate the deep pride which still exists within the Acadian community. Generations later, people still want to talk about their roots.

People's roots are often entangled with those of others, and I find it fascinating that in almost every tale I write (*Tides of Honour* is an exception), I am obliged to research the native people of the place I'm writing about. Here it was the Mi'kmaq, the native people of Canada's Maritime provinces. Since I do not know their language, I got in touch with a Mi'kmaq translator named Pemaptoq (https://twitter.com/Pemaptoq or www.mikmaqonline. org), and he told me *Me'tekw* means "does not speak" or "he is silent." I'm grateful for his help; Me'tekw's journey meant so much to the book.

My research often leads me to places which do not make it into the actual book. Regardless, they are all a part of the story, immersing me in the setting so I can better understand the characters and situations. An example: last summer I dragged my family to the Fortress of Louisbourg. In the beginning the drive may have seemed a chore to our teenage daughters, but they quickly fell in love with Cape Breton and the historic site. (A special thank you to the informative and very entertaining "Bassigny," our living history guide at the Fortress of Louisbourg.) As a result of our visit, I wrote pages and pages of story about the arrival of the British via Louisbourg, relating how that remote, rocky shore became a strategic point of entry, how the troops lived, and how they fought. Once I had tens of thousands of words written, I cut them all out of the manuscript—but not out of my thoughts. Even though the fort was not discussed in *Promises to Keep*, through re-creating that story I learned how the British troops were able to eventually travel to the Acadians' little world and turn it upside down.

Speaking of travelling, through the generosity and faith of the people at Simon & Schuster Canada, I had the privilege in April

2015 of touring select Canadian cities with one of my historical fiction idols, Susanna Kearsley. I shall never forget showing up in our hotel lobby in Victoria and greeting her . . . in a whisper. Yes, laryngitis had struck the night before my debut on a speaking tour! Ms. Kearsley was gracious and supportive, ensuring I had microphones wherever we went and translating my husky words when needed. She had her own difficulties to overcome, since she had broken her foot badly that winter—parkour, right, Susanna?—so I was glad I could help a little, pushing her wheelchair through the airport and holding doors. I dubbed ours the "She Can't Walk, and I Can't Talk" tour, and it was an enlightening experience. Susanna taught me a lot, from where to dig up three-hundred-year-old journals to the best social media practices. I am glad to be able to call her my friend—and I admit I am still a major fan girl. Everywhere we went, we were hosted by welcoming booksellers and introduced to enthusiastic readers. I never would have thought I'd be comfortable in front of a microphone, but this experience showed me I could do it—even better, I enjoyed it!

One highlight of my trip was our evening in Calgary, since I was able to spend time with my mother. She is a tireless and generous cheerleader, and I am always grateful for every mention she makes of my books, whether it's to friends or complete strangers. After supper, Susanna and I were taken to the Fish Creek Library. I stepped up to the microphone but had to wait when our Simon & Schuster Canada representative made an unexpected announcement. I was looking directly at my mom when it was announced that *Tides of Honour* had just hit the *Globe and Mail* Top Ten Bestsellers list. I had never imagined that might happen! And things just kept getting better: I never could have predicted that my dear Danny and Audrey Baker would remain on that prestigious list for eight precious weeks!

That success had everything to do with you.

Before I thank the team behind me, I would like to thank the audience in front of me. Thank you, thank you, thank you for picking up one of my books. From there you might have chosen to pick up another and another, and I am beyond grateful for that. When you take a few moments to share a review on Amazon or Goodreads or any other forum—even if it's just a brief mention—you introduce my books to new readers, for which I am truly appreciative. I was particularly excited when the Halifax Regional School Board, prompted by a number of recommendation letters from local teachers, put *Tides of Honour* on their Teachers' Recommended Reading list, meaning it may soon be in the hands of high school students. Thank you to everyone who has read and recommended my books. I promise to keep writing stories which will inspire more of your reviews!

Now to the people behind the scenes: first of all, to my gracious, insightful editors, Nita Pronovost and Sarah St. Pierre, my incredible cover artist Liz, and the rest of the eager, efficient team. They have been a joy to work with, and I look forward to a long, prolific partnership. Simon & Schuster Canada's president, Kevin Hanson, has a fantastic group of people over there.

Jacques de Spoelberch, my chevalier and perspicacious agent, continues to amaze me: always in my corner, always the consummate professional and gentleman, always inspiring.

Every one of my books is dedicated to my family, because without their support I would not do what I do. My little girls are now beautiful young women who are putting their imagination, intellect, talent, and compassion to good use. I am proud of who they are becoming and love them more than they'll ever know.

Finally, my anchor in any stormy sea, my light at the end of every tunnel, my one M&M in a trail mix full of nuts: my beloved husband, Dwayne. He takes care of me and everything around me when I sink so deep into my books that I forget what day it is. He understands me as no one ever has, and my love for him inspires every romantic moment I write. Bonus: he is an insightful and creative editor. When I write myself into a corner, I go to him. He patiently leads me back out, offering suggestions that are . . . well, actually sometimes they're pretty silly, but *most* of the time they are brilliant. He has an uncanny ability to tie all my loose ends together into a perfect bow. Before I send my manuscripts to anyone else, they go through him. We were both very pleasantly surprised to learn how good he is at this, but really, we shouldn't have been. Anyone who knows us knows we're a perfect team in every way. Always have been, always will be.

Also by
GENEVIEVE GRAHAM

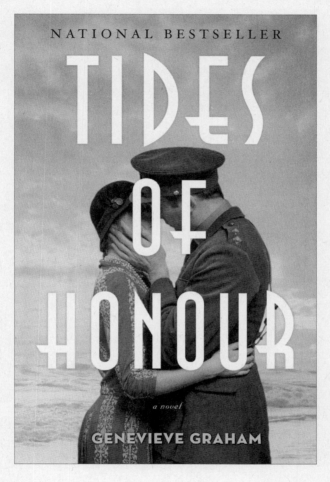

NATIONAL BESTSELLER

TIDES
OF
HONOUR

a novel

GENEVIEVE GRAHAM

"Fans of Gabaldon and other historical fiction/romance writers
will lap this up for the classy, fast-moving, easy-to-read and
absorbing book that it is—with some Canadian history to boot."
—*Winnipeg Free Press*

SIMON &
SCHUSTER